NO TEST FOR
THE WICKED

Previously published Worldwide Mystery title by
JULIE MOFFETT

NO ONE LIVES TWICE

NO TEST FOR THE WICKED

JULIE MOFFETT

W❂RLDWIDE®

TORONTO • NEW YORK • LONDON
AMSTERDAM • PARIS • SYDNEY • HAMBURG
STOCKHOLM • ATHENS • TOKYO • MILAN
MADRID • WARSAW • BUDAPEST • AUCKLAND

"A mother understands what a child doesn't say."
~Old Proverb

To my mother, Donna B. Moffett, because she always understands me. I love you, Mom!

Recycling programs
for this product may
not exist in your area.

No Test for the Wicked

A Worldwide Mystery/January 2016

First published by Carina Press.

ISBN-13: 978-0-373-26976-1

Copyright © 2014 by Julie Moffett

Printed in U.S.A.

Acknowledgments

A book is never a singular effort, so I would like to acknowledge the excellent assistance of my wonderful, insightful, (insert your favorite spectacular modifier here) editor, Alissa Davis, as well as my terrific beta readers, Sandy Parks (a fantastic author in her own right), Bill Moffett and Donna Moffett. I also owe a big gratitude of debt to my brother, Brad Moffett, for his excellent brainstorming sessions on the plotline for the story, and my niece, Katy Moffett, for her great suggestions. I also want to thank security experts John McBrien and Kevin Hodges for their helpful insights on SWAT teams, police procedure and other security issues. Finally, much thanks is due to my supersmart techie nephew Kyle and his lovely fiancé, Julia, for their important assistance and patience with my numerous technical questions. However, any imaginative use or outright mistakes of any of the technology in the story is on me alone.

I would also like to thank the many fans and friends who entered my Facebook contest to help me decide on a title for this book. It was great fun and I saved several of them for potential future use. However, it was high school pal Alicia Stepp-Starnes's son Brandon who came up with the title *No Test for the Wicked*. As a result, he won having a character in the book named after him. Congratulations, Brandon! I hope you enjoy your namesake.

ONE

HOW IS IT POSSIBLE that even though I graduated with a double degree in mathematics and computer science from Georgetown University, saved the Vatican millions of euros, and caught a reality television-obsessed hacker while posing as a dating contestant in Hollywood, I still can't figure out how to tell my mother I have a boyfriend?

I can visualize it now. I'll blurt out the news, she'll hug me and shriek in my ear for a while, and then the analysis will commence. My mother will ask me if he's rich, if he comes from a good family, and if he has a respectable job.

I don't know the details of his bank account and, in terms of his family, I've only met his grandmother. But regarding the job… Would a supersecret hacker spy who may (or may not) work for the Vatican, but is definitely working for the National Security Agency, qualify as respectable? I'm afraid that would be iffy.

Then my mom would want me to tell her all the gory details of how we met, whether or not he's a foreigner (he is, so that may not go over well), and if he has some weird religion. Maybe I shouldn't tell her he's on a first-name basis with the Pope.

After I've been forced to give her specifics about my boyfriend's career, ethnicity and religion, she will take my hand and tell me that a June wedding would be just lovely. Besides, if we held it at the ultra-expensive Willard Hotel in Washington D.C., we could invite up to several hundred guests. By that point, I'd be so panicky and nauseated I'd upchuck on her three-hundred-dollar Manolo Blahnik leather pumps.

That's my life. My name is Lexi Carmichael and I'm a twenty-five-year-old hacker, gamer and fangirl who isn't planning on getting within spitting distance of a white dress anytime soon. Normal relationships are murky waters to navigate even if one is emotionally astute and socially capable. For those of us with less than stellar skills on these fronts, entering into a romantic relationship can be exhausting, not to mention terrifying, especially if my mother is involved.

It's hard enough for me to manage the few relationships I have outside of my boyfriend. I can count the number of close friends I have on one hand. Add in the work relationships I have to navigate, and things really get complicated. Now that I'm the Director of Information Security at X-Corp—a cyberintelligence firm right outside of Washington, D.C.—I have employees to manage and staff to keep busy. It wouldn't be a stretch to say it's all a bit overwhelming.

It didn't used to be that way. I once lived a relatively quiet life working as a tech head for the NSA. Not too long ago, the agency operated in relative obscurity with less than five percent of the American population even knowing that we existed. That anonymity was blown out of the water by the Edward Snowden scandal—he's the guy that filched an enormous amount of top-secret cyber information from the NSA, implicating the agency in questionable privacy actions. Now everyone in the world knows about the NSA. Although I'll be the first to admit my life has been anything *except* quiet since I joined X-Corp, at least I got out of the NSA before the scandal broke. Still, I know a few decent people who continue to work at the agency in one capacity or the other, including my new boyfriend. Slash is a master hacker, one of the best I've ever met, and he also supports the NSA in other intelligence efforts, including terrorism and cyberterrorism. He is a man of many, many talents.

My office phone rang and I picked it up.

"Carmichael."

"Buon giorno, cara."

His voice was so sexy it almost made me forget how much I hated talking on the phone.

It weirded me out that my stomach felt all tingly. "Hey, Slash. *Si deframmenta la mia vita.*"

There was silence and then a soft laugh. "You are studying Italian now?"

"Isn't that a practical thing to do when one has an Italian boyfriend?"

"Not necessarily, but I'm pleased. Did you mean to say that I defragment your life?"

"Yes. Is that inappropriate?"

"No. It's perfect."

"Okay. Good. I know I have to work on the accent. I'd like to be able to say at least a few words to your grandmother in Italian the next time we meet."

"She'd love that. That reminds me, I owe you another trip to Italy, this time for pleasure. Perhaps you can meet some more of my family."

He said it casually, but my stomach flipped. He wanted me to meet more of his family.

Intellectually I knew this was part of the boyfriend-girlfriend dynamic, but it scared the heck out of me. I mean, Slash had a mother. He'd mentioned her when we were in Rome. What would I say to her? What if she couldn't speak English? And how could I look her in the eye after having engaged in sexual intercourse with her son? Oh jeez, who knew what would come out of my mouth!

Even worse, it was logical to extrapolate that if I met Slash's family, it meant he would have to meet *my* family. And that brought me back to the fact that I hadn't even *told* my family I was dating anyone. The mere thought of it made me so unnerved that I had to recite the first three lines of Fermat's Last Theorem in order to calm down. My mother had been planning my wedding since the day I was born. If I brought Slash home for dinner, there was a statistically significant chance she'd have him measured for his tuxedo before we finished the first course. Or worse, she'd pull me aside at dessert and give me the dreaded sex talk.

I started to hyperventilate. "Um, sure, Slash. That would be great someday."

He chuckled. "I didn't mean to scare you."

"Why do you think I'm scared?"

"You paused for a bit too long and then your voice quavered. Don't worry, I'm teasing you again."

"I knew that."

But I hadn't really. Slash was a geek, but he was able to read people in ways I never could. He was pretty clever and talented, that boyfriend of mine.

I heard an electronic beeping sound in the background over the phone. Where was he? Before I could ask, he spoke.

"I just called to say good morning and that I miss you. I'm not sure how my day will shape up, but I'm going to figure out a way to make sure it ends with you. Are you available?"

"Yes."

"That's my girl."

"Slash?"

"Si?"

"I think I like being your girl."

"Ah, that makes me very happy." I could hear the smile in his voice. "See you soon."

"Okay. Bye."

I hung up the phone and stared at it. I'd just made casual plans with my boyfriend. This was going to take some getting used to. I'd never had a boyfriend before. Not even in high school. In fact, I'd never even had a *date* in high school. Slash has been my significant other for just a few days. A couple of wow-I-can't believe-he-can-do-that days, mind you, but I still haven't adjusted to our relationship yet. It may take me some time to get used to it. Maybe forever. That's hard to calculate in real-time terms.

While our relationship is still new, I couldn't spend all day thinking about it. Especially since I was on the clock. So I took one more sip of my coffee, straightened the glasses on my nose and hunched over my keyboard, hoping today would be a quiet day in the office so that I could catch up on paperwork. A glance out the window confirmed the December weather in the nation's capital remained crappy—snow, ice and freezing rain. Most of the area schools had closed and more than a few X-Corp employees had called in. But hackers don't take snow days, so neither do I. Somehow I skidded and slid my red Miata all the way to Crystal City, Virginia, about a forty-five-minute drive from my apartment in

Jessup, Maryland, to show up for work. I was a bit disappointed to see the continued snowfall because I had hoped the weather would ease up a bit so I could go for a late-morning donut and coffee run. Unfortunately, it would have to wait.

It was nearly noon and my stomach had started to growl when the phone rang. Internal number.

I picked up the phone and jammed it between my shoulder and ear while I continued to type. "Carmichael."

"Lexi, we have a client here. Can you meet me in conference room two?"

I stopped typing. It was Finn, my boss and onetime romantic interest. I liked Finn a lot and he liked me, but the possibility of a romantic liaison had come to a screeching halt because I couldn't handle the boss/employee aspect of our relationship. Luckily for me, Finn had been taking it well, although I wasn't sure what he'd think about me and Slash. Not that I intended to tell him about it any time soon.

"Sure, Finn. Be right there."

I logged out, then snatched my laptop in one hand and my coffee mug in the other. I swung by the kitchen, poured exactly three-fourths of a cup of coffee, added exactly two teaspoons of creamer and one-and-a-half teaspoons of sugar in the mug and stirred it four times counterclockwise. Then I snatched a couple of Christmas cookies off a tray. Stuffing the cookies in my mouth, I walked toward the conference room.

As I passed through the outer office, where white lights twinkled on a lovely floor-to-ceiling Christmas tree, I could hear the strains of "Joy to the World" playing softly over the loudspeaker. It made me feel warm and cozy.

I walked into the conference room. Finn sat across the table from a pretty young woman in a red suit. She had shoulder-length blonde hair that curled around her chin. Her face was perfectly made-up, with just the hint of a rosy glow to her cheeks. Her hands rested atop the table and, although they were devoid of any jewelry, they were perfectly manicured with red nail polish. Next to her sat a very distinguished-looking man with gray hair and sideburns, dressed in a three-piece suit and steel-blue tie. I felt like an outlier in my purple sweater, black slacks and ponytail.

I set my laptop down on the table as both men rose.

Finn swept out his hand. "Glad you could make it. Lexi, I'd like you to meet the Honorable Percival O'Neill, Ambassador of Ireland to the United States."

Jeez, I *was* underdressed. An ambassador? I hoped I'd brushed the cookie crumbs off my sweater.

The older gentleman extended a hand and I shook it firmly.

Finn nodded to the young woman, who remained seated. "This is Bonnie Swanson, Headmistress of the Excalibur Academy for the Technologically Gifted in Washington, D.C."

I leaned across the table to shake her hand and she smiled at me.

"Glad to meet you." Although she looked young, she had a firm grip and a no-nonsense look to her.

After the introductions were finished, we all sat down. Finn leaned forward, consulting what looked like several pages of notes.

He shuffled them around and then placed his hands

on top of the small stack. "Ambassador O'Neill and I have been talking over the phone for a couple of days. In the spirit of full disclosure, our families have been close friends for years in Ireland. He recommended X-Corp to Ms. Swanson to see if we can assist with her current situation."

I looked between the ambassador and the headmistress, wondering what kind of situation would bring the two of them together via X-Corp.

Finn leaned back in his chair and pressed his fingertips together. "I'll go ahead and let Ms. Swanson explain her situation to us."

Bonnie smiled at us around the table. "I greatly appreciate the ambassador's assistance in bringing me here to discuss this confidential matter. His daughter, Piper, is a junior at our Academy, so it goes without saying that he is personally invested in helping us come to a satisfactory solution. Actually, I'm not sure whether to be embarrassed or proud of our problem, but..." She paused. "There is no easy way to say this. We can't seem to keep our students out of the school's computer system."

I grinned before quickly fashioning my face into a somber expression. Bonnie caught my smile, but to my surprise, I didn't see disapproval in her eyes, only amusement.

She looked at Finn. "So, do you think X-Corp can help us?"

Finn glanced down the table at me. "I'm sure of it. This kind of situation is Lexi's specialty."

I hadn't realized I had a specialty, but if Finn said so I wasn't going to contradict him.

Bonnie studied me. "I've seen you before."

"I'm pretty ordinary looking. A lot of people say that."

She stared at me a moment more. "No, I'm sure of it. Have you ever been on television?"

I cleared my throat. "Ah, briefly. Very briefly."

"I *knew* I'd seen you before. I rarely forget a face. Well, glad to make your acquaintance."

I mumbled and looked down at my laptop, pretending to search the web for something.

Finn spoke. "Well, if we are in agreement, we can have Lexi accompany you back to the school or come at your convenience to determine a solution to the problem."

Bonnie nodded. "Actually, today would be excellent if she is available. There are no students there now because of the weather. I'll be happy to sign the paperwork as soon as it's ready."

"Of course." Finn reached into his briefcase and pulled out a sheaf of papers. "It will take me just a few minutes to prepare them."

I stood. Both men rose to their feet.

"I, ah, thought I'd just get my things together so I'm ready to go when Ms. Swanson is."

"Call me Bonnie, please."

"Sure, Bonnie. Then you should call me Lexi."

I left the room and went to get my laptop case, a notepad, my coat and purse. The rest of my tools were either in my head or at my fingertips online.

I returned to the conference room as Finn and Bonnie were signing papers. The ambassador stood at one of the windows looking out at the city below. I walked up and stood beside him.

"It looks festive with the snow," he said.

"People around here can't drive for beans in weather like this. Adverse weather conditions, such as snow and ice, are present in nearly thirty-four percent of total vehicular crashes and nearly twenty-eight percent of highway fatalities in America. Or in other words, Americans can't drive in such conditions."

He chuckled and glanced at me sideways. "Bloody truer words I've never heard. None of them has ever seen an Irish snow. Have you ever been to Ireland?"

"No, but Finn speaks quite fondly of it."

We stood in silence for a bit before he spoke again. "So, Ms. Carmichael, did you go to a school like that?"

"Excuse me?"

"The Excalibur Academy. Did you attend a school like that?"

"No. I attended public school. My parents thought it important I get the full experience of a diverse student population."

"Did they make the right decision?"

I sighed. "Probably not. It was a waste of my time, academically speaking. But I survived."

"You look quite young. Have you been out of school long?"

I bristled, ready to snap out my list of academic and workplace accomplishments. *Wait.* I paused, then watched him. He looked curious, so maybe he hadn't meant it disparagingly. Per Basia's advice, I'd started trying to assess my conversational partner's facial expressions before I responded to any remark that seemed contentious.

I kept my tone neutral. "I graduated from Georgetown a couple of years ago. But age is not an indicator of ability. I am fully capable of handling this assignment."

He smiled. "I don't doubt that and I certainly didn't mean to imply otherwise. I've known Finn for a long time and he has impeccable taste in people. I just wondered how long you've been into computers."

I stared at him for a moment. Where was he going with these questions?

"Truthfully? I've been into computers since I could type on the keyboard. I also had an early aptitude for math. The two subjects meshed quite well for me."

He nodded. "It's been the same for my daughter. She is obsessed with math, code, and computers. Her mother and I are worried. She has no outside interests, including friends or boys."

I stiffened, feeling an immediate kinship with Piper even though I'd never met her. I wanted to leap to her defense, but didn't have a clue what to say.

Before I could say anything, Finn and Bonnie stood up and shook hands. Bonnie walked over to me. "Are you ready, Lexi?"

"Sure. Give me the address so I can plug it into my GPS."

She handed me her business card. "Here you go. See you there."

"Okay."

Just like that, I was on my way back to high school.

TWO

As I was driving, my cell rang. I turned off the Christmas music and punched it on, putting it on speaker so I could keep both hands on the wheel and my eyes on Bonnie, who drove a dark blue sedan in front of me.

"Hello?"

"Hey, Lexi."

I grinned. "Hey, Basia. It's great to hear your voice. How's Hollywood treating you?"

Basia had recently ended up on a television reality dating show in Hollywood. To make a long story short, she saved me by agreeing to take my place in the cast after my undercover operation to catch a hacker had ended. I'll be happy when she's back at work as a translator for X-Corp in a few weeks.

"Oh, Lexi, Hollywood is amazing. Haven't you caught the show lately?"

I grimaced and was glad Basia couldn't see it. "Ah, I'm sorry to report I haven't."

"I shouldn't be surprised."

"No, you shouldn't. I'm sure you're a superstar. How are the guys?"

The "guys" were the nerdy male contestants on the show, all of whom I'd made friends with when I was out in California.

"They're doing wonderfully. They all say 'hi.'"

"Tell them I say hi back. Glad things are well with them and you."

I heard a squeaking noise in the background. Basia was sitting down in the big, black makeup chair on the set. I'd sat there a few times myself and recognized the sound.

"So, Lexi, I'm going to skip the rest of the small talk and get right down to the important stuff. How are things with Slash?"

"Huh?" I hadn't seen that coming. "Slash? What do you mean?"

She clucked her tongue. "I've seen the way Slash has been looking at you lately. Then he shows up in California and tries to sweep you off your feet on national television. I would presume he's either made his move or is about to do it. So, what's going on with you two?"

How she was able to interpret our social interactions to come to that scarily accurate conclusion was beyond me. Still, I tried to fake ignorance.

"What makes you so sure anything is going on?"

"Because you got really nervous when I asked you that question. Plus, you're doing what you always do when you don't want to answer. You ask me a question."

Well, she had me there. "Guess you're not my friend for nothing. Things are going fine."

"That's so *not* an answer."

"Okay, okay. You win. He's my boyfriend."

"What?"

"What, what? Don't freak out on me. You asked. I figured the jig was up."

It was quiet for a moment before Basia spoke. "Okay. I'm breathing now. I am not freaking out. Much. What exactly do you mean by boyfriend?"

"Wait. Why are you asking me that? You're the expert on relationships. You know the definition of boyfriend inside and out."

"True, but I believe there's a distinct possibility your definition of boyfriend may be significantly different from mine. I need to know for sure."

"Fine. We're an item. You know…together."

"How together is together?"

"Seriously? You want details?"

"Absolutely."

I couldn't help it, my cheeks heated. "Well, he's officially my boyfriend. We're going to go on dates and stuff. We're a couple."

Silence. "I see. Are you still *talking* about this or are you sleeping with him yet?"

"Sleeping as in spending the night or—"

"For heaven's sake, Lexi! Have you had sex with him?"

It was my turn to be silent.

"Lexi?"

I sighed. "Is it really normal for girls to tell each other the details of their sex lives?"

"Just tell me you *have* a sex life."

"Okay, I have a sex life."

She screeched. "Really? OMG!"

"Well, sex *is* part of the adult boyfriend-girlfriend dynamic as long as they agree that it's morally acceptable within the bounds of their personal beliefs, right?"

"You did it? You really slept with Slash?"

"Look, I know you don't approve. I also realize this is a big risk for me. It's okay. I'm taking this slowly and figuring it out as I go along. I do think he cares about me. Actually, he said he loves me. I didn't say it back, but I'm working on it."

"Wow. Just slow down. Slash said he *loves* you?"

"Yes. When we were in Rome."

"Okay, now I can't breathe. That's just…astonishing."

"That I had sex or that he loves me?"

"Both. For crying out loud, give me a second to recover." She took some audible breaths. "Okay, look, Lexi, it's not that I don't like Slash. I do. I just want you to be careful with your heart."

"Jeez."

"That being said, let's get to the juicy part."

"What juicy part?"

"How's the sex?"

I laughed. "Well, I assure you, all the parts involved are definitely in working order."

"I figured that much. What I really want to know is how *was* it?"

"How am I supposed to answer that? I'm not sure how to categorize something like sex. It's subjective."

"Okay, smarty-pants, let me put it this way. On a scale from one to ten, how was it?"

Math. Now that was something to which I could relate. "Well, on a scale of one to ten, sex with Slash was… one hundred."

She squealed. "No way!"

"Way. Not that I have a lot of experience with which to form a solid comparison. But I'm pretty sure a lot of what he does is fairly innovative."

She giggled. "Oh. My. God. That's amazing. I'm going to need more details soon. And, since we're in a sharing mood, I guess I should admit I'm seeing someone, too."

"You're *always* seeing someone."

"I mean on an exclusive basis."

Now I was surprised. "Exclusive? You?"

"I don't want you to get all worried or invested, but it's Xavier."

I felt like she had punched me in the stomach. As long as I have known Basia, she's *never* been exclusive with anyone. She has adeptly dated multiple guys without breaking a sweat. Xavier Zimmerman is the identical twin of my other best friend, Elvis, and a fellow geek first-class. Basia had been dating him off and on for a while, but that she'd now actually gone exclusive with him was huge. Xavier is like a brother to me. Whether she wanted me to be or not, I *was* invested and worried what might happen if she got bored.

I managed to get my voice to work. "Xavier? Exclusive? Why him?"

I could hear the smile in her voice. "I know it's crazy, but he's so sweet, I can't help it. We both know he's not my usual type, but he sees me like no other guy ever has. I'm not saying this is *it* or anything. It's just I want to give it a go and see what happens. I was going to tell you while we were in Hollywood, but I didn't have a chance. Look, I know you care a lot about Xavier, so I want to promise that this is not just a fling or a casual thing. I'm really into him."

"Okay." I really hoped she meant it, because I was worried how Xavier might react to getting dumped by Basia. It wouldn't be pretty.

"I'm going to Greece with him for Christmas. Filming on the show takes a hiatus for the Christmas holiday, so it fits into my schedule."

I already knew the twins had booked a villa for three

weeks because Elvis had told me. "Wow. That's a big step, Basia. Greece with Xavier. Wow."

"I know, right? Elvis isn't coming until later so that we can have some alone time. It's really sweet of him. So, we're just going to veg, sightsee, and get to know each other a little better." I heard her take a deep breath. "Actually, I can't believe I'm doing this."

"You sound excited."

"I am."

A car honked as a minivan slid on the slippery asphalt. I swerved to avoid a collision. "Jeez."

"Where are you?" Basia asked.

"On I-95, heading to a new client's place. A private high school for technologically gifted kids in D.C. The students keep hacking into the school's system, so they've hired X-Corp to keep them out."

"Sounds like it's right up your alley. So, you think high school will be any better the second time around?"

"We'll see. I make it a point to never underestimate smart kids."

She chuckled. "You still *are* a smart kid. Anyway, Mandy needs to put on my makeup, so I've got to go."

"Okay. Tell Mandy I said hi. I'll try to talk to you before you head out for Greece. Good luck."

"You, too. Keep me posted on developments with Slash, and, damn it, Lexi, text me once in a while."

I hated texting with a passion and texting wasn't too fond of me either. "Not likely, but I'll think of you. I promise."

We hung up and I made it in one piece to the Excalibur Academy. I followed Bonnie into a gated parking lot with an attendant who waved us both through. Bonnie parked in a spot reserved for the headmistress, but the parking lot was essentially empty so I had my pick of spots. She waited for me by her car.

I pulled the collar of my jacket up and walked toward her, wishing I had a hat. The wind was cold and the ground icy with a light dusting of snow.

I looked up at the building as I walked. The school was situated in a nice part of D.C., in the northwest section surrounded by trees. The parking lot was large, which was unheard of in the city, and the building looked modern and brand-new. It was at least four stories high and had what looked like two flanking wings with a small covered walkway between each wing to the main building. Huge glass windows were centered on the third floor, sparkling like jewels against the gray winter sky.

When we got closer, I stopped and stared. "Wow. This is a high school?"

Bonnie nodded, blowing on her bare hands. "Yes. A very exclusive one. I won't lie to you. It costs more than an arm and a leg to go here."

"Wow. Just wow."

"We finished building the school just two years ago. Razed and rebuilt. We have the best of everything here."

"Looks like it."

"Come on. Let's go in. I want to introduce you to Ron Boland, our part-time technology guy. We have a Code Green situation, which means while students are not here because of the weather, the staff is."

"Okay."

We walked up to the school and Bonnie waved a badge at an access terminal. The door buzzed and she pulled it open.

"Security badges?"

"Every student has one. We don't mess with security

at our school. It's top-notch. Now if we could just protect ourselves from our students."

I shrugged. "Insider threats are almost always the hardest to stop."

I followed her down a gleaming hallway. Rows of steel lockers glistened under modern track lighting, and solid oak doors shone as if just polished. My high school sure hadn't looked like this.

Bonnie led me into a huge office area fronted by a woman with short brown hair who sat behind a marble counter typing something on her laptop. To her left was a large sitting area with a sky-blue couch and three matching padded chairs. A coffee table with a few child development and teaching magazines completed the look. Framed sketches, perhaps made by students, adorned the walls. I couldn't imagine sitting in this kind of comfort while waiting to be called into the principal's office.

The woman looked up and smiled when Bonnie and I walked in.

"Any problems, Marge?" Bonnie asked her. The woman shook her head.

"Nope. All quiet on the Western front."

"Just the way we like it. Can you page Ron and have him meet us in my office?"

"Absolutely." She picked up a phone and dialed something.

Bonnie motioned for me to follow her down a corridor, then ushered me into a large office with glass windows. She shrugged out of her coat and held out her hand to take mine. Opening a small closet, she hung both our coats in it and then sat down behind her desk.

It had been a few years since I'd been in a principal's office, but I still felt uneasy when she motioned me to sit in one of the visitor chairs. My palms began to sweat as I perched on the end of the chair and tried not to look uncomfortable.

Bonnie pulled on a pair of dark-rimmed glasses and folded her hands on top of some papers on her desk. "I hope this doesn't sound intrusive, Lexi, but I wondered if I could ask how old you are."

I leaned back in my chair and kept my gaze on her. "Only if you answer in turn."

She smiled. "Fair enough. I'll start. I'm thirty."

I raised an eyebrow. "Which is pretty young to be a headmistress of an expensive private school in the middle of D.C."

"Not if your grandfather owns said school." She narrowed her eyes. "But that's not the only reason I'm the headmistress. I have a PhD in Education from Dartmouth and I'm damn good at my job. Now, your turn."

"Okay. I'm twenty-five. My first job was at the NSA in the InfoSec Department. This is my second job. I've been into computers and code for as long as I can remember. I'm damn good at my job, too, if that's what you are worried about."

She considered me and then nodded. "Glad we're clear on that. I like a confident woman. You just look really young, which is why I asked. But I want you to know I got a good impression of you from the start."

"Likewise. But thanks, I guess."

A knock sounded on the door and a tall guy with black hair and a beard stepped in.

"You called, Bonnie?"

"Yes, I did. Ron, this is Lexi Carmichael."

I stood and shook his hand. He looked puzzled as his gaze darted from me to Bonnie. "A new student?"

Bonnie smiled. "No, she's here to help us with our, ah, computer problem."

He studied me, the light dawning in his eyes. "*You're* the infosec expert? Oh, I apologize."

"No need. It's okay. Apparently I look young for my age. I get it."

He sat down. "So, did Bonnie give you the rundown?"

"Can you bring me up to speed?"

"Sure. You want the basics?"

"Always the best place to start."

"Okay. Well, we've got a classic setup with a decent firewall. I'll show it to you in a minute. Unfortunately, the kiddies keep getting in no matter what steps we take to stop them. Kind of hard to keep them out when they're essentially plugged in to our network 24/7 for school-work."

"What have you done so far to lock them out?"

"As much as I can. Isolated the network, but the in-structors must have access to postgrades, make an-nouncements, and monitor discussion boards. They're the weakest link. I've separated the administrative func-tions and protected them to the best of my ability, but once the students are in the system, it's not much of a leap to hack if you're clever enough. And trust me, the students here are clever enough."

He sighed and stroked his fingers through his beard. "But that's not all. It's not just individual kids doing this. They've created a core group."

"A group?"

"Yes. They're calling themselves the WOMBATs."

I snorted and Bonnie looked at me. "You know what that means?"

I nodded, tried not to smile. "Well, yeah. It stands for

Waste of Money, Brains and Time. It sounds like the students are taking this to a political level."

Bonnie leaned forward. "A political level? Why?"

"Apparently they're voicing their disapproval of the grading system, extracurricular activities, the cafeteria food or authority in general. Who knows?"

Her eyes narrowed. "What they're doing is illegal. I could not only suspend them, but have charges brought against them."

"Yes, you could. However, I suspect the kids just don't realize the dangers of what they are doing. That being said, there's no better time than the present to teach them before they get the wrong kind of taste for it."

This job would test my loyalties. I would get it done, no question, but it would not be a simple seal and lock. Not only did I understand these kids, I'd *been* one of these kids not that long ago. I'd have to find a creative solution that would help them understand there was more at stake here than just their egos and need for a challenge.

Bonnie leaned back in her chair, steepled her fingers and studied me. "You sound like you understand them."

"I had my moments in high school."

"Did you do anything like this?"

I paused. It probably wouldn't be appropriate to tell her how I'd signed the principal up for Watch Your Weight Anonymous using his credit card after he told my mother the tech field wasn't for girls and I needed to try out for cheerleading in order to improve my social interaction.

"This isn't about me."

Bonnie smiled. "Ah, but in a way it is. It might make a difference in the way you approach them."

"Yes it might, but that's a good thing for you. Truthfully, I don't know enough about your system yet to know how I'll approach it or them. This isn't going to be an easy fix. Figuring out how to stop them is the easy part. *Keeping* them out is a lot harder and much more important."

Ron cocked his head. "Any thoughts on how you might do that?"

"Not yet. I've got a lot of questions. Tell me more about the teachers and staff. What kinds of things have you done to make them more aware of their behavior?"

"As much as I can. I make them change their passwords every couple of weeks. I insisted they create stricter passwords—longer, and more complicated ones involving additional letters and special characters. I also required them to stay after school for a couple of training sessions on computer security."

"Bet that went over well."

"Yeah, as you can well imagine. We even put up numerous signs and posters around the school about network security and the illegality of hacking, which the students promptly stole or vandalized."

I winced. "Ouch."

"Yeah, so I'm going nowhere fast."

I thought for a moment, studying his school access badge, which hung around his neck. "How about the school's security system? Is it tied in to the network?"

Ron shook his head. "No. A separate company runs the system, which may actually be a blessing in this case. That's all we'd need, the kids messing with the security system."

"Phone system?"

"Separate, as well," Bonnie said. "The school went massively over budget on a new phone system and we still haven't figured it all out. It was part of the plan before I came on board."

"So, you have three separate systems?"

"Exactly. Crazy, I know."

"How long have you been headmistress?" I asked her.

"Nearly two years. I came on just after we reopened."

I stood. "I think this might be more complicated than I expected. But still doable. If you'd show me the computer room now, Ron, I'd appreciate it."

"Sure. Come on, Lexi. I'll have to get you a badge in the outer office first."

"Okay."

We walked out to the office and Marge signed out a badge to me. "Are the badges only for the front door?"

"No. It can be programmed to open the restricted access areas. The Server Room and the Server Administrator's office—two adjoining rooms we affectionately call Computer Central—is one. Others are the elevator, the teachers' lounge and the planetarium."

"Whoa. Did you just say planetarium?"

"Yes. We have one located on the roof. It's pretty impressive. But the expensive equipment means students need a specially programmed badge to get in."

"Wow. Just wow."

"Wait until you see our computer setup."

"Can't wait."

I hung the badge around my neck as we headed down the hallway with rows of lockers on either side. It was almost creepily silent.

Ron led me to a stairwell. "Computer Central is on the third floor. It's flanked on either side by the distance learning labs and the foreign language multimedia learning center."

"A multimedia foreign language center? Jeez. We had Latin class in a regular classroom with Mr. Dodd, if he was awake."

"I assure you, there's nothing regular about this school."

"So I'm discovering."

We climbed the three flights of stairs and Ron led me into another hallway. We walked a bit farther before he stopped in front of a door with a keypad. He waved his badge and a green light flashed. He pushed down on the handle and opened the door.

I stepped into a pretty sweet setup. The area consisted of two large rooms divided by a spectacular glass wall with a doorway but no door. Despite the recessed lighting, the area was dim. Neither room had a window. The interior location was meant to protect the equipment. Pipes could burst on an exterior wall and windows could leak or break and damage expensive computers, cables and electrical wiring. An interior positioning made the lab safer and more secure for the equipment and wiring.

I whistled. "Nice. You got antistatic finishing on the floor?"

"Of course. We also have an excellent fire suppression system and all the latest bells and whistles." He swept out a hand toward a desk. "This is my station…well, at least for the three days a week I'm here."

I liked the setup. Convenient to have the system administrator's office next to the Server Room. Some offices use separate rooms, as there are some IT employees who can't stand working in an office without windows. I wasn't one of them. When I was in the virtual zone, I didn't notice any of my surroundings, so a window wasn't important to me.

A glance through the glass wall into the Server Room explained why Ron was a part-time employee. A school this well funded would certainly operate on a headless system. That meant most of the computer functions could be operated remotely by administrative software as needed. Ron could easily handle routine maintenance three times a week at a school like this.

I stepped through the opening in the glass partition and into a significantly colder area. The servers had been stacked neatly in a tower, with one server rack mounted on the wall to the left of a long table holding a couple of laptops. A security camera mounted to the back wall could see most of the server room and the system administrator's office. Beneath the camera in the corner of the room was a thin vertical cable closet, jammed with wires and cables. I took a quick peek at the closet and then stood beneath the camera, looking up.

"Can you do a manual override of the security system from here?"

"Yes." He pointed to a desk in one corner that had been angled to have a view of the door. The table held two laptops. "The first laptop is tied in to the security system. The second one is for our phones. I can do a manual override on the security system from here and monitor it myself if I want. But I rarely do since I'm only here three times a week, and who has time to sit and watch a security camera anyway? It loads to a file that I can review later as needed. Right now we have nine cameras mounted at various locations in the school, including one right here in Computer Central. Unfortunately, it's not directly tied in to our system, which makes it a pain for me to operate remotely. Most of the time, I'll just call and request that the security company adjust camera angles or run routine checks rather than do them myself if something needs to be done on a day I'm not here. It's the same setup with our phones."

I shrugged. "Kind of poor planning to have three separate systems, but in this case, it probably saved you some grief from the students. So far, no kids have hacked in to the phone or security systems?"

"Well, we've had some trouble with kids setting off the fire and tornado alarms, but those controls are also available within our general system. So, no, not that I know of."

I tried not to smile. "Can you provide me with a laptop and passwords so I can have a look around?"

"Sure." He set up a laptop for me on the table with the security and phone laptops and got me started.

"I'm going to help some teachers who've asked for assistance, so I'll be back in a bit."

"Take your time. I don't need any hand-holding."

"That's good to know."

After he was gone, I logged in to the system and took a look around. Top-notch system with a solid firewall and good protection. Unfortunately there were a lot of ins to the system. A slew of teacher, student and administrator accounts, as well as general accounts from the math lab, the English lab, the fine arts lab, six different science and engineering labs, the weather lab and several computer labs. Ugh. This wouldn't be easy by any stretch of the imagination. And I had a big imagination.

I leaned back in the chair and flexed my fingers. Now came the real work.

Fingers on the keyboard.

Head in the game.

Just the way I liked it.

THREE

THE NEXT MORNING I went in to work as usual at X-Corp. My sniffing around the high school's network and system had given me an idea and I'd pinged Finn the night before to see if he was available in the morning. He asked me to come down to his office at nine thirty. So, at nine twenty-five, I refreshed my coffee in the break room and headed to his office.

His door sat half-open and he was talking to someone. I peeked in and Finn saw me.

"Come in, come in." He gestured for me to enter. I closed the door behind me.

A man with balding hair and a bit of a paunch sat in one of Finn's chairs. Ben Steinhouser, the other bigwig of X-Corp and a legend at the NSA where he used to work before he retired and got picked up by Finn for a job. Even after working together for several months, it was weird for me to talk to Ben like a normal person because he was freaking legendary within our field. But he treated me like I had a brain, and I appreciated him for it.

"Hello, Lexi." Ben balanced a laptop on his knees and didn't look up. "Finn was just telling me about your new assignment. Going to take on some kids, I hear."

I plopped into the chair next to Ben. "Yeah, lucky me."

Ben lifted his gaze to look at me from above his spectacles. "Do I detect a hint of concern in your tone?"

"More than just a hint. One of the more unfortunate trends in cybersecurity is that it is becoming less of a tech problem and more a people-centric issue."

"Ah." Ben snapped his laptop shut. "Let me guess. The students are getting in through the teachers and professional staff."

"They're smart. The school has a part-time IT guy who is capable, but honestly, he's no match for these kids."

Finn came around his desk and perched on the front edge. "Well, that's why they hired us."

"Yes. But the solution isn't going to be a simple one. This is largely a people-centric problem. I can see already it's going to have to be a combination approach, which is going to be difficult for me to balance."

"Because?" Finn crossed his legs out in front of him.

I rotated my neck to release the tension that was building there. "Because I have to convince the kids that what they're doing is wrong."

"Teenagers. Good luck with that."

"I appreciate your vote of confidence, Ben. Not."

"Just being realistic. So what's your strategy, Lexi?"

I forced myself to continue before I chickened out. "Well, it's a bit of an unorthodox approach, and I'm not sure Bonnie, the headmistress of the school, will approve. Technically, I'm not even sure I approve and it's *my* idea. But after turning it over in my head for a while, I think it's our best shot of solving this problem for the school once and for all."

Ben lifted an eyebrow. "Okay, I'm intrigued. You have my full attention."

"Mine, as well," Finn added.

I took a deep breath. "Well, I think the best way to

figure out exactly how and why they are getting in is for me to become one of them. A student, I mean."

Finn blinked, clearly in shock. He held up a hand in a stopping motion. "Wait. *What*? Did you just say you want to pose as a high school student?"

"Well, let me make it perfectly clear. I don't *want* to pose as a high school student. Technically, I'd rather face down a post-apocalyptic zombie swarm with nothing more than a nail file than go back to high school again. High school was one of the worst periods of my life. Ever. But I think the best solution lies within this plan."

Finn stared at me in disbelief, so I tried another approach.

"I actually got the idea from Ron, the school's IT guy. He mistook me for a student when he first met me. Even Bonnie asked me how old I am. I think I could pull it off."

"Clever." Ben regarded me thoughtfully. "Really clever. I think it's a solid idea."

I looked at him. "You do?"

Finn pushed off the desk. "Seriously, Ben? You think this would work?"

"I do. It's creative and innovative."

Finn began to pace the office. "But she's twenty-five years old."

I held up a hand. "Hey. Hello. I'm in the room here."

They ignored me.

Ben leaned back in his chair. "So what if she's really twenty-five? We both know she could easily pass for seventeen or eighteen. Put her in a ripped pair of jeans and a T-shirt, keep her hair up in that ponytail she likes to wear, and slap a backpack on her. She'd fit right in. I'm serious. Look at her."

Both men turned to stare at me. Self-conscious, I reached up and touched my ponytail. While I appreciated Ben's full support, I wasn't sure I was thrilled with his utter certainty that I could pass as seventeen or eighteen. I had expected at least a *bit* more resistance.

I cleared my throat. "Um, the students wear uniforms. Technically, I'd be in a green-and-white plaid skirt, white polo shirt and green sweater, not ripped jeans."

"Hell, that's even better." Ben slapped his thigh. "She'll blend in perfectly."

"I'm not sure about this," Finn said.

"Why?" Ben shifted in his seat. "Lexi has accurately described the situation. We all know it's going to be near impossible to stop the hacking because every damn student at the school is an insider threat. These are smart kids. Lexi can isolate the networks and the system all she wants, but all the kids need is one teacher who forgets to shut down or leaves their password taped to their desk. This is an organized group with a leader. Finding the ringleader and teaching the group a lesson from the inside—one hacker to another—is *exactly* the way to shut this group down and keep it down. We don't want these kids to get a taste for what it's like to cross the line from a little harmless hacking to illegal cracking. In order to get the kids to listen, she has to become one of them. Her talent alone will be enough to get her noticed by the best and the brightest in the school and they should bring her right into the group. Once she's in, the hard part is done."

I decided it was time for me take control of the conversation.

"Well, I don't know if it would be *that* simple, Ben,

but it would definitely be a start to determining how and why they're cracking, and what I can do about it."

I glanced over at Finn and rubbed my temples. "Look, Finn, the group at the school is apparently quite well organized and has a ringleader. I need to find out who it is and give him or her a lesson from the inside. This is exactly the way to shut this group down. Ben gets it. In order to get them to listen to me and understand what I'm saying, I have to become one of them to show them I *am* one of them."

"So, you're certain going undercover like this will help you shut them down just like that?"

"Not just like that, but I have a plan."

"What if someone recognizes you? You've been on a television show. Bonnie recognized you."

I shrugged. "Plausible deniability. If I'm recognized I can say I'm sometimes mistaken for that woman on the television show. No biggie, really. I can handle it. It will take me all of thirty minutes to create an alternate identity that Bonnie or Ron can upload to the school system. The kids that matter will check me out there."

"Agreed," Ben said emphatically. "Not to mention that I hardly recognized you on that show and I *know* you. The clothes and hairstyles made you look really different—in a good way, of course. Not that you don't look good now. I didn't mean that to be an insult. Just you don't look good in that glamorous, really pretty way on a daily basis. Except I didn't mean that in a sexually harassing way."

"Jeez. I know, Ben."

"Good, because these days a guy can't say a thing about a woman without getting into trouble. That being said, I'd suggest changing your hair color as an extra precaution. Go blonde. I guarantee no one would recognize you then."

My mouth fell open. "Blonde?"

"No one on this planet, perhaps in the entire universe, would recognize you then."

"I don't know if that's necessary." My stomach lurched queasily.

He chuckled. "Going undercover as a high school student is less extreme than dyeing your hair?"

"Totally."

Finn looked between Ben and me. "Do you think you can really pull this off, Lexi?"

"I don't know. Maybe. I'm definitely on the fence about the blonde thing. But, regardless of whether I could actually pull it off, I still think it's the right approach, in spite of my anxiety about reliving the absolute worst period of my life."

He gave me a small smile. "You're not the same girl you were then."

"No, thank God, I'm not."

Finn pushed his fingers through his hair, paced a few steps more. "This is all a bit tricky. Do you think we can we convince Ms. Swanson this is the right path?"

I lifted my hands. "You're the lawyer with the wicked persuasive skills. You tell me."

"Is there no other way?"

"Well, there are lots of other ways, but none of them will keep the kids out permanently. This may not work either, but I believe it has the best chance. They'll take me more seriously, especially from the inside. Besides, I know what to say and how to say it in their language in order to explain the gravity of the situation. Been there, done that, if you know what I mean."

Ben gripped his laptop and stood, pushing himself up on one arm of the chair. "She's right. It's a good plan, Finn. Do as she says. Work your magic on Ms. Swanson."

"Easy for you to say. The boss always has to do the dirty work."

I rose, as well. "No pity party for you. At least *you're* not dyeing your hair blonde—not that I've agreed to that—or going back to high school."

"There's that." He sighed. "All right, team. I trust your instincts. Guess I'm the last on board. Let's do this."

Just like that I was headed back to high school. Maybe this time around, geek girls would rule.

FOUR

I PICKED UP my phone and saw I had a text from an unknown number. I punched the button.

First real date tonight. Dinner. Dress casual. Pick you up at seven o'clock.

Slash. He wanted to go to dinner. On a date. I blew out a breath. Jeez, now the real relationship stuff started. In comparison, sex suddenly seemed easy.

I read the text again. Dress casual. What the heck did that mean? Jeans, sweatpants, or just not an evening gown? Why couldn't he have been more specific?

I tried to calm down. I had until seven o'clock to figure it out.

I did some work and then strolled out of my office and stopped by the cubicle of Ken Kurisu, one of my assistants.

"Hey, Ken."

He looked up. "Hey, Lexi. What's up?"

"I have a question to ask you."

"Ask away."

"It's not work-related."

"Okay. So what is it?"

My cheeks felt warm. "Well, um, if you were to ask a girl to dress casual, what would that mean?"

"This is a girl I like?"

"Yes."

"Do you want me to be completely candid? I mean, you are my boss after all and this might be awkward."

"Oh." I hesitated. "I don't want you to feel as awkward as I feel right now, but I really could use some advice."

He laughed. "Okay, then I would want her dressed in some fancy lingerie."

"Lingerie is considered casual?"

"Yeah, it sure is."

My cheeks got even hotter. "To go out to dinner?"

"Okay, I was just kidding. Sort of."

"Sort of?"

He stared at something over my shoulder and smiled.

"Ken."

Silence.

"Ken!"

He blinked. "Huh?"

"I can't wear lingerie to a restaurant. Well, I guess I could, but it would have to be under some kind of clothes. Casual clothes. Define *casual* in this setting."

He blinked. "This is for you? *You*? You're going on a date?"

"What? Is that so hard to believe?"

"Ah, no. Not really."

I sighed. "Look, just tell me what I'm supposed to wear."

"Damn, you *are* going on a date." He grinned. "That's pretty cool. Well, I guess casual depends on which restaurant he's taking you to. Do you know where?"

"No."

"Okay. Just to play it safe, I'd wear a nice pair of slacks with heels and a slinky little blouse."

"I don't have a slinky little blouse."

"Just put some lingerie beneath an ordinary blouse. Then unbutton the blouse a bit. Voilà, you have slinky."

"Unbuttoning it makes it slinky?"

"Hell, yes."

I hesitated. "I'm not sure I could do that."

"Sure you could. You asked me to define casual. That would definitely meet his requirement of casual."

"You're sure?"

"Of course, I'm sure. I'm a guy, aren't I?"

"That's true. Okay, thanks, Ken."

"Anytime."

I SHOWERED, THEN dried my hair. Time for the hard part. I had a clean pair of black slacks, but I couldn't figure out which blouse I should pick to go with it. I laid out my lingerie on the bed. Other than the standard white and nude cotton bras and panties, I had only a black bra with no matching undies, a red padded bra and four matching thongs (long story how I got those) and a purple bra with sequins and matching underwear as a result of my one disastrous foray as a stripper (an even longer story). After a long consideration, I chose the purple ensemble and picked my purple blouse to go on top. I unfastened the top button, but you could only see a glimpse of my throat. I should have asked Ken whether the bra was supposed to show a little bit or a lot. I unbuttoned one more. My neck was visible, but no hint of the bra. Jeez, why couldn't there be some sort of manual to determine the correct procedure?

Thank God for the Internet. I sat down in front of my laptop and Googled how many buttons was standard to unbutton on a woman's blouse. Unfortunately, all the answers referred to men and how many buttons they could politely unfasten once they took off a tie. Apparently men needed all the fashion advice. Unbuttoning blouses was left completely in the hands of women who—with the exception of me—knew exactly how many to unbutton to define casual. Standing in front of the mirror, I unbuttoned one more. Now I could see the edge of the purple bra.

Sighing, I decided to leave it for the time being and worry about the rest of me. My hair was long and loose. Remembering Ben's words about how young I looked with my hair in a ponytail, I left it down. I went to the bathroom and swiped on some mascara and lip gloss. I probably should have done more, but I'd already started to get cranky. What I really wanted to do was put on my sweatpants and play Hollow Realm while eating cornflakes. I was emotionally exhausted and I hadn't even set one foot out of my apartment yet.

There was a soft knock at the door. I peeked out the peephole and saw Slash standing there. I opened the door.

"So, now that we're dating you knock on the door?"

Slash was a master at entering rooms without needing a key or an invitation. He had conquered my door a long time ago, despite my fancy alarm system.

He lifted an eyebrow. "You're giving me permission to enter at will?"

"You've *always* entered at will."

"But not with the same purpose."

"What purpose is that?"

He leaned across the threshold and kissed me. "This." He murmured something in Italian against my lips. I felt my knees getting weak as he deepened the kiss.

A throat cleared and I opened my eyes. My neighbor

Jan Walton and her seven-year-old son, Jaime, stood at their door, staring openmouthed at me.

I stepped back from Slash, my cheeks heating. "Ah, hey, Jan. Jaime. How are you guys? Um, this is Slash."

"Lexi?" Jan seemed shocked to see me kissing a guy. Okay, it *was* kind of shocking, given the fact that it was me and I was engaging in a public display of affection in the hallway of my apartment complex. I hadn't been thinking, which happened to me a lot when he kissed me.

Jaime, who was high-functioning autistic, only had eyes for Slash. "Did you know that human bodies contain ten times more bacteria than human cells? Up to five hundred differing kinds of bacteria can live on our skin at any given time. By putting your mouth on her like that you have likely exchanged no fewer than one hundred thousand germs, many of which have the potential to turn into something dangerous."

Jan snapped her mouth shut. "Jaime! Oh, I'm sorry, Lexi."

I glanced over at Slash, who didn't seem perturbed or embarrassed by Jaime's comments. I tried to think of a quick way to alert Slash to Jaime's autism, but before I could say anything, he took two steps and knelt down in front of the boy.

"True. But did you also know that kissing is a critical way to strengthen our immune system? The germs we exchange by kissing are usually so weak and varied that, instead of harming us, they help us build our resistance so when we encounter truly dangerous germs, our bodies are better prepared to fight them."

Jaime's eyes widened. "You were making Lexi stronger?"

"Exactly."

Jaime looked over at me. "I like Lexi. Can you do it again?"

Jan stifled a laugh. "Not right now, he can't." She held out a hand. "Nice to meet you, Slash."

Slash rose and took her hand, lifting it to his lips and kissing it. "I assure you, the pleasure is all mine."

Jan shot me a questioning glance. As Slash returned to me, she fanned herself behind his back. I tried not to roll my eyes, but I couldn't help the little smile that rose to my lips.

"Lexi, we need to have coffee. *Soon.*"

"Sure, Jan," I called out as Slash and I entered my apartment.

After he closed the door behind us, I turned to him. "Did you know Jaime was autistic?"

He nodded. "*Si,* I'm familiar with autism."

"How?"

He kissed my cheek. "That's a story for another time. Are you ready for dinner?"

I looked down at my outfit. "I'm not sure. Do I look okay?"

He took a step back and studied me. Then he reached out and fingered the edge of my bra. "Pretty."

"Well, Ken said lingerie defined casual."

His hand dropped. "Ken?"

"Kenji Kurisu. My assistant at work. I asked him to define casual dress and he said lingerie."

"Ah, I see. *Cara,* if you have any questions about what to wear for me, you can always come straight to the source."

"I know. I just…"

"Just what?"

"Well, this stuff doesn't come intuitively to me. You're

my boyfriend now. I just can't ask you about *everything*. In my own defense, I went online, but I couldn't find out how many buttons were proper to unbutton and still be considered casual. Ken said I had to unbutton some of them to make it slinky…"

Slash let out a low growl and pulled me into him again. "Let's stop talking about Ken." He glanced down at my unbuttoned shirt and then back up to my face. A smile touched his lips. "You look just right."

"I unbuttoned the proper number?"

He started walking me backward, holding me in his arms the whole time. "You unbuttoned perfectly. So perfectly that we are going to be late to dinner."

I turned my wrist and glanced at my watch. "Actually, unless we're going somewhere really far away, we should have plenty of time."

He started nuzzling my neck as he walked me into my bedroom. "Trust me. Dinner will be late."

I felt the edge of the bed behind my legs. I fell back on it when Slash released me. He shrugged out of his leather jacket.

"Oh." It took me a moment to get there. "Oh!"

He unfastened his shoulder holster and set it and his gun on my dresser. "We're going to have our appetizer first." Reaching out, he unfastened another button on my blouse and then another.

I looked up at him. "Okay. So, what's on the menu for our appetizer tonight?"

He smiled, lifting my chin with his fingertips. "Something delicious."

FIVE

WE WERE TWO hours late. Totally worth it.

Slash assisted me with re-dressing. He buttoned my blouse one higher than I had done myself.

When I looked at him questioningly, he kissed the tip of my nose. "I have to maintain some level of decorum at dinner."

I tried to smooth my rumpled hair. "I had no idea that unbuttoning a blouse would lead to that. However, I believe that continued field research—the kind we are currently engaging in—is important to broaden our knowledge on this subject. We should do it again and soon."

He chuckled. "I've created a vixen. Let's go eat. I'm starving."

"What? The appetizer wasn't filling enough?"

He growled, pulling me to my feet. "Don't tempt me. When it comes to you, I'm discovering I have less willpower than I thought."

I laughed, pleased by my witty comeback.

Slash drove to an Indian restaurant called Royal Tandoor Indian Cuisine, located in Laurel, Maryland, not too far from my apartment. Despite our late arrival and the fact that the place was packed, the maître d' led us to a small table in the corner of the restaurant near the window. The restaurant was lovely with Indian décor and what looked like gorgeous handcrafted furniture. Our table was set away from the main area and in a semiprivate alcove. Slash, as always, claimed the seat facing the entrance. He held out my chair as I sat and the maître d' handed us menus. As we read the offerings by candle-light, Slash asked if I'd like to try a glass of Indian wine.

"Sure."

A few minutes later a waiter appeared with two glasses and a bottle. He poured a bit in Slash's glass. Slash swirled it and took a taste, then nodded. The waiter poured more in our glasses, then asked us if we were ready to order. I ordered tandoori chicken while Slash asked for the vegetable biryani.

I glanced around the restaurant. "So, where is the FBI tonight?"

It was kind of a running joke between us. Slash apparently knew so much sensitive information he had an FBI detail around the clock. I knew it wasn't an easy thing for him to be constantly followed by government agents, but I thought he'd done a good job living with it the best he could.

"I told them to blend."

I looked around the room, but didn't notice anyone out of place. That was the idea, I guess.

Slash followed my gaze and smiled. "They're outside in a vehicle. We're alone in here."

I was glad for at least a little privacy.

Slash lifted his glass. "To our first official date."

I raised mine and clinked it against his. "May it be as memorable as the appetizer."

"Indeed." He smiled and took a sip. "So, what's new?"

"With what?"

"With whatever you want to talk about. Work, friends, whatever."

"Oh, this is the part where I have to talk. Okay, let me

think. Well, X-Corp caught a case at a D.C. high school for gifted kids today. I'll be the lead on it."

"Interesting. What's up?"

"Kids keep hacking in to the computer system and changing grades and schedules, among other things."

"Sounds like fun."

"Yeah, for the kids. Not so much for the adults. The kids have created a clandestine group called the WOM-BATs and they're causing havoc."

I didn't have to explain WOMBAT to Slash. He chuckled. "Creative."

"I know, right? My mission is to keep the students out permanently. Given the fact that everyone is so plugged in to the system, including these kids, I won't be able to rely on a simple tech solution."

He nodded, lifting the glass to his lips and sipping. "The adults are the weak link."

"Exactly."

"So, what's your approach?"

"I'm thinking to go undercover as a student at the school to see if I can figure out who, why, and how they are breaking in."

He choked, nearly spewing his wine.

I looked at him with concern. "Slash? Are you okay?"

He coughed and pressed his napkin to his mouth. "I'm okay, *cara*. Come again. You're going undercover at a high school?"

"That's the plan. Slash, do you think I look eighteen?"

He stared at me for a long moment. "I *think* that's a trick question."

"Well, the reason I ask is because I wasn't prepared for the enthusiasm with which Ben Steinhouser agreed I could pull this off. He said all I had to do was to wear the school uniform, dye my hair blonde and wear a back-pack, and I'd look eighteen all over again. Easy as pie, he says. Finn didn't seem to think I could make it work."

Slash just stared at me.

"Slash? Are you listening?" I snapped my fingers in front of his face.

"You never cease to surprise me."

"You mean that in a good way, right?"

He let out a breath. "It means that right now I'm still trying to follow this conversation."

"Why? Going back to high school is not a complex subject."

"The problem is I didn't hear anything you said after that part about wearing a schoolgirl uniform and going blonde."

I rolled my eyes. "I didn't say I was going to go blonde. I said Ben suggested it to help disguise me in case anyone recognizes me from my abbreviated stint on television."

Slash chuckled and reached across the table, cover-ing my hand with his. "Okay, I'm focused now. Let's go back to the beginning. First, there's nothing wrong with a woman looking young for her age."

"So you *do* think I look eighteen."

"I *think* that you can make people believe almost any-thing with the right attitude, effort and disguise, even if it's just jeans and a backpack. I speak from experience."

"Okay, I guess you're right. It's just that both Bonnie and Rob asked me how old I was when I went to check out the school. Now that I think about it, so did the am-bassador during our initial meeting. No one could believe I was old enough to handle their problem."

"Good thing we know better." He squeezed my hand.

"So who is this ambassador? I think you'd better tell me the whole story."

I gave him the quick rundown of the situation. He listened, sipping his wine until I'd finished. "Hmmm. I can see how you came to the conclusion that becoming one of them would be the right approach."

"Do you have any better ideas?"

"In this particular case, no. But how comfortable are you with the prospect of going back to high school?"

"Truthfully, I'm dreading it. I'm hoping it will take no more than a week or two. First, Finn has to convince Bonnie Swanson, the headmistress, that this is the best way to solve her problem. If she agrees, I'll have to consult with Ron to determine which kids are the most likely to be involved. Then I'll have to make sure I'm in some of their classes so I can catch their attention."

"Who's Ron?"

"The IT guy at the school."

"Okay."

The waiter brought us our soup. It was spicy.

"Oh, my God. This soup is so good."

Slash tried his. "It's always excellent here."

I spooned in another mouthful and swallowed. "Is it still my turn to talk?"

"There don't have to be turns. If you have something to say, just say it. Whenever you want."

"I feel like I'm monopolizing the conversation. Surprisingly, it's not that hard to talk to you."

"Why is that surprising? We've never had a problem with conversation."

"That was before we were dating."

"Dating isn't going to change that." He lifted his wine-glass. "What else is on your mind?"

"Well, I told Basia about us."

The glass paused midway to his lips. "Really?"

"Really. She didn't freak out as much as I expected."

"That's good, I guess."

"She's also dating Xavier."

"I thought she was already dating him."

"She is. Well, was. I mean she's usually dating a lot of guys at the same time. Don't ask me how she does it, but it works for her. Anyway, she decided to be exclusive with Xavier."

Slash set his glass down without taking a drink. "Why?"

"I guess she likes him. A lot."

"Interesting."

"My thought exactly." I played with my napkin. "The thing is, I'm not sure how I feel about it. I just hope she's careful with his feelings. It would be terrible if she hurt Xavier, and she could *really* hurt him. I don't want that to happen."

"He's a big boy."

"He's also my friend."

Slash ran his finger across the rim of his wineglass. "You're unusually protective of the Zimmerman twins. You've known them for some time."

"Well, not as long as Basia, but long enough. We're pretty darn close. Other than Basia, they're my best friends in the world. I don't have the greatest social skills, but Xavier and Elvis—especially Elvis—take me the way I am. They understand me on an intuitive level. I get them in the same way."

Something had changed in the atmosphere, but I couldn't figure it out. I picked up my glass, took a sip, and then set it down.

"Slash, we're exclusive, right?"

His eyes narrowed. "Utterly."

The predatory way he looked at me made my breath hitch in my throat. "Okay. Just checking."

"That's nonnegotiable."

"I didn't intend to negotiate. We just hadn't exactly talked about it. Besides, it's not like you have to worry about that with me. You're my first boyfriend *ever*. I barely know what I'm doing with you. That I could figure it out with someone else, potentially at the same time, is unimaginable."

"Good." He smiled, but it seemed forced, like he was actually worried I might want to start dating around, which, if he took a minute to think about it, was beyond ridiculous. Unless he was worried about Finn, which he shouldn't be because I'd already told him I wasn't capable of working for and dating the same guy. Besides, Finn had been cool about the whole sort-of-break-up thing, which I really, really appreciated.

I opened my mouth to say something else when Slash started staring at something over my shoulder. I began to turn around and follow his gaze when he said, "Don't."

I froze. "What is it?"

He fiddled with a ring on his right hand. It was silver with an antique setting that held a large black stone. "Stay here. I'll let you know in a minute."

He rose from the table. Unable to stop myself, I glanced over my shoulder and saw him walk slowly past the maître d', who was speaking to a man with cropped black hair and a dusky complexion. The man was maybe of Indian or Middle Eastern descent. It was hard to tell from there.

I watched as the maître d' handed the man a bag that

looked like carryout food. In return the dark-haired man handed him some cash. It all appeared harmless enough.

Slash crossed his arms casually as he walked past them again. Neither man seemed to notice. I turned around in my seat just as Slash returned to the table and threw a bunch of bills down.

"I told you not to look."

"I just took a peek. Sorry. I couldn't help myself."

He rolled his eyes. "Come on, *cara*, let's go."

"Where are we going?"

"I'll tell you on the way."

SIX

IT'S NOT LIKE I've been on a lot of dates, but on the few I've had, I actually *ate* dinner before leaving.

Whenever I was with Slash, normal seemed never to be the norm.

"What about the rest of our dinner?" I asked, taking a last whiff of the delectable smells.

"We'll eat later. I'll talk to the maître d'."

Slash left and spoke quietly to him. Moments later our waiter magically appeared with our coats. I tugged mine on as Slash pulled me out the door and into the cold December air.

"Hurry, *cara*."

"Who was that guy?" I zipped up my coat.

"I'm not sure yet. I sent a picture to be analyzed."

"You took a picture of him?"

Slash tapped his ring. "I've got a miniature camera in here. I think I may have recognized him."

"So that's what you were doing when you passed by him with your arms crossed."

"Exactly."

"Optimum. Can I see how the ring works?"

"Later. I don't want to lose him."

The man walked quickly ahead of us, holding his bag of takeout food and hurrying into the night. "He's headed for that car."

Slash quickly detoured us to his SUV and we hopped

in. He reached into his jacket pocket, pulled out an ear-bud, and then pushed it in his ear as he pulled away from the curb.

"Tango Charlie two-two-four. I'm following a POI. Male, possibly Middle-Eastern, six feet, black hair, wearing a tan jacket and dark pants. At this time, identity is unknown. I sent a facial scan to UFW minutes ago. Concealed pursuit only. I just want to know where he's going. Car is a gold, four-door Honda Civic. License plate reads…"

I leaned forward in the seat. "KEF 7700. Maryland plates."

Slash repeated the license plate number and then listened.

"Affirmative."

The Honda took a right turn and Slash calmly followed from a slight distance, keeping two cars between us. He tapped his ear. "Right on Montgomery Avenue."

"What's a POI?" I asked, keeping my eyes on the Honda.

"Person of interest."

We drove for a minute before I asked, "So, who is this guy?"

Slash shrugged. "I'm not sure. He looks remarkably similar to a man named Mazhar Zogby. Zogby is originally from Pakistan. He came to the United States with his parents in 2001, shortly before 9/11. He was about fourteen at that time. Eight months after the Twin Towers went down, his parents were arrested for laundering money for the *Shahid*, a splinter terrorist group in Pakistan. *Shahid* is a pretty radical group and openly supports al Qaeda. A year later, during the trial where their parents were convicted, Mazhar and his younger brother, Ansari, vanished. We think they may be sleepers."

"Sleepers?"

"Agents sent underground until they are called to action within the U.S."

"I know what sleepers are. But they were just teens when their parents were arrested."

"*Si*, but they aren't kids anymore."

I frowned. "So, you think they may be acting on the orders of these *Shahid* terrorists?"

"It's possible."

"They could be totally innocent."

"They could. But I'm playing it safe. I can't just pass it off as a coincidence when we have recent intelligence this group may be up to something in our area. Just call it a gut feeling."

"I trust your gut, Slash."

"So do I." He smiled as the Honda took a left. "Left on Gorman."

The Honda drove about a minute more and then pulled into a parking lot in front of a complex of multiple three-story apartment buildings. Slash quickly pulled over a half a block back and turned off the lights. He hopped out, just as the man in the Honda emerged carrying his bag of takeout.

"Stay here."

"Okay."

Slash left the ignition running so the car stayed warm. He followed the man on foot until they both disappeared from sight. Minutes ticked by and nothing. I ran a series of long division problems in my head using Vedic mathematics.

Still nothing.

I was fiddling with the radio when I saw the man in the tan jacket return without the food. He looked over his shoulder and then around the parking lot. After yanking on the car door, he scrambled into the Honda and started it. I looked around for Slash. He was nowhere in sight. The FBI was nowhere in sight. Where was a police car when you needed one?

I started to hyperventilate. Should I get out of the car and look for Slash? Follow the guy in the Honda? Sit and wait?

I saw the reverse lights of the Honda come on as the guy pulled out of his spot. I took another look around. No Slash and no FBI-looking car in sight.

Crap.

Before I could talk myself out of it, I slid into the driver's seat. I adjusted the seat so I could reach the pedals better, and pulled away from the curb. When the Honda took a right out of the parking lot, I waited a couple of beats so it wouldn't appear too obvious I was following, then drove after him. Hands shaking, I fumbled in my coat pocket for my phone and tapped in my password.

I pulled up Slash's number and punched it. I could hear it ringing, but there was no answer.

"Okay," I said aloud in an effort to calm myself. "This isn't rocket science, Carmichael. You're just going to follow this guy and see where he goes. No apprehension, no takedown, no biggie. I'm sure Slash wouldn't want to lose him."

Why isn't he answering his phone?

I tried to relax by inhaling deep breaths, holding for five seconds and exhaling. But my heart was beating so hard I thought it might leap out of my chest.

Remembering how Slash had driven, I stayed as far

back as possible without losing sight of the taillights. The Honda went straight and then took a left at the next traffic light. I sped up a bit so I wouldn't miss it and turned left, as well. Two blocks up, the guy pulled the Honda to the curb and got out. I drove past him, took a right at the next corner and then immediately pulled the SUV over at the curb. I hopped out of the SUV, locked it up and pocketed the key. We were in downtown Laurel, Maryland. I jogged around the corner and saw the man in the tan jacket walking toward another building.

I raised the collar on my jacket to shield myself from the cold wind and walked in his general direction. He disappeared between two buildings. I strolled past a defunct fountain and then approached the alley where I'd last seen the guy.

I peeked around the corner to see where he'd gone and looked directly into his face. He yanked me forward into the alley and slammed me backward against a brick wall.

"Who are you? Why are you following me?"

Guess I wouldn't pass my secret agent test anytime soon.

I tried to catch my breath. It wasn't easy. His forearm was pressed up against my windpipe and he had a gun pointed at my head.

"I...was just out for a walk." My voice wavered. Having a gun next to my brain does that to me, I guess.

He pushed harder against my windpipe and I gagged while he reached under my coat and felt up my sides and back.

"Hey!" I managed.

"You don't have a weapon on you."

"Why would I?"

Frowning, he grabbed my purse and stepped back.

Relieved the gun was no longer pointed at my head, I took a couple gulps of air. He pulled the stun gun out of my purse and held it up.

"You use this for protection?"

"Sometimes. I should have thought of it before stepping into the alley. Well, you know what they say about hindsight."

He dropped the stun gun back in my purse and retrieved my wallet. He slid out my license, angling it at the streetlight outside the alley so he could read it. "Lexi Carmichael. I saw you. You were at the restaurant. You *are* following me. Why?"

"Coincidence?"

"What happened to that guy you were with?"

"What guy?"

"Don't play me. Who do you work for? DHS? CIA? DoD?"

"X-Corp in Crystal City. You can check my badge if you don't believe me. It's in my purse."

He fished around in my purse and pulled out my work badge. "X-Corp Global Security and Intelligence? You're the Director of Information Security?"

"At your service. We can solve your cybersecurity issues and have reasonable prices in case you are interested."

He took a step back, his eyes suddenly wide. "Computers. You work in computers. What did you find out?"

"I don't know what you are talking about. Seriously. My brother lives around here, so I was headed out to visit him and…"

He slammed me back against the wall and put the gun to my head. The cold barrel pressed painfully into my scalp. "I'll ask you one more time, and then I shoot. What have you discovered about our plan? I must know."

I opened my mouth to say something when a shadow blocked the light from the streetlight behind his shoulder. "Drop the gun nice and slow."

There was a pause and then the guy lifted the gun from my head. The pressure from my neck disappeared and I saw Slash come into view as he whipped the guy's hands behind his back and cuffed him. Two more men in dark clothes came running and hauled the guy to his feet. The scream of sirens filled the night and I saw no less than a half-dozen police cars screech to a stop.

Slash turned to me. "*Cara*, are you all right? Did he hurt you?"

My legs were shaky, but I steadied myself by holding on to Slash's arm. "I'm fine. Where *were* you?"

He pulled me into a hug. "I got hit from behind. Knocked out for a short time."

"When you didn't answer your phone, I got worried. Are you okay?"

"Fine, now that you are safe. What the hell were you thinking, chasing him?"

"I wasn't chasing him. Just following at a discreet distance, until he parked and got out. I was just going to see where he was going and let you know. But he must have spotted me."

Slash let out a breath. "Before our next date I'm going to give you a lesson in Surveillance 101."

"Maybe we can just eat at home on our next date." My stomach growled.

He smiled and then winced, rubbing the back of his head. "I'll make it up to you. I promise."

"I was just kidding. You need some ibuprofen."

"I'm good as long as you're with me." He slung an arm around me, then steered me to the car. "Let's go."

I pointed at the two guys who were loading the man who'd accosted me into a dark sedan. "Are those the FBI agents?"

"*Si.* They're taking him to the police station. They'll need an official statement from us on what happened."

"Okay. How did you find me?"

"There's a tracker on my car. We weren't far behind you. I toyed with calling you, but I didn't want to distract you."

"I'm just glad you showed up in time."

Slash kissed the top of my head. "You keep bringing me years closer to my grave. We're going to have to talk about that. Did he say anything to you?"

I reached up to touch my neck. "There wasn't much talking. He just kept asking me what I knew. He also freaked out when he saw my work badge and discovered I'm the director of Information Security for X-Corp."

Slash stopped, studied my face. "That bothered him?"

"Yes. He asked me what I knew of their plan."

"What plan?"

"I don't know. You came just after that."

He thought for a moment and we resumed walking toward the car. "Okay. Gives us something to question him about."

"I'm sorry. I should have stayed in the car like you told me."

"No, it pains me greatly to say it, but you did exactly the right thing. Do you know who he is?"

I shook my head.

"Ansari Zogby. Just as I suspected."

"The youngest of those two brothers from Pakistan?"

"*Si*. The results from my photo came back while we were following you in my SUV, which has a tracking device."

"So you were right."

"I was. I followed him to a ground-level apartment. I went around the back and was able to see inside the living room through a gap in the curtains on the patio door. Guess what they were doing inside?"

"I bet playing poker isn't the answer."

"Making bombs. I reported my findings to the FBI and shortly afterward, I got hit from behind." He rubbed the back of his head again.

I gasped. "Holy cow. Did they capture the people in the apartment?"

"While the FBI came to my rescue, they got away. Except for Ansari Zogby, thanks to you. But we got most of the materials and the bombs they left behind. There were a great deal of materials there, but not many bombs."

"Maybe they didn't have time to make them yet."

"Perhaps, but we can't assume that. I'm afraid we have to prepare ourselves for the possibility they made many and have them stored somewhere else."

"Wow. That's scary. But at least you have Ansari."

"*Si*. We will question him hard. But it will be very important for you to remember every word he said to you if you can."

"You know I can. I've got a pretty good memory even under duress."

"That's my girl." He hugged me. "After that I'm going to feed you."

"Promises, promises." Then I sighed. "Don't bother. I'll just have something from the vending machine at the police station."

"That's an appalling thought."

"The peanut butter crackers are sometimes edible."

"By whose definition?"

"I'll treat you to a package and then you'll see."

"You will not. We're going to have to work on those taste buds of yours, *cara*."

"Thank goodness. I've been hoping you'd say that."

SEVEN

SLASH AND I SPENT several hours at the police station. While I sipped bitter coffee and ate stale crackers, police officers, the FBI and agents from the Department of Homeland Security questioned me. I didn't have much further to say, as my encounter with Ansari Zogby was pretty short. But I was able to recite every bit of our conversation by heart and was required to do so several times for each different agency.

Finally the police released Slash and me. By the time I got back to my apartment, it was five-twenty in the morning. Slash walked me to the door and I keyed myself in.

"Ugh. I can't believe I have to go to work in a few hours." I punched the code on my alarm. "I have a massive headache from all the talking and no sleep."

"I can speak to your boss if you want. I'll tell him you were involved in matters of national security."

"He's heard that one before." I stood on tiptoe and kissed the tip of his nose. "I can handle Finn. But thanks anyway. Good night...or morning, Slash. It was a memorable first date. I'm going to hit the shower and get dressed for work. A nap at this stage will just make me groggy."

He seemed hesitant to leave, but he gave me a quick kiss. "Be careful, *cara*. I'll check in with you later."

After he left, I showered and got dressed for work. I made a stop at Dunkin' Donuts for an extra-large coffee and a couple of chocolate donuts. I needed the caffeine and sugar rush to keep me awake as I drove to work.

No one was in the office yet, so I sat at my desk, listening to Christmas music while answering email and browsing the daily news on cybersecurity. Finn strolled into my office about seven forty-five.

"Good morning, Lexi. You're in early. I was surprised to get that email from you a half hour ago."

"Well, the early bird catches the worm or, in my case, the hacker. Did you have a chance to talk to Bonnie about our plan yet?"

He took a seat in my visitor's chair and stretched out his legs. "I did. She thought it a bit unorthodox—well, truthfully a *lot* unorthodox—but she likes you. Therefore, like all of us, she trusts you and your judgment. She agreed to it. You must have made a good impression."

"There's a first time for everything."

"Very funny. Anyway, there are some ground rules for you posing as a student, but I'll be drawing them up later. They will protect the school from any liability issues. It's just legal mumbo jumbo and I've got it all taken care of."

"Did you really just say mumbo jumbo?"

"Why? Is that not an appropriate American phrase?"

"It's fine, Mr. Irish. It's just kind of cute how you slipped it into conversation so effortlessly. I think you're becoming quite Americanized."

He rolled his eyes. "Anyway, the point is that I've got the bloody legal side handled. You just stop those kid hackers, okay?"

"Ah, better." My smile faded. "Look, Finn, before you

go, I want to tell you what happened to me last night. I don't want you to hear it from anyone else."

His expression became serious. "Hear what? What happened? Are you okay, Lexi?"

"I'm fine."

I gave him a brief rundown and then sat back in my swivel chair. "I just wanted you to know in case anyone comes here looking for me. I don't want this to reflect badly on X-Corp in any way."

"Reflect badly? You helped stop a group of potential terrorists. I don't see how that could reflect badly on X-Corp."

"Well, unfortunately, they didn't capture the people making the bombs, except for one. That one guy happens to know I work at X-Corp."

Finn frowned. "Are you worried for your safety?"

"Not so much mine as others'. I won't even be here for the next week or so."

Finn nodded. "Right. Just in case, I'll check with Brian and make sure our security procedures are up-to-date. You should make sure your home alarm is working. Don't go out alone anywhere for a while."

"All of that is very good advice. But Finn, there is one more thing I need to do today. It's work related. Sort of."

"What is it?"

"I've got a hair appointment for two thirty."

His eyes widened. "A hair appointment? You're going to do it?"

I sighed. "If I can go back to high school, I can dye my hair. It's all about resolve."

He chuckled. "Hot damn, I can't wait to see this. Text me a selfie, okay?"

"Not in a million years."

THE CLOSER IT GOT to my hair appointment, the more convinced I became that I couldn't do it. I picked up the phone and dialed the hair salon to cancel before slamming down the receiver. Three times. The last time I hung up my hands were shaking so badly I had to put my head between my knees and breathe deeply. I couldn't concentrate on my work or think intelligently. I was a freaking nervous wreck. All because of some stupid hair dye.

Maybe it was exacerbated because I hadn't slept. Or maybe because I'd just faced down a potential terrorist who had held a gun to my head. Or maybe hair dye just freaking terrified me on some primal level.

Whatever the case, I felt extremely anxious.

I began to pace the office. I considered all angles of hair dye from an intellectual perspective. I tried to separate the emotional components from the practical ones. After careful analysis, I didn't think I could go through with it. Desperate, I picked up the receiver and dialed. This time I let it ring through.

"Hello?"

"Hi, Elvis. It's me, Lexi. Do you have a minute?"

"For you, always."

"Thanks. I wondered if you could talk me into something I don't want to do."

"If you don't want to do it, then don't. It's pretty simple."

"I wish it were that easy. See, it's job related."

"My former statement still stands. If you feel like it's against your principles, either work or personal, then don't do it."

"It's just… I… I have to dye my hair blonde in order to disguise myself so I can go undercover at a high school to penetrate a group of hacking students and hope that no one recognizes me from my brief stint on television."

"Silence."

"Hello?"

Silence.

"Elvis, are you still there?"

"Uh…yes. I'm here."

"So, what do you think? Should I dye my hair or not?"

"I think… I think I need more data. You'd better start at the beginning."

I quickly explained my plan for the school, then waited. Elvis listened without interrupting once. I imagined the expression he got on his face when he was thinking. That calmed me.

Finally, he spoke.

"It's a novel approach, Lexi. Oddly ingenious. It might take longer than you think to penetrate the group, but I agree this might be your best bet for putting a permanent end to the student-hacking revolt."

"Thanks. It means a lot to hear you say that. Give me the big picture. Do I have to emotionally and intellectually be prepared to be a blonde longer than a couple of weeks? Because I don't know if I can do that."

"It doesn't matter. This isn't about you being blonde. Think of your hair as nothing more than an accessory or a piece of equipment you need to work this case."

I sat down in my chair. "You mean like a cable or a thumb drive?"

"Exactly. It doesn't matter what color your hair is. It doesn't define you."

"Right. You're absolutely right. Hair color doesn't define me. It disguises me."

"Yes. When it's over, change your hair back if you

want. It's a pretty simple thing, and it's not permanent. You've got this."

I sat up straight. "I've got this. Right. My hair is an accessory to solve this problem. Simple. Logical. Except…"

"Except?"

"I'm freaking scared out of my mind. What if I don't recognize myself when it's said and done?"

"You will. Want me to come along for moral support?"

"Would you? Oh, jeez, Elvis, that would be prime. I'd really appreciate it. I have an appointment at two thirty. Are you sure?"

"Absolutely. Give me the address and I'll meet you there."

"OPEN YOUR EYES."

I shook my head. "I can't."

"Come on, Lexi. Open your eyes. You look great."

I peeked open one eye and saw Elvis leaning over me, his nose almost touching mine. I sat cringing in the stylist's chair, afraid to look in the mirror after an hour of really smelly chemicals, a hair wash, a blow-dry and style.

I felt thoroughly traumatized.

Elvis smiled. I felt better having him here. "It's okay, Lexi. Trust me. You can look now."

I opened the other eye. "How bad is it?"

"It isn't bad at all. It's very pretty."

"But it's blonde."

"Yes, that was the idea, right? Think accessory. You can do this. Just look."

I gulped a breath. "Okay. You're right. I can do this. Besides, it's too late to turn back now."

"Ready?"

I nodded, so Elvis swirled the chair around until it faced the mirror. I blinked. I absolutely didn't recognize myself.

I was blonde. Totally blonde.

It wasn't a platinum blonde, but a darker, warmer blonde with a golden hue. It didn't look as bad as I expected, but it was utterly, totally different from the usual me. It looked like a completely different person looking back at me. There were a couple of people staring at me in the salon and I blushed self-consciously.

I turned my head and my hair swished softly around my shoulders. I was convinced that there was no way on God's green earth that anyone would recognize me, and that made me feel a lot better even if it still freaked me out.

Elvis held out a hand and I took it. He pulled me out of the chair. "You did great, Lexi. A walk in the park, right?"

"Not hardly. But I did it...thanks to you." I gave him a big hug. "You are the best, Elvis. Really. I couldn't have done it without you. You're my rock. Thank you."

His cheeks reddened. "Glad I could help."

"You always do. I guess that's what friends are for."

"I guess so."

EIGHT

AFTER THE HAIR appointment, I went straight home. I checked my email and saw that Finn had sent me confirmation that all the necessary paperwork had been signed with Bonnie and she had created a dossier for me as a new student named Lara Carson. She had also sent a courier to my apartment with a school uniform and shoes in my size. I tried them on and as much as I felt like an idiot, they did make me look significantly younger. Add in the blonde hair and I was statistically confident no one would recognize me.

Lara Carson had been born. We were a go for the undercover operation.

I appreciated Bonnie's foresight in giving me the same initials. The name was also short and sweet, which would make it easier for me to remember. I spent the next hour or so creating Lara Carson and uploading my information to the school's system. When I was done, I sat back and examined my work. It wasn't perfection, but it was good enough to fool any curious kids who might try to check me out.

I'd texted Slash that I was going to bed early as I had school in the morning. He texted me back that he'd come over tomorrow. He was involved in the questioning of Ansari Zogby anyway and would update me when he had the chance.

Despite my nervousness about returning to high school, I was out as soon as my head hit the pillow.

The next morning, I took a shower and got dressed in the school uniform—a green, white and black plaid skirt, a white polo with the school emblem, a green school sweater and black shoes. I looked really…young. My stomach felt shaky just imagining myself in high school again, so I didn't spend too much time looking in the mirror.

I grabbed my backpack and drove to school. It all felt a bit surreal. Returning to high school wasn't at the top of my bucket list, but since this had been my idea, I had no one to blame but myself if it didn't work out.

I joined a group of students entering the school, hunching my shoulders and shoving my hands into my pockets. The wind was biting cold.

I stepped inside the building and headed for the office. My nerves jangled. I'd met the secretary, Marge, on my earlier visit to the school. She wasn't in on the deception—only Bonnie and Ron were—so I hoped she wouldn't recognize me.

The office was really busy. I sat in one of the visitor's chairs and read a teacher magazine, waiting until things calmed down. After the first bell rang, I stood and walked over to her desk. It was empty. She must have stepped out when I wasn't looking. I was standing there indecisively when a tall kid with brown hair, piercing green eyes and a mischievous smile strolled into the office.

He came right up to me. "Well, hello there. I haven't seen you before and I *always* notice the blonde girls."

I tried not to roll my eyes. "I'm the new kid on the block."

"Well, welcome, New Kid on the Block. Where's Ms. Eder?"

"Who's Ms. Eder?"

He dipped his head at the empty desk. "The secretary."

I knew her as Marge. "Oh, her. I think she stepped out."

"Excellent." He grinned, slid into her chair and began typing on the keyboard.

My mouth fell open. "What are you doing?"

"Fire alarm at eleven-fifteen. Liven up the day a bit."

He hit a final key with a flourish and bounced into a chair next to me seconds before Ms. Eder stepped into the office. Her gaze locked onto him and she frowned.

"Brandon, seriously? You're in here again? The day just started. What has happened now?"

"A minor misunderstanding between me and Mr. Jouret."

"It's *always* just a misunderstanding."

"It's truly unfortunate. I'm one misunderstood guy."

Marge turned to me and I had my first moment of panic. I let out a breath when I didn't see any recognition in her eyes.

Instead, she sighed. "Go sit down, Brandon. I'll tell Ms. Swanson you're here for the fourth time this week." Her gaze shifted back to me. "Now who are you, exactly?"

Brandon winked. "Yeah, Blondie, you got a name?"

I cleared my throat. Even though I had permission for this deception, I felt quite anxious, which I didn't think was a positive attribute for a master of disguise. "Um, Lara Carson."

Ms. Eder sat at her desk, her fingers poised over the

keyboard. "Ah, yes, here you are. A transfer student. Just a moment and I'll print out your schedule."

A printer chattered in the background and she stood, retrieving a couple pieces of paper. I pulled my winter cap down tighter across my hair and kept my eyes lowered as she approached me.

"Here you go, Lara. I've included a map of the school to help you find your classes, but the teachers will be forgiving for a couple of days while you figure out where to go." She tapped one of the sheets. "Your locker number and combination is here. Your teachers will have the books you require for most of your classes. Here is a tardy slip for today. Would you like me to find someone to walk you to class?"

Brandon stood up. "I volunteer."

Ms. Eder stared at him. "Sit down, Brandon."

"Hey, it was worth a shot."

"I'll find my way just fine," I mumbled.

"Okay. Well, you'll need this, too." She handed me an access badge. I hung it around my neck like I'd seen the other students do. Bonnie had told me she'd have one ready for me and that Ron would have it programmed to be able to enter Computer Central and other rooms typically closed to students so I could come and go as needed.

"You need it to enter the school. Some rooms with expensive equipment are off-limits and specially coded for staff only. Okay?"

"Okay."

"Good. Don't lose it. It will cost you twenty-five dollars to replace it."

"Thanks. I'll be careful."

Ms. Eder rolled her eyes. "Stay away from this one, Lara. He's the resident troublemaker."

Brandon gave an exaggerated sigh. "Ms. Eder tells all the girls that. Sure takes the fun out of school."

I turned to leave when Brandon called out, "Hey, Blondie, take your hat off. School policy. Looks like you're trying to hide under that thing."

Ms. Eder nodded. "He's right. I'm afraid you'll have to leave it with your coat in your locker."

"Sure." I pulled off the hat as I slipped into the corridor.

My stomach felt full of butterflies as I walked down the empty hallway. This wasn't really high school. This was a job and I was an adult. I could easily handle it. I stopped in front of locker 266. I twirled the combination and it opened on the first try. I hung my coat on the metal hook and then added the hat and school sweater. Despite the freezing weather outside, sweat trickled down the back of my neck.

Nerves.

Sighing, I pulled out a notebook, a couple of pens and a scientific calculator out of my backpack. I stuffed my backpack in the locker, closed it and spun the combination.

I took a minute to study my schedule. I'd stacked it with a full array of computer tech and security classes. There was no question the mastermind of WOMBAT was going to be in at least one of these classes, if not all of them. If I were to catch the attention of the leader or other members of this group, I'd have to prove myself in one of these courses and do it quickly. But first I needed a little time to adjust and get the lay of the land, so to speak.

My first class was System Vulnerabilities. I hustled to the classroom, my ponytail swishing back and forth, took a breath and opened the door. The teacher stopped mid-sentence and looked at me in surprise. I felt every eye in the room on me and tried not to cringe.

"Ah, sorry I'm late." I handed him the tardy slip and he looked down at it.

"You're a new student, Miss Carson?"

"Yes."

"You've had some computer classes before?"

"Yes."

"Good. Try to keep up. Welcome to Excalibur Academy. Our course work is quite rigorous here. I'm Mr. Fitzgerald. Sit down."

I took an empty chair in the back of the classroom, pulled out my notebook and pencil and pretended to listen as the teacher began to talk about distributed denial-of-service attacks. I found myself nodding off and had to pinch my leg a couple of times to stay awake. It really felt like old times.

The bell finally rang. Mr. Fitzgerald handed me the class textbook. Expensive, but really heavy. Not wanting to carry it to my next class, I made a beeline for my locker. I turned a corner just in time to see a short, chubby kid being cornered by the drinking fountain by a bunch of tall guys. Other students were crowding around.

A big guy with a brown crew cut got in the kid's face, maneuvering him backward. One of his buddies slipped in behind the kid and got on all fours. The kid took one more step backward and promptly fell over the kneeling guy. He landed on his rear, his books and papers scattering across the floor.

Jeez. Some things never changed.

Crew Cut started laughing along with his buddies. "You're such a damn klutz, Wally. Why don't you look where you're going?"

Although my mind calculated the odds at 3 million to 1 that I'd be successful in stopping him, I darted forward and stood between Crew Cut and Wally. The poor kid was now on his hands and knees, crawling around the floor behind me, trying to retrieve his papers.

I put my hand on Crew Cut's chest. I never would have been this brave when I was really in high school. But in the ensuing years, I'd been threatened, stalked, kidnapped, knifed, held at gunpoint and shot, so frankly, I had no more patience for bullies.

"Back off."

Crew Cut looked surprised at the seriousness of my voice and then his eyes went to his chest where my hand still rested. "Who the hell are you?"

"Someone who is telling you to stop."

His eyes narrowed. "I haven't seen you before."

Before I could say anything, a guy strode out from the crowd and stood next to me. It was Brandon, the kid from the office. "Stand down, Mack. It's her first day. Cut her a break."

Mack looked down at my hand. I still held it against his chest as if I could physically stop a six-foot-two beefed-up guy from advancing on me.

His mouth stretched into a cruel grin. "You do realize you're still touching me. You like it, new girl, don't you? You want me?"

"I *want* you to leave him alone."

He narrowed his eyes as he studied me. "Haven't I seen you before?"

"Yeah, last Thursday. I work as a part-time reception-

ist at the health clinic for sexually transmitted diseases."
I'd once heard Basia say that to a guy she'd wanted to
leave her alone. It seemed rude, but it was the best I could
come up with on a moment's notice.

I scored a hit. The kids laughed and Mack's face reddened. "I'm going to say it again. Move out of my way
or else."

His two friends tried to crowd us. Neither Brandon
nor I budged.

Brandon stiffened beside me. "Come on, Mack. Stand
down."

Mack clenched his fist. "Last chance, Brandon. Move
aside or you become a part of this."

I heard Wally stand up behind us. He might have
whimpered.

I crossed my arms against my chest, figuring they'd
be closer to my face if Mack actually decided to take
a swing, which was looking more and more likely. "I
don't know about Brandon, but I'm not moving. Leave
the kid alone."

I saw disbelief in his eyes. Hadn't anyone in the entire
freaking school stood up to him even once?

"Are you for real, girl? Do you know who I am?"

"Other than a first-class jerk?"

His face flushed purple. "Do you know who my father
is? You'll be kicked out of school by tomorrow. Think
about it." He stuck his finger in my face.

Angrier than I should have been, I slapped his finger
away and saw the surprise in his eyes. "No thinking required, Mack. I'm not engaging in a battle of wits with
you, especially when you're unarmed."

There were some more snickers and then a teacher
appeared. The crowd instantly dispersed.

The teacher looked between Mack, Brandon and me. "Is everything okay here? What's going on?"

I turned around. Wally had disappeared.

Mack shrugged. "Nothing at all, Mr. Jouret. Brandon and I were just getting to know the new girl. Right, Bran?"

Brandon met my eyes. "Yeah. That's just what we were doing."

Mack hoisted his backpack on his shoulder. "Well, see you around, new girl. Glad you're here. Looking forward to knowing you better." He smirked at me and then walked down the hall with his friends.

Mr. Jouret turned to Brandon with a frown on his face. "I would urge you to move on to your next class immediately, Mr. Steppe. No more loitering and no causing trouble. I don't want to have to send you to the office twice in one morning."

Brandon winked at me. "Hey, I wasn't even here, Mr. Jouret." He disappeared down the hallway.

The teacher appraised me. "You're new?" He had a faint accent but I couldn't place it.

"Yes. My name is, um, Lara."

"Well, welcome, Lara." He glanced over his shoulder at a girl who was closing her locker. "Would you mind showing Lara to her next class? She's new here."

The girl twirled the dial on her lock, then walked over to me. "Sure, what class do you have?"

The bell rang as I fumbled in my backpack. "I don't know. Shoot. I'm late again."

"Don't worry." Mr. Jouret pulled two pieces of green paper out of his pocket and scribbled on them. "Here are your tardy slips. Where's your schedule?"

I handed it to him.

"Hmmm...you've got Digital Investigations and Forensics. Second floor. That's a pretty advanced computer class. You got some background to go with that?"

"Yes."

"That's the class I've got, too," the girl said. "Come on."

"Make haste, ladies."

"We will, Mr. Jouret," the girl called out as we hurried down the hallway.

I followed her to a stairwell and up a set of stairs.

She looked over her shoulder. "I saw what you did for Wally."

"Who was that jerk with the crew cut?"

"Mack? He's an idiot. Thinks he's God's gift to women now that he's captain of the wrestling team. But everyone's afraid of him. He's going to target you now, and no one is going to help you."

"Except for Brandon."

She sighed. "Yes, except for Brandon. He has a knack for getting into all kinds of trouble."

"I thought this was a school for technologically gifted and talented kids. Mack hardly seems the type."

She laughed. "Technologically gifted. Sure, that's the public face. But look around. You aren't going to find this level of equipment and instruction via funds provided through the state or the District of Columbia."

For the first time I wondered. Bonnie had said it was a private school, not a state-funded one. Apparently I'd made an inaccurate assumption about admissions standards. "I guess you're right."

"Well, there is a decent percentage of gifted and talented kids that get in, some on their own merit and some subsidized by scholarships or the city. But if your family has the money and you want to come here—trust me, you're in. Which explains why we are chock-full of self-important rich kids."

"What about you?"

"Me? Well, I could have got in here on my brain alone, but I didn't. I'm here because of my dad. He's the Irish ambassador."

"You're Piper?" I blurted it out without thinking.

She turned around, stared at me. "How did you know my name?"

"Ah, I heard someone talking about the Irish ambassador's kid this morning in the office while I was waiting for my schedule. You...you don't have an accent."

"I can turn it on and off at will. Don't want to draw too much attention to myself. What were they saying about me in the office this time?"

"This time?"

"Yeah, they're always blaming me for something."

"That sucks."

"Tell me about it." We reached the classroom door and Piper reached for the handle. "You'll have to tell me later what they were saying."

Jeez. At least I had a whole class period to make something up.

NINE

It seemed like the day would never end. I questioned myself at least a hundred times as to whether my approach would be successful. I had hoped to talk more with Piper, but the unexpected fire drill (thanks, Brandon) ate up most of the class time. Then Piper disappeared from the classroom the minute the bell rang. I checked my schedule and saw it was time for lunch. My heart sank. Great, now I had to suffer through gross cafeteria food.

I returned to my locker, deposited my books and notebooks, then followed the crowd until I found the cafeteria. I waited in line. This was not the cafeteria food of my youth. This food actually looked *and* smelled good.

"Wow," I said, staring at the choices behind the glass.

"It's catered," the girl in front of me said. "I'm a freshman and I've already gained five pounds this year."

She looked skinny as a stick, but I kept silent. I took a ham-and-cheese sandwich, an apple, bottled water and some curly fries and loaded them on a tray. I paid cash and then headed into the cafeteria. I felt the same sinking in my stomach as I'd felt every day in high school—where to sit and with whom. I looked around the room and fell upon a lone figure sitting alone at a table.

Wally.

I made a beeline for his table. He looked up when I arrived and didn't seem happy to see me.

"Hey, Wally. Can I sit here?"

"I wouldn't if I were you."

"Why?"

He jerked his head toward another table where Mack, his friends and a couple of girls sat eating and laughing.

I sat down anyway. "What's their deal?"

"They're jerks."

"That goes without saying. Why do they have it in for you?"

"I keep killing the curve in English."

"That's it?"

"That's not enough?"

I sighed. "You're scared of them?"

He took a bite of a sandwich, then dabbed his mouth with a napkin. "In the sense that they make my life miserable, yes."

"Why do you let them?"

He laughed. "How do I stop them? I'm clearly unable to validate myself to their standards and therefore, I don't fit in. High school is what it is. A nightmare of viciousness, exclusivity and myopic vision."

Since I couldn't argue with that, I didn't. I focused instead on eating my lunch. For a while we sat chewing in silence. After a bit, I forced myself to continue the conversation.

"What kind of activities do you do at school?"

He frowned. "Activities?"

"As in extracurricular."

"Oh, those. Well, I—"

Before he could finish, I saw a horrified expression cross his face. I glanced over my shoulder just in time to see Mack lunging toward me. He faked tripping and then dumped his soda—ice and all—on top of my head.

I gasped, leaping to my feet, soda dripping down my hair and cheeks, and off my chin.

Mack grinned. "Whoops. I am *so* sorry, new girl. I guess I can be a klutz, too. It's so unfortunate this had to happen to you on your first day of school. My bad."

I stood there dripping wet, glaring at him.

He flicked a piece of ice off my head. "Better go see the nurse. You're all wet." He strode past me. As he passed Wally, he hissed, "You're next, loser."

After he left, Wally stood up, handing me some napkins. "I told you to stay away from me. Now you know why."

Without another word, he picked up his tray and walked away.

Sighing, I wiped off some of the mess with a napkin and then dumped the remains of my lunch in the trash. I then went to my locker and retrieved my school sweater. In the bathroom, I used paper towels to rinse my hair and wash my face and arms the best I could. It had been a sugary drink, so no matter how much I wiped, I was still sticky…and mad. I took off my wet shirt, rinsed it, wrung it out, and put it back on. It was uncomfortable, but I pulled my sweater on over it and sucked it up.

I checked to see what class I had next—Red Teaming and Deception Analysis. I found the room before the bell rang this time. When I came in, I saw Brandon and Piper sitting near the back of the room. I headed toward them and took an empty seat behind Piper and across from Brandon.

"Surprise. We're in the same class," Brandon said, twirling his pencil.

"Looks like it."

"You must be pretty capable on the keyboard. There're only a few of us permitted in here."

I looked around and realized he was right. I counted six students including myself. "I can handle a keyboard."

"We'll see."

"Guess we will."

He studied me. "I saw the stunt Mack pulled in lunch, dumping his drink on you. That was shark-cage level shit."

I shrugged. "It is what it is."

"Why didn't you tell on him?"

"On my first day? Hopefully I've got more grit than that."

He grinned. "Good for you. Want to get revenge?"

"Brandon," Piper hissed. "Knock it off."

Brandon kept his eyes on me, and I didn't look away. After a moment, I spoke. "Logically speaking, taking revenge on the likes of Mack is a royal waste of time."

"Truth…to a certain extent. Could be fun."

"Could be. What did you have in mind?"

Before he could answer the teacher strolled in. I looked up and saw Mr. Jouret, the teacher I'd met earlier in the hallway. His gaze locked on mine and he cocked his head, puzzled.

"Wait. You're the new girl. Are you sure you're in the right classroom?"

I held up my schedule. "Red Teaming and Deception Analysis."

"This is a very advanced computer class. Most students have to be cleared by me first."

"The headmistress approved. She saw my transcripts and felt I'd be a good fit here."

He frowned. "She didn't consult with me. I'll have to speak with her later."

I didn't say anything, so he closed the door. "So, what's your name again?"

"Lex—ah, Lara. Lara Carson. Yes, that's it."

He looked at me like I was an idiot. Maybe I was. This master of deception thing was a lot harder than I'd thought.

"Well, Miss Carson, I suppose it's a good thing you're here today since we're having a pop quiz. It will give me a chance to measure your knowledge."

Brandon groaned and knocked his head against the desk while the other kids sighed. I reached into my backpack and pulled out a pencil. Mr. Jouret went to his desk to retrieve the quiz when Brandon leaned toward me, whispering.

"He's a self-indulgent, puffed-up excuse for a teacher who doesn't know jack about anything. He's new here, but acts like he's God's gift to the keyboard. Don't let him intimidate you. Just do your best."

"I'm not intimidated," I whispered back.

"Good."

Mr. Jouret handed out the quiz. I glanced at it and saw there were ten questions. He told us to get to work, so I did. I finished the quiz in about four minutes and peeked over at Brandon. He was on question number two. Jeez, maybe I should have gotten one wrong or something.

I looked over at Mr. Jouret and saw him staring at me.

"Miss Carson, are you having trouble?"

"Ah, no."

"Then why are you just sitting there?"

"Well… I'm done."

Brandon and Piper glanced up, their eyes widening.

Mr. Jouret stood and walked over, picking up my quiz. He glanced at my answers and then at me. "Just exactly where did you transfer from?"

"Um, a small private school in Switzerland." Maybe I'd overdone that part.

He stroked his chin. "I see."

He frowned and, keeping my quiz, walked back to his desk. After another twenty minutes, everyone else had finished. Mr. Jouret collected the rest of the quizzes and stacked them on his desk.

"How the hell did you finish so quickly?" Brandon whispered.

"I'm smart?"

He laughed. "Damn, that's pretty cool."

"Hush, you two," Piper hissed at us over her shoulder. "Here he comes."

Mr. Jouret began strolling through the class, discussing how to discern and counter a cyber opponent's deceptions. I tried to appear interested, but it was really basic stuff and my mind began to wander. I began trying to think like a student. I didn't like my grade. I wanted to adjust it, so what would be the optimum way to plug in to change it?

The kids had obviously been doing it from the inside by stealing the teachers' passwords and then using any remote or school terminal they wanted. But once they were in, they had to have a system or a method to bridge the network in order to slide in surreptitiously and make the changes.

"Miss Carson?"

A hand slapped down on my desk.

Crap. Mr. Jouret had asked me a question and I hadn't heard him. It really *was* like I was back in high school again. Drifting, daydreaming and solving tech problems in my head that had nothing to do with the class I was in.

I swallowed and tried not to look guilty. "Um, could you repeat the question, please?"

It was evident he knew I wasn't paying attention. Still, he gamely repeated it.

"Seeing as how you apparently have had some exposure to the concept of red teaming, explain to me the theoretical importance of deception analysis in cybersecurity."

It was a ridiculously hard question for a high school student, but for some reason he had his hackles up. He probably didn't like the way I'd breezed through his test. Now he wanted to reestablish his dominance in the classroom. The best way to do that was to humiliate me in front of the students.

I considered my approach. He didn't realize it, but he'd given me the perfect opportunity to shine in front of my peers. But I had to handle it carefully. I didn't want to come off as *too* smart or cocky. I had to answer this question just right, so I chose my words carefully.

"That's a really hard question, Mr. Jouret, and I'm just learning about this concept, but I once heard a story from a teacher that may help explain how I understand deception analysis. The story went like this…there was a judge who had several law interns. He decided to task them with determining the answer to a specific question. He told the interns he wanted them to figure out why jurors in his courthouse were taking an inordinately longer time to come to a verdict in comparison to other juries in the same county."

I looked around and saw the students watching me

intently. So was Mr. Jouret, a frown furrowing between his eyes.

I took a deep breath and continued. "So, the interns set about their task with great enthusiasm. They studied everything starting with the jurors, the way they were selected, the lawyers, the physical organization of the courtroom and the layout of the jury room. Finally after spending about a month or more analyzing all the data and information, the interns told the judge they'd figured out why the jury in his courthouse took so much longer to come to a verdict."

It was so quiet in the classroom, you could hear a pin drop. Mr. Jouret perched on the corner of an empty desk. "Please continue, Miss Carson."

"Well, the interns told the judge the round tables in his jury rooms were the issue. Their analysis determined that juries who were seated around a round table took nearly twice as long to come to a verdict than those who sat at rectangular tables. The interns, quite pleased with themselves, then asked the judge if he wanted them to replace the round tables with rectangular ones."

Brandon leaned forward so far he almost tipped his desk over. "So, what did the judge say?"

"The judge told them absolutely not. He wanted to keep the round tables. Of course, the interns were quite surprised. They thought the judge wanted them to figure out how to get the juries to come to a quicker decision. But that wasn't the case at all. The judge's instructions to the interns were simply to find out why juries took longer in deliberation in his courtroom. The interns, *on their own*, perceived that the judge wanted to improve the speed of his juries. That was a faulty assumption. In fact, the judge tasked the interns because he wanted to know how to *keep* his juries deliberating for longer periods of time. He knew that statistics have shown that juries who take more time make better and more thorough decisions. That's the kind of jury he wanted in his courtroom."

"While that's fascinating, the point is?" Mr. Jouret asked with a raised eyebrow.

"The point is you have to be careful in your assumptions about what *you* think your cyber adversary is after. That is the core of deception analysis. A good adversary will trick you into thinking you know what he wants when, in reality, he's going after the exact opposite."

Mr. Jouret's mouth fell open. After a moment the students started clapping. Brandon stared at me with wide eyes. Jeez. I'd probably overdone it.

Well, my plan was to get in with the tech kids, and I didn't have time to fool around with false modesty. Only time would tell if I'd overplayed it. I'd definitely proven to my peers that I had the smarts to, at the very least, be included in a hacker's group. It would be most unfortunate—although given my track record with people, not inconceivable—if I were excluded from my own peers.

Class ended shortly after that, and after two more classes, so did the school day. Thank God, I'd survived another day at high school.

Barely.

Sighing, I returned to my locker, sorted through the books I'd need for my homework, then stuffed them in my backpack. I slipped on my coat and smashed the cap back over my blonde ponytail before heading out to the parking lot. Before I got to my car, I ran into Piper, Brandon and Wally. They were huddled together, talking. They stopped when they saw me.

"Hey, Lara." Wally lifted a gloved hand.

I almost corrected him on my name and literally had to bite my tongue. I winced and pressed my hand against my mouth.

"Hey, you were awesome today in Jouret's Red Teaming class," Brandon asked. "He almost crapped a brick. He's probably in fear for his job now."

"I wasn't that impressive. It was just a story."

"No, seriously, it was way prime."

Piper nodded. "You totally stunned him into silence. I've never seen him like that. It was a great story."

"Well, thanks, I guess." I gingerly rolled my tongue where I had bit it. "What are you guys doing?"

Wally shrugged. "Just talking. Getting ready to head home soon."

"Okay, well, I'll see you tomorrow."

"Sure. See you tomorrow, Lara."

I walked past them and keyed open my car. I heard Wally whistle. "What? You drive a Miata? Did the 'rents buy that for you?"

"No, I paid for it by myself by, ah, working during the summer and on the weekends."

"Really?" Piper looked surprised. "Your parents made you do that?"

"My parents didn't *make* me do anything. But if I wanted a car, I had to get it myself."

Brandon blinked. "Radical."

I smiled. "Actually, I think it's called good parenting."

TEN

I FOUGHT RUSH-HOUR traffic and got home about forty-five minutes later. I tossed my backpack on the couch and got a bottle of water from the refrigerator. I drank the entire thing while standing at my kitchen counter and then tossed it in the recycle bin.

I was headed to the bedroom when I heard the knock on the door. I checked the peek hole and then opened the door to let Slash in.

He immediately pulled me in for a kiss. "Twenty-four hours is too long to be without you," he murmured against my lips. Then he leaned back and looked at me with eyes widening.

"You're blonde."

My hair was still in the ponytail. I reached up to it and touched it. "You're not going to freak out, are you? It's totally weird."

"No, it's lovely. And you're…in a schoolgirl uniform."

I blushed. "Jeez. I forgot. It's really embarrassing."

He shook his head. "No, it's an entirely different look for you."

"I'll go change."

He put a hand on my arm. "No, please don't."

"Why not?"

He reached out, winding a strand of my ponytail around his finger. "Because I have something in mind for later involving that skirt."

"Yowza."

He leaned over and pressed a kiss against my neck. "Hey, I didn't even have to tell you that was a sexual innuendo."

"I must be improving. You're a good influence on me."

"Glad to hear that."

He sniffed. "Why do you smell like Coke?"

"It's a long story."

"Hmmm." He put his arm around me. "I take it that all of this means your high school operation is underway."

"It sure is."

"I can't wait to hear about it. But first, food. I still feel guilty about the other night."

"Don't. It was a sacrifice in the name of national security."

"Ah, I adore you." He grinned and walked over to my refrigerator. "What do you have in here that I can whip into our dinner?"

"You're going to cook?"

He glanced at me over his shoulder. "I told you I could cook."

"I know, but wow. I never thought I'd say this, but your ability to cook is really turning me on. Is that weird?"

He chuckled. "I'm not protesting. Just remind me to cook more often for you."

"Anytime."

Opening the door, he rattled off the contents. "Mustard, wine, milk, soda, beer, butter, grated cheese, eggs, baloney and bottled water." He frowned at me over his shoulder. "Where are the vegetables?"

"I've got a cucumber, tomato and carrot in the top drawer. I usually have lettuce, but I finished it off a couple of days ago on a baloney sandwich."

He straightened and closed the refrigerator door. "Really? That's it?"

"That's it." I crossed my arms defensively. "It's not like I'm starving. There are also cornflakes, Cheerios, peanut butter, trail mix, bananas and crackers in the cabinet along with a loaf of mostly mold-free bread. I also have a bag of oranges and apples in the pantry. But most importantly, I have Christmas biscotti and hot cocoa from the all-important holiday food group. I'm actually pretty well stocked. For me."

He sighed. "Let's go out to eat."

"Remember what happened last time we went out to eat? Besides, after the day I've had, I'd rather eat at home."

"Fine. But let's make a quick stop to get you some more groceries first. I'll make you dinner, okay? It will be one of Nonna's recipes."

I loved Slash's Italian grandmother. She was the best cook in the world. Perhaps in the entire universe. "Really? Do I get to watch you cook?"

"Absolutely. You can participate, too."

"Deal."

A quick trip to the grocery store netted me all kinds of items I had no idea even existed. Within the hour we had Christmas music on the stereo, a delicious-smelling minestrone soup simmering on the stove and a loaf of crusty French bread warming in the oven. We sat on the couch, sipping a nice red wine and enjoying the holiday music, my little twinkling tree and each other's company.

"So, how did the questioning go with Ansari?" I asked, pulling my legs up onto the couch. I was still in my school skirt, but I wrapped my arms around my legs anyway and rested my chin on my knees.

Slash set his wineglass down and took my stockinged feet into his lap.

I leaned back, closing my eyes as he rubbed. "Oh, my God. Really, that feels amazing. Your hands…they are magical."

"Good to know." He continued his ministrations. "Well, Ansari isn't talking. He completely shut down. We still don't know the whereabouts of his brother, the others in that apartment or the rest of the bombs. The only person he talked to was you."

"Couldn't you search his apartment or something?"

"He's a ghost. He had no driver's license or identification on him. No home address, no credit card, no known presence online that we can find. We don't know where he's been living. That apartment was rented two months ago and the rent was paid in cash. The name and information on the lease was completely bogus. We traced Zogby's gun to a batch that was stolen from a police station in southern Virginia and then purchased illegally. We're currently trying to trace the bomb materials and going through the apartment. So far nothing. The only thing we know for sure is that he is Ansari Zogby. We matched his fingerprints to those on documents provided when he first entered the United States."

"Tough break. What more do you know about his parents' background?"

"We're researching the *Shahid* organization pretty extensively right now. The police arrested Ansari's parents and convicted them of money laundering for them. It's interesting because the group has been in the news lately."

"What did they do?"

"Several minor bombings in Pakistan and one rather high-profile assassination of a popular Pakistani politician who was supporting peace efforts to bring a group called the *Mehsuds* to the table to stop the violence in the country."

"So, what does the *Shahid* have against the *Mehsuds*?"

"The *Shahid* is actually a splinter group of the *Mehsuds*. They broke apart in the late 1990s. Both groups are terrorist organizations by our definition. The *Shahids'* violent actions and support of al Qaeda's activities has netted them a top spot on our watch list."

"That's not good news."

"No, it's not. Finding Zogby in the presence of bomb-making materials in such close vicinity to Washington, D.C. has a lot of people at Homeland Security and the FBI quite worried."

"That's probably why they kept us so long at the police station."

"*Si.* That's part of it. We have a team of agents at the prison now, interviewing the parents, but I doubt we'll find out anything. As far as we know, they haven't made contact with their children since they were incarcerated. They've also had no visitors."

I blew out a breath. "This is getting ugly. It was a lucky break you recognized Zogby."

He tapped his head. "Photographic memory. Just like you." Setting my feet aside, he stood. "The soup should be ready. Hungry?"

"Famished."

Slash served up the soup while I cut the bread into

thick slices and put butter on the table. We sat at my kitchen table, eating in quiet contentment.

Slash buttered a piece of bread. "Now, let's hear about your day. How was high school?"

"Well, I'm *trying* to fit in."

He chuckled. "How's that working for you?"

"Ugh. Some jerk spilled his drink on me in the cafeteria." I gave him a quick rundown.

He raised an eyebrow. "He did it on purpose?"

"Yeah. Resident bully and all."

His mouth hardened. "Do I need to pay said bully a visit?"

"God, no. I'm not worried. He's just a kid. A royal jerk, but still a kid. I've got this."

Slash didn't look satisfied, but he nodded. "If you say so."

I sighed. "Anyway, I hope I get invited into the hackers group sooner than later. Jeez, that reminds me, I still have to do my homework."

Slash handed me the bread he'd just buttered and smiled. "Need any help?"

I punched him lightly in the arm. "Hardly."

We finished our soup and I stacked the dishes in the sink to wash later. Carrying our wineglasses, we headed into the living room where the Christmas music was still playing. I tapped my foot to "God Rest Ye Merry Gentlemen."

Comfortably full, I leaned back against the cushions. "Slash, can I ask you something?"

"Of course."

"Remember how you said I could come straight to the source if I needed more information on our relationship?"

"What's on your mind?"

"Well, I don't know what to get you for a Christmas present."

"I don't want you to buy me anything for Christmas."

"Are you going to give me a present?"

He was silent.

I threw up my hands. "See. I *have* to get you something. Reciprocity in a relationship is important."

"But I don't *need* anything."

"That's exactly my problem. What in the world do I get the man who has everything?"

"I've already got what I want."

"That's not fair. Unless you promise you aren't going to give me anything, then I *have* to give you something."

He reached out, wound a strand of my hair around his finger. "Okay, take me to dinner the next time we go out."

"That's a gesture, not a gift."

"Now you're arguing semantics."

"In this case, semantics is important. Help me out here. Please."

"Okay. Let me think about it."

"Promise?"

"I promise."

I blew out a breath. "Thank you. I sincerely mean that. But don't take too long, okay? I have to order it and then wrap it. Do I have to get a card, too? This is really stressing me out."

He reached over and took my wineglass, setting it on the coffee table. "Forget about the present. How about we relax instead? I find that certain activities enhance my cerebral function, leading to more creative thoughts."

"You're referring to sex again, right?"

Slash smiled and pulled me to my feet. "If you insist."

I leaned into him. "That was a pretty tricky segue."

He began nuzzling my neck. "I can be a pretty tricky guy."

"So I see. Slash, can I ask you something else?"

"Hmmmm…"

"Can you recite a recipe from memory? That cooking thing…it's pretty sexy."

He pulled back from my neck and stared at me, his eyes darkening. "Can you wear that skirt to bed?"

I looked down at my skirt. "Done."

A slow smile crossed his face. "So, would you like that recipe in Italian?"

"Wow." My breath caught in my throat. "I sure would."

ELEVEN

THE NEXT MORNING I returned to school reinvigorated and ready to get the hacker. I felt like I'd made some progress yesterday, so I'd see what today would bring.

As soon as I entered the corridor, the stench of rotting flesh hit me hard. Everyone around me held their noses. A custodian walked around, hunting the source without any luck.

Breathing through my mouth, I headed for my locker. When I spun the combination and opened the door, a large rat fell out and splatted on the floor at my feet. I jumped back. A girl two lockers down began shrieking, which caused a mini-stampede of students running away from me and screaming so loudly my ears rang.

I bent over and peered at the animal. Definitely a rat.

The custodian ran over and knelt next to it.

"Ah-ha!" He glared at me. "Is this yours?"

"You're asking me if I own a dead rat?"

"You won't believe what some kids keep in their locker."

I pinched my nose shut. "I assure you this rat does not belong to me."

"But this is your locker?"

"*Was* my locker. I'm definitely asking for a new one."

He frowned at me. "Why do you have a dead rat in your locker?"

"Good question. Because someone put it there?"

"Like some kind of joke?"

"Well, I'm certainly not laughing."

"Do you know who did it?"

I did, but I wasn't going to rat...pun intended. "Not a clue. I'm new here."

He stared at me and then stood. "Okay. Don't touch it."

"Seriously, that's not going to be a problem."

He marched off and I studied my locker, trying to figure out the physics of getting the book for my next class out without touching the dead rat on the floor or the gooey stuff covering the book at the top of the pile. If someone had done this to me when I was actually in high school, I'd have skipped school for three days while plotting my online revenge. Now I just found it annoying and disgusting. And I felt sorry for the rat.

"You shouldn't have stood up for me."

I turned around and saw Wally. He looked at the rat. "That's gross even for him."

"Mack?"

"Who else? He's a jerk first-class. Because of your association with me, intended or not, you're now marked. Good thing you're a senior. It's going to be several long months for you."

"How did you know I was a senior?"

"Your class load."

"How do you know what my class load is?"

"There's a lot I know. Come on, let's get out of here."

"Wait." I reached into my locker and carefully slid a book from the middle of the pile. I carried my coat and backpack with me. No way was I leaving them near that dead rat smell.

"I don't know where I'm going," I said, fumbling for my course schedule.

"You have Systems Forensics."

"Glad to know you're so familiar with my schedule."

"Don't mention it."

Without a word he showed me where my next class was and then disappeared down the hall. I sat in the class and made a concerted effort to answer a bunch of questions to hopefully get noticed by other tech students. Unfortunately, all I did was attract the puzzled attention of the teacher, who probably wondered if I was secretly plotting to take over her job.

On the way to my next class, Ron, the IT guy, caught up with me and told me Bonnie wanted to talk to me. I entered the office and started to walk back to Bonnie's room when Marge—um, Ms. Eder—stopped me.

"Excuse me. Just where do you think you are going?"

I turned around slowly. Crap. I'd forgotten I was a student.

"Ah, I was told Ms. Swanson wanted to see me."

"Then you tell me and I tell her."

"Right. Sorry." I returned to the main office and sat down on one of the comfy chairs. After a few minutes, Ms. Eder returned. "You can see her now."

"Thanks."

Bonnie was sitting behind her desk when I came in. "Shut the door behind you."

I did as I was told and sat down.

She slid her glasses off her nose and looked at me. "How's it going?"

"It's going. I'm meeting the kids, trying to figure out who is who. I'm just getting started."

"What's this I hear about a dead rat being found in your locker?"

"Yeah, about that… I think I raised the hackles of the resident school bully."

She looked surprised. "Our school has a bully?"

"Yes."

I'd never really understood how adults could be so clueless about this. Of course there were bullies. I'd been bullied incessantly in high school and it had gone largely unnoticed by any of the school staff. There had been bullies since the beginning of mankind when one caveman hit another one over the head with a club and stole his bison leg for dinner. The severity of the problem was the issue. Apparently no one at this school had reported on Mack yet.

"Who is it?"

"I'll give you all the details later. Besides, I can't be certain he was the one who put the rat there. But he is definitely the leading contender."

She sighed. "Okay. By the way, a couple of the teachers have mentioned your unusual smarts. Mr. Fitzgerald said you appear to have exceptional skills."

I winced. "It's a fine line I'm walking. I want to catch the attention of my peers. In order to do so, I have to show off a little. But I don't want to be too flashy or cocky so I raise anyone's suspicions. I'm working on it."

"I understand. This is a very unusual approach to solving our problem, but after assessing it, I think it's a pretty good one. Ron liked it, too, so I trust the school is in good hands."

"I'll do my best."

"I believe that or I wouldn't have agreed to this."

I studied her for a moment and decided I liked her.

It certainly couldn't be easy managing a school full of talented kids and yet she'd gone out on a limb to help me figure a creative way to stop the students without insisting on punitive or harsh consequences. It made me wish I'd had a principal like her to come to when I was in high school.

"Thanks again, Bonnie."

She stood. "Sure. Let me know if you need anything."

"Will do."

I left her office and realized it was lunchtime. I headed for the cafeteria, filled my tray with probably the best food I'd eat all day, then looked for a place to sit.

I made a beeline for Wally, who sat at his usual spot.

He sighed when I sat down. "Why are you doing this?"

"Doing what?"

"Being nice to me. I can't take the stress of being responsible for you."

My sandwich stopped halfway to my mouth. "Whoa. Stop right there. You're *not* responsible for me. I've got a lock on that all by myself."

"Then why can't you be nice to me when no one is looking?"

"Because that's letting them win."

"So what? They win anyway. You're just asking for trouble."

I put down my sandwich and leaned forward. "Wrong, Wally. Big-time. No one *asks* to get bullied. That's an important distinction."

He sighed. "Okay, you're right. I just can't wait to get out of this hellhole. Another year and a half."

I pushed my sandwich aside. I'd lost my appetite. I saw more of myself in Wally than I felt ready to acknowledge. I felt like I should do something about it and about him, but I didn't know what. Right now what I really needed to remember was my true goal here, which was figuring out what was going on with the renegade kids. I'd hand over the bullying stuff to Bonnie when I left.

"Look, you'll make it, Wally. Trust me."

"We'll see."

"Just hang in there. College is awesome…or so I've heard."

"It better be."

I fiddled with the bread on my sandwich. "So, Wally, you didn't have a chance to tell me what you do for fun around here."

"There's supposed to be fun in high school?"

"Ha, ha. I meant extracurricular activities."

"Oh, those. I'd hardly call them fun. Well, I belong to the Latin Club, the Astronomy Club and the Computer Club. Wouldn't have joined any of them, but it's crucial for the college application."

My eyes lit up. "Hey, I'm interested in the Computer Club. How often do you meet and what do you do?"

He shrugged. "We meet once a week and do some language prototyping, application creation and play with the networks. Sometimes we pick a platform and go through the development process. A couple of the kids are into circuit design. It's a mishmash group."

"Does this club have a teacher sponsor?"

"Yeah, Mr. Jouret. He doesn't know the half of what we do."

"Which is?"

"Just stuff. Hey, why are you so interested?"

Whoops. Time to back off a little. "I'm looking for something to do after school. There are only so many hours in the day I can spend playing Realm and pretending to do my homework."

He studied me for a moment. "We meet today. Want to come?"

"Gee, I don't know. I'll have to check my social calendar."

"Smart-ass."

I grinned. "Which is why I like you, Wally."

"That's what all the girls say. If you're serious, meet me in front of the computer lab after the last bell."

"I'll be there."

TWELVE

I MET WALLY in front of the computer lab after the last bell rang. He stood in the hallway, looking around uncertainly. His face lit up when he saw me.

"Hey, Lara. You made it."

"Of course. Did you think I'd bail?"

He pushed his glasses up on his nose. "It's happened before. Come on and I'll introduce you to the Nerd Herd."

We walked into Mr. Jouret's classroom. He was nowhere to be seen. I counted eleven kids. Four of them appeared to be working on a circuit board. Piper and Brandon were sitting together in front of a monitor doing something. Several other kids had linked their laptops and were talking about a PHP programming language. I looked around, wondering if the leader of the WOMBATs was in this very room and how many kids were involved in the group.

Wally led me over to Piper and Brandon. They glanced up.

"Hey, Lara, Wally. Pull up a couple of chairs." Brandon grinned. "Want to see what we're working on?"

I peered over his shoulder. "Sure."

Wally dragged two chairs over and we sat.

I scooted to the edge of the chair. "You're in the school's system?"

Piper clicked around. "Sort of. It's Chalkboard, the school's e-learning management system. Mr. Jouret wants us to get more familiar with it so we can write a tutorial for the student body."

"Sounds…interesting."

Brandon laughed. "Not. You don't have to fake interest in something so mundane, Lara. Come on, Piper. Enough of the boring crap. Let's show her where the real fun is."

Piper hesitated. "Brandon…"

He paused his fingers over the keyboard. "Anyone who can show up Mr. Jouret like she did is prime in my book. I say she's in."

Piper glanced and Wally who shrugged.

"Oh, for God's sake, come on." Brandon stole the mouse from her and started clicking. He angled the monitor toward us and laughed.

I looked at the screen. "A desktop?"

"It's our fearless leader's, Mr. Jouret's. He has no idea how easy it is to remotely access his computer."

"Don't be stupid," Wally hissed. "He could walk in here any minute."

"Which makes it all the more exciting." Brandon typed faster. "We could shock some sense into his prissy, South African ass. What's wrong with you guys? I thought you all liked a little cyber deviance."

I looked up. "Mr. Jouret is from South Africa?"

"Yeah. You didn't know? He transferred from some swanky university there and never ceases to remind us that he took a step down to teach the likes of us."

South African. That was why I hadn't recognized the accent—a mixture of British English, Dutch and Australian English.

Brandon hopped around Mr. Jouret's desktop, clicking on random folders. "Hey, guess what? We're having another pop quiz on Friday. Want an advance copy of the semester exam? It's yours…for a price. Ha! The world at my fingertips."

As he was clicking around, I noticed something strange. "Wait, Brandon. Stop for a minute. Go back."

He glanced over his shoulder as he clicked. "What?"

"Just go back. There's something…there. Stop."

Brandon stopped and we all leaned forward to look at the screen.

Wally whistled. "What is that?"

I shook my head. "I don't know. It's odd."

Piper tapped the monitor. "What kind of weird encryption is on that file?"

I frowned. "I have no idea. It looks a bit like KeyPass, but it's not. I haven't seen it before."

I was just about to ask Brandon to click on it for a closer look, when Wally leaned over and blanked out the screen. Mr. Jouret strolled into the classroom.

"So, how are things going, kids?" He saw me and raised an eyebrow. "Oh, the new student, Lara Carson. You've taken an interest in the Computer Club?"

I shrugged. "Sure, why not? I like computers."

He dismissed me and turned to Piper. "What are you working on, Miss O'Neill?"

She lifted her chin. "Ah, Chalkboard. We're figuring out the best way to write the tutorial, just like you asked us to, Mr. Jouret."

"Good. I expect it by the end of the quarter."

"Of course. We should be done with it by then."

Mr. Jouret walked over to his desk and sat down. Brandon turned on the screen and quickly got out of his desktop.

Wally gave an audible sigh. "Too close for comfort."

Brandon just grinned. "YOLO."

You only live once. Sure, a good mantra if you *weren't* going back to high school for the second time.

Wally, Brandon and Piper returned to Chalkboard and started maneuvering around the system. I was bored, so I looked around the room. A movement at one of the empty computer terminals caught my eye. I stood, stretched and nonchalantly walked over to check it out.

The cursor on the screen was moving around, clicking on system administrator functions. I frowned. The school's system wasn't supposed to be connected to anything. Any remote access had to be done by permission and would be logged in. It could have been Ron, but I wanted to check it out just in case.

I walked over to Wally. "I'm going to use the bathroom. Be back in a few."

He nodded. I went out into the hallway and then headed up to the third floor. I took a surreptitious glance both ways to make sure the hall was empty, and then used my badge to access Computer Central. I slipped inside, but the room was empty.

I sat down at Ron's terminal and logged in. I checked the system logs and noted that no remote access had been approved or noted. Definitely odd. If Ron was in the system, he'd be logged in remotely. From what I could tell right now, he wasn't. In fact, no one, other than myself, was logged in to the system admin's account. So who had been looking around and why hadn't they left a trace? I'd seen it. Someone had come into the system, done something and gone.

So, who? It wasn't Wally, Brandon or Piper. I'd been watching them for the past hour or so. It could have been another student, but somehow I didn't get that vibe. From what I'd seen, someone had been tweaking the system functions. I didn't like that one little bit.

I wanted to do a more thorough search, but I didn't have time. Instead, I ran a quick virus scan and did one more search through the remote system logs.

Nada.

I stood. I needed time to think. I left Computer Central and headed back to Mr. Jouret's classroom. Wally was waiting impatiently.

"What took you so long? We're just wrapping up things."

"Sorry. Ah, it must have been the cafeteria food."

"I thought you might have skipped. I figured you were probably bored. We usually do more interesting things."

"It wasn't boring at all. Thanks for inviting me, Wally. I'm definitely coming back."

"Great. I'll walk you to your car."

"Okay. If you want to."

We said goodbye to Piper and Brandon and headed toward the parking lot. As we went out the front door, Wally put a hand on my arm.

"Wait. Lara, can I ask you something?"

"Sure."

He shifted nervously on one foot. "Will you go to the Christmas Ball with me? It's next Friday."

My eyes widened. It was the first time I'd been asked to a high school dance, and I wasn't even really in high school. Such is the life of a geek girl. Except now I had to turn Wally down in a way that wouldn't damage him, and there wasn't time to Google how to do that.

Crap.

Okay, I'd have to make this up as I went along. I could do this. I'd just break it into easy steps.

Step One: Attempt To Be Tactful.

I took a deep breath. "Me? A dance with you? Oh, God, no."

Wait, that wasn't what I'd meant. Try again, this time with tact.

"I mean, not *God*, no. Just a regular, polite *no*. No, no, no. I can't go to the dance with you. But thanks for asking. Really."

I winced at the expression on his face. I'd have to hurry to Step Two: Say Something Positive.

"Look, Wally, you are a great kid…guy. Really nice and obviously intelligent. Those are terrific traits. Seriously. Any girl would be lucky to go out with you."

"You *are* any girl."

"Any girl *except* me."

"Just say yes, Lara. It's easy to do. Open your mouth and out pops the word *yes*."

"I can't, Wally. Besides, you don't want to ask me to a dance. I can't even dance. In fact, I hate dancing."

He brightened. "Awesome. Me, too. We can just drink punch, eat the cookies and stand in the corner talking about multi-factor authentication."

Jeez. It actually sounded like fun. Why couldn't someone have asked me out like this when I was *really* in high school?

Okay, on to Step Three: Lie Madly Through the Teeth.

"Well, I wasn't going to tell you, but I can't go to the dance with you because…because… I'm a lesbian."

He blinked. I'd surprised him. Thank God. Maybe now he'd leave me alone.

I started walking again. Wally caught up with me. "Hey, Lara, that's not a problem. Can I go to the dance with you and your girlfriend? I'd be like the hypothetical fly on the wall. Not a bother at all."

"Wally!"

"Okay. Fine. It's cool with me. I'm all for tolerance and equal rights. I just want you to know I'm here for you and your girlfriend anytime you need me."

THIRTEEN

By the time I got home, I was exhausted. No kidding, high school was mentally draining even the second time around. I slipped on sweatpants and a T-shirt and tucked my hair into the ball cap even though there was no one there to see me. It was just hard walking by a mirror and not being freaked out by my blonde reflection. I heard my cell make a noise, so I dug in my purse and pulled it out. I had a text from an unknown number.

Slash. He rarely called me from the same phone. He changed phones like I changed underwear. Guess it was all part of the national security gig.

Am in the middle of something and won't be able to come by tonight. Miss you.

Slash.

I thought for a moment, typed back ok and then sent it. I probably should have said more, but I didn't know what was appropriate. I could have said I wasn't exactly expecting him so it was no problem, but what if I was *supposed* to expect him now that we were dating? Jeez. I had no mental capacity to deal with this tonight.

Sighing, I set down my phone and went in the kitchen. Although Slash had bought all kinds of wonderful groceries, I wasn't sure what to do with them. So instead, I grabbed some crackers, the jar of peanut butter and a banana. I made myself a plate and took it into the bedroom where my laptop was set up. I needed a break from school, so I did a cursory glance at all the gaming websites, but saw neither Xavier nor Elvis were active.

I slid my banana through a glob of peanut butter and chewed it while I checked my progress on Hollow Realm. Not good. I didn't feel like facing a group of frenetic ogres by myself, so I retrieved my phone and called Elvis.

"Hey, Lexi."

"Hey, Elvis. You and Xavier busy?"

"Xavier's not here. He's already in Greece. I'm just hanging by myself."

"Oh, yeah, that's right. Basia told me Xavier was heading out. When did he leave?"

"Last night. He's going to get the place ready for Basia."

"Cool. It sounds like it's going to be a prime vacation. Basia told me she's excited to spend time with him. How about you? Are you looking forward to Greece?"

"I guess it will be okay." His voice sounded kind of funny.

I continued. "Well, I was going to ask if you wanted to play Hollow Realm online, but if you're all by yourself, would you be up for a visitor, some pizza and Quake?"

"You want to come here? To my house? By yourself?"

"Of course I want to come there. I *always* come there. Elvis, is everything okay?"

"Uh, sure. If you want to come over, you can. It's your decision."

I frowned. What was wrong with him?

"Okay. Then it's my *decision* to swing by and pick up the pizza. You get the laptops ready."

"Fine. Okay. If that's what you want to do, consider it done. I've got beer, too."

He was acting really strange. "Excellent."

It took me half an hour to pick up the pizza from Avanti's and drive over to his house. The pizza smelled fantastic and I had to restrain myself from having a bite in the car at the stoplight.

I rang the bell and Elvis opened the door. He was dressed in a blue flannel shirt and jeans. His feet were bare. He smiled when he saw me, his blue eyes lighting up.

"Anchovies. I thought I smelled something good."

"The usual, of course."

"Of course. You're sure this is what you want to do, right?"

"Elvis, is everything okay?"

He twisted his flannel shirt between his fingers. "Fine. Everything is fine. Come in, if you want."

I stepped through the door and he took the pizza.

"I'm really glad you came, Lexi. I'm ready to game when you are."

"You know I'm *always* ready to game. But I'm also starving. Let's eat first."

"As you wish." He gave me a funny little smile and I laughed.

"*The Princess Bride*, right? I love that movie."

"The best lines ever."

"Agreed. Ever."

Elvis fetched some paper plates and napkins and then brought us a couple of open beers.

I opened the box and piled the pizza on the plates. Elvis took a bite and sighed. "Damn. This is the most delicious pizza in the universe."

"Is that a scientific certainty?"

"Indisputably."

We both laughed and licked our fingers. After three pieces each, we started to clean up.

"So, how's high school?" Elvis asked, taking my empty beer bottle.

"About the same."

"Is Operation Undercover High School Student working out?"

"So far, so good. Which reminds me, have you ever seen an encryption program that kind of looks like Key-Pass, but isn't?"

"I'd need a better visual."

"Okay, let me show you."

I sat down at one of his terminals and called up the school system. I had all the passwords and information in my head, so I was in within two minutes. It took me another minute or so to pull up Mr. Jouret's desktop and find the unusual file.

"I didn't have any time for more than a cursory glance when I was at the school, but it raised a red flag with me. What do you think?"

I vacated the chair so Elvis could sit down.

He sat and studied the file. "Never seen anything like this. It's definitely strange."

"My exact sentiments."

"Shall we?"

He was asking for permission to hack in to the file. I hesitated. Hacking in to the file of a teacher was outside the boundaries of what I'd been hired to do on this job, not to mention illegal without permission from the school.

"No. Can't. Damn."

"Understood. Doesn't mean we can't check out the encryption software though."

I brightened. "True."

Elvis began cross-referencing it with his considerable database. In about six minutes he got a hit.

I leaned over and rested my chin on his shoulder while we stared at the information scrolling across the screen. "What is it?"

"Bad stuff. Looks like it's a tailored software used almost exclusively by a group called the Veiled Knights."

"The who?"

"Veiled Knights. An international group of cyber mercenaries."

"Really? Jeez, what kind of name is Veiled Knights? Someone should be shot for a lack of imagination. What do we know about these cyber mercenaries, other than their presumed willingness to sell their services to the highest bidder?"

Elvis pulled up the file and started reading. "There isn't much. The suspected leader is a guy named Johannes Broodryk."

"What's his deal?"

"Well, Broodryk and his group have ties to just about every illegal operation in the world. Drugs, guns, human trafficking, industrial espionage and cyberwarfare. It's all a game for them, but apparently a lucrative one."

"Where are they located?"

"They're phantoms, of course, but Broodryk is originally from South Africa."

I blinked. "South Africa? Wait. My computer teacher, Mr. Jouret…this is his desktop. He's from South Africa, too."

Elvis met my gaze. "That's a significant coincidence."

"Agreed. But what in the world would a high school computer teacher be doing with a file from the Veiled Knights?"

"That's a good question, isn't it?"

"Sure is. Looks like I need to do a lot more research on Mr. Jouret and the Veiled Knights."

"Want to get started?"

I put my hand on his arm. "I appreciate your help, Elvis. Always. But not tonight. I seriously need some downtime to clear my head. High school is not for the faint of heart, even the second time around. I came over for some pizza and gaming. School and work can wait until tomorrow. Let's just game."

He studied me. "You look really tired, Lexi."

"Don't get too hopeful. I'm not too tired to beat you at Quake."

He bumped his shoulder against mine. "Now you're on."

After several hours of playing, I had relaxed considerably and we were at a happy stalemate. I stretched and got a piece of cold pizza.

Elvis sipped a beer, leaned back in his chair and studied me. "Good game, as usual. I can't figure out how you keep finding ways past me. We've played so many times I should be able to anticipate your moves by now."

"That's my strategy. Do the unexpected, except when you expect that."

"Well, that helps."

We laughed and then Elvis lifted his feet and placed them on the desk, cradling the beer in his lap. "So, I hear you're, um, dating Slash."

"Oh. You heard about that?" I grabbed another beer

from the fridge and popped the top. "Let me guess. Basia told Xavier."

"Exactly. Why didn't you say something?"

I looked at him in surprise. "You're interested in my love life?"

His cheeks reddened. "Ah—"

I sighed. "I know. You're right. It's just way too weird."

"What's weird?"

"It's weird that someone like Slash would want to date someone like me. It's pretty out there."

"I don't think it's out there. He's had his eye on you for some time."

"Really? You knew?"

"Everyone knew…except you."

I thought about that. "Why didn't you say something to me?"

He paused and looked down. "I don't know. I just didn't."

"Well, you should have. I'm not good at figuring those things out on my own. How could you tell he was interested?" I guess it didn't really matter now, but I was still curious.

"It was the way he acted around you—kind of territorial." He shrugged.

"That's *so* not indicative of sexual interest. This is Slash we're talking about. He's territorial with everyone."

"He was different with you."

"Different is not an established scientific criteria, Elvis."

"Okay, maybe I was guessing a bit." He ran his fingers through his hair. "But I had a feeling. Maybe it's a guy thing. I'm not disagreeing that attraction is a hard thing to define, especially by observation only. I just had a feeling. In the end, I can't say I'm surprised you're dating him. Guys like Slash typically tend to get what they're after."

There was something in his tone… "You almost make it sound as if I had no say in the matter."

He lifted the beer to his lips. "Did you?"

"Of course I did. Do you think I went into this relationship against my will?"

The color in his cheeks deepened. "No, of course not. I'm just saying that it would be hard to resist a full package like that."

"Like what?"

"I don't know…rich, suave, handsome, intelligent and able conversationalist. You know, the full package."

I took another bite of pizza and sat in a swivel chair across from him. "Well, he's the first guy to ever express a genuine interest in dating me. I mean, other than Finn, but that's a complicated situation. Anyway, I'll admit it's an odd pairing, but I have no other experience with which to make a comparison. Slash is my first boyfriend *ever*. I'm still in the initial stages of data collection."

"Yeah, well, let me know how it goes."

"Of course, I will. Other than Basia, who else would I tell?"

I set the pizza aside, glanced at my watch. "Crapola. It's already one thirty. Man, it's going to be a tough morning and I have to go to school."

"That sucks. I'm sleeping in. Bonus perk of setting my own hours."

"Show-off."

"Not too proud to admit it. Thanks for coming over, Lexi. I'm really glad you came."

"Sure, why wouldn't I?"

"I… I don't know."

I studied him for a moment. "Okay, well, thanks for a fun evening, Elvis."

I gave him a fist bump and drove home. I was bone tired by the time I opened the door to my apartment. Once inside, I stopped. My alarm had been turned off.

Then the light in the hallway clicked on, nearly blinding me. Slash stood there, leaning against my wall, his arms crossed and an angry expression on his face.

"Where have you been?"

FOURTEEN

I WHIRLED AROUND, pressing a hand to my heart. "Jeez. You scared me to death. I thought you weren't coming over."

"I got off earlier than expected. I was worried sick when you weren't here. Don't you ever check your phone?"

I glanced at my purse. "Ah, not much."

He ran his fingers through his hair. "Were you at your parents'?"

"No. I was at the Zimmermans'."

"I thought they were in Greece."

"No, Xavier is in Greece, getting the villa ready for Basia. Elvis will go sometime after Christmas."

"So, you were with Elvis?"

"Yes. Gaming and eating pizza with anchovies, which is why I'd better go brush my teeth before you kiss me. You are going to kiss me, right?"

He closed his eyes and sighed. "Of course I'm going to kiss you."

I paused for a moment, looking at him. "Okay. Tell me the truth. Is it the hair?"

"What?"

"Well, all of a sudden everyone is treating me differently. Elvis is acting all weird, and now you're talking to me in a strange tone of voice. Ever since I dyed my hair blonde, people have been interacting with me in odd ways. I knew something like this would happen. Hair dye is evil."

Slash exhaled. "No, *cara*, it's not your hair. I'm sorry, it's just been a long couple of days. Go brush your teeth."

"Okay then, I'll be right back."

I slipped past him and headed for the bathroom. What in the *freaking* world was wrong with everyone lately? If it wasn't my hair, what was it?

I brushed my teeth and returned to the living room. Slash sat on the couch reading something on his phone. He looked really tired.

I stood there uncertainly. "Um, do you want something to drink?"

He put his phone in his pocket and wagged a finger at me. "No. Come here."

I went and sat next to him. He put his arm around me and leaned in for a kiss.

"You taste like toothpaste."

"Better than anchovies."

"Indeed."

I pulled back. "Slash, what's wrong? You seem worried about something, and I mean more than not being able to reach me tonight."

He rested his head back against the cushions, closing his eyes. "*Si*, I am. I'm limited in what I can say, but the arrest of Zogby, the discovery of the bombs in the apartment and additional intelligence strongly indicates that something big may be going down. I'm worried about it, so by extension, I'm worried about you."

"I take it the agents didn't get any useful information from Zogby's parents."

"No. We're still working on tracing the materials from the bombs, but it is tediously slow work."

I put my hand on his arm. "I'll be careful, Slash. I promise."

He covered my hand with his. "Stay out of public spots like malls, movie theaters, high-target tourist areas and restaurants. Be aware of your surroundings and don't follow any more suspicious characters, okay?"

"Okay."

"And for God's sake, check your phone once in a while and let me know your whereabouts. I need to know you're safe or I can't concentrate."

He sounded like my mom. "Look, Slash, you can relax. You know me well enough to realize I don't normally go to any of those places, but if it will make you feel better, I won't start going now. You don't have to worry about me."

"I'm *always* worried about you." His arm tightened around me. "Trouble follows you like a stalker. Besides, you talked to Zogby. He knows who you are and where you work."

"Zogby is in custody. Finn is reviewing the company's security policies. Besides, I don't *know* anything."

"But he doesn't know that."

I shifted on the couch. "I'll keep my eyes open, okay?"

"It's just, now that I've found you, I don't want to lose you."

"You aren't going to lose me."

"No, I'm not." He fingered my hair. "Who knew you could look so sexy as a blonde?"

"Sexy? Me? Really? This undercover stuff is harder than I anticipated. I can hardly remember my real name anymore."

He relaxed, chuckling. "Ah, welcome to the club. So, how is high school?"

"Well, I'm making progress. I got invited to the Computer Club today. Already saw some suspicious things. Now I need to find some time to follow up. Oh, and someone put a dead rat in my locker."

Slash straightened. "What?"

"I stood up for a kid who was getting some mouth from one of the bullies. Actually got between them. Said bully has decided I'm on his hit list now."

His eyes narrowed. "Does he need a little straightening out?"

"Nothing I can't handle. He's just a dumb jerk who thinks he's something special. On the upside, I got a new locker while they fumigate mine."

"You certainly make an impression on people."

"Did I mention I really hate the high school social dynamic?"

Slash looked like he was going to say something and then closed his mouth.

I touched his hand. "So, you ready to hit the sheets?"

He raised an eyebrow. "Is that an invitation to stay the night?"

"Well, it's after two o'clock in the morning. Technically the night is almost over. We're both exhausted and a bit wired. Since sex relieves tension, it seemed logical. We can just go to sleep if you'd prefer."

A slow smile crossed his mouth. "Damn. I have the best girlfriend."

"So, does that mean you're ready for bed?"

"*Cara*, I'm *always* ready."

FIFTEEN

I ARRIVED AT school rested and satisfied. Having a boyfriend did have its benefits and I was beginning to appreciate the comfort and companionship we were slowly building. When I'd agreed to be in a relationship with Slash, I'd never expected to enjoy it so much.

Bonnie had made sure to build a study hall into my schedule, giving me time to snoop, which was good because I needed some time to do research on Willem Jouret and the Veiled Knights. I slipped my laptop out of my backpack and set it up. Just in case anyone was monitoring the school's system, I'd be anonymous in my movements. Ron was off today, which gave me free rein of Computer Central for at least this class period.

I started with Jouret and then moved to his application to the school. He was an only child born in Cape Town to a South African father and American mother. He held dual citizenship, and had attended the University of Cape Town, where he studied math and computer science. Jouret was thirty-eight and he'd held eleven computer-related jobs. That implied he was a crappy employee or had really bad luck choosing solvent companies. Interestingly enough, he'd shown no interest in teaching until the past year.

I began taking a closer look at his more recent employment history. The year prior to coming to the school, he'd worked part-time at a local cybersecurity firm,

Maxim Security Solutions in Washington, D.C., while he got his teaching credentials in order. He put in his application to Excalibur Academy in the late fall and had been accepted for the new school year in March.

It all seemed to check out, but something kept bugging me. Teaching seemed out-of-character for a man like him, and there was a significant decrease in earning potential from the kind of money he *could* make with his credentials. Maybe that's just who Willem Jouret was, but it didn't feel right to me.

I decided to investigate Maxim Security Solutions. I certainly didn't know the name of every cybersecurity outfit in town, but this one didn't even ring a bell. A quick check indicated the company had been founded and registered in Washington, D.C., a year earlier and then gone under about two months after Jouret left. Not that unusual, given a lot of start-up firms went under after a year. But what *was* unusual was the dearth of information I could find on the company.

I ran a trace on the name of the CEO and came to a dead end in about six minutes. It was bogus.

My spidey sense was tingling. Something was definitely off about Willem Jouret. But what, if anything, did it have to do with the strange encrypted file and the unusual anomaly I had witnessed during the Computer Club yesterday?

What I really wanted was to have someone run a face recognition program on Jouret so I could be sure he was who he said he was. Since I no longer worked at the NSA, I no longer had access to that software or database. But luckily I had a boyfriend who did.

I shot Slash a quick email asking if he would be willing to run a scan on Willem Jouret for me. I gave him all the information I had, but figured he wouldn't need even that much.

I checked my watch and realized I had about ten minutes until my next class. I wouldn't have a break until lunch, so I picked up the phone and called Elvis. He picked up on the third ring.

"Hello?"

His voice sounded sleepy. Jeez. I'd forgotten he was sleeping in. Good friend, I was not.

"I forgot. I woke you. Crap."

"Lexi?"

"I'm sorry, Elvis. I got so focused on work, I spaced on the sleeping-in thing. I'll call back later."

He sounded more awake. "No, it's okay. Really. I can't think of a better way to wake up."

"Really?"

"Really. What's up?"

"The usual. Would you mind being my sounding board?"

"Not at all. Shoot."

"Well, I'm trying to trace any other incidents where the Veiled Knight encryption software might have been used to see if I could tie it to Jouret, but I'm not sure which method is the right approach. Any thoughts?"

He was silent, thinking. "That's a tough one. I'd need another look."

"I can come by after school."

"As it turns out, I'm mostly free today. I'm just tying up some loose ends at work before I leave for Greece next week. How about I stop by the school?"

"I don't want to bother you."

"No bother at all. Actually, I'm stuck with a code I'm

working on. Getting my mind busy on something else might help."

"Are you sure?"

"I'm sure."

"Thanks, Elvis, that would be great. But let me clear it with the principal, okay? Then I'll send you the address. I've got lunch at twelve forty. That might be a good time to rendezvous."

"I could make that."

"Thanks, Elvis. I really appreciate it."

I swung by the main office and gave Bonnie a rundown of the situation and my concerns about the file on Mr. Jouret's desktop. She, too, was conflicted about breaking in to the file without his permission and wanted to ask him directly what was in it. I convinced her to let me research it first. I worried if he got wind of our suspicions, he might destroy or remove the file before we could get more information on it. As a result, she cleared Elvis on the condition that she got to meet him first.

We were waiting for him in her office when Margaret—Ms. Eder—led him in and then left. She gave me a curious look but didn't say anything. Elvis was dressed in a long, dark winter coat with no hat and gloves. He had snowflakes in his hair and smiled when he saw me.

"Hey, Lexi. Wow. You look really…different in that uniform."

"I know. That's the idea. By the way, don't forget to call me Lara while I'm here. Part of the cover and all. Thanks for coming, Elvis."

"Sure, I'm happy to help out."

Bonnie set aside her glasses and stood. "I'm Bonnie Swanson, the headmistress of Excalibur Academy."

She extended a hand to Elvis. "Lexi has spoken highly of you."

Elvis took it and shook it. "Elvis Zimmerman. Nice to meet you."

"You've got a nice name. I'm a big Elvis fan. As in Presley."

"Yeah. I figured."

She smiled. "Well, Lexi says that you're going to consult with her on an anomaly she's come across on a teacher's computer."

"Yes, ma'am."

I patted Elvis on the shoulder and felt the melting snowflakes beneath my fingers. "No one knows anomalies like Elvis."

"Well, I appreciate your assistance, Mr. Zimmerman."

"No problem, but please call me Elvis."

"Certainly, if you call me Bonnie."

Elvis nodded, then turned to me. "Now what?"

"Now we go to Computer Central. Bonnie has cleared me for my next few classes, so I have some time to work on it with you."

"Okay. I need to make a quick stop in the bathroom first."

"I'll show you where it is," Bonnie offered, and they left the office. After a minute she came back smiling.

"So, that's Elvis." She leaned back against her desk. "Are you and he dating?"

"What? Me and Elvis? No. We're just friends. Why would you ask that?"

"I just wondered. Does that mean he's single?"

"Why would that matter?"

She shrugged. "It doesn't really, I guess."

I tried to imagine Elvis on a date and failed. Somehow, it just didn't compute. But before I could say anything else, Elvis returned. With a final, puzzled look at Bonnie, I led Elvis from her office. I walked down the hall, carrying my backpack slung over one shoulder, still needing to appear as if I were a student.

"Where's your badge?" I asked when I didn't see him wearing one.

He shrugged. "No one gave me anything. I didn't even sign in. I think the secretary was in a hurry to get to lunch. I suppose she figured I was only going to the principal's office."

"It's okay. My badge will get us most everywhere."

He looked at the gleaming lockers as we passed. "Nice setup here. Way better than what I had in high school."

"Me, too."

"Does the better environment make it any more bearable?"

"No. It's only better the second time around because I know it's just temporary. Overall, it still sucks."

"I figured as much."

We stopped in front of Computer Central. I made sure the hallway was empty before waving my badge in front of the access panel. A green light came on and the door clicked open. I stepped in and Elvis followed.

I led him to Ron's desk and dropped my backpack on the floor. Elvis shrugged out of his coat and hung it on the back of one of the chairs. I pulled a rolling chair over next to mine and patted it.

"Sit here and I'll show you the file."

"Any chance I can have a peek at the general landscape first?"

"Sure." I pulled up a screen. "So, here's the deal. The school has three separate systems. There's the security system—which controls access to the school and various rooms in the school—the phone system and the electrical system. The security system has computerized-controlled access and television screens on all major entrances and exits and is linked to an external security company that monitors the school and will call appropriate authorities in case of danger, fire or other disaster. The phone system is also linked to an external company. Although the external companies maintain routine control, the school can take charge of any system at any time with a manual override. This is unfortunate because if the kids hack in, they can overwrite controls and take charge. The upside is that they would have to break into three separate systems, as none of them are linked."

"That's pretty decent. They've got wireless here, I presume."

"Yes. Cell phones, however, don't work in the building. That was intended. Staff and students have to use the school phones or go outside to use their cells."

"Makes sense these days, I guess."

"I guess." I tapped the monitor. "Anyway, neither the security system, the phone nor the general system is connected, so imagine my surprise when I'm sitting in the Computer Club chatting with some of the kids yesterday and I see the cursor moving around the screen all by itself and clicking on items."

"Remote access?"

"Well, that's what I thought. I checked the logs. No remote management was noted. But last night when I accessed the system from your place, it registered me. So, I know it's working. I asked Ron, the IT guy, what was the deal on that and he told me external companies must request to connect to any one of the systems to do any administration work. They absolutely cannot access our system on their own."

"Let me guess, no requests were made."

"No. But someone was definitely playing around with the admin controls. I saw it with my own eyes."

"Students?"

"Maybe, but it felt different. Can't explain it better than that. Later I ran a virus scan. It was clean. It was like I'd imagined the whole thing."

"But you didn't."

"No, I didn't."

"Interesting. Let me have a look."

I rolled to the side so he could be front and center at the monitor.

He had just started to engage when I heard a noise. It sounded like someone was making popcorn.

"Did you hear that?" I asked Elvis.

He looked up, listened. "Yes."

"Popcorn?"

"No. I think…gunfire."

"What?"

We cautiously approached the door. The popping sounds were louder now, accompanied by screaming.

He grabbed my hand, yanking me against the wall with him. "I think the school has an active shooter."

"An active shooter? Here?"

"Yes." Elvis leaned over and glanced at the doorknob. "This room locks automatically, right?"

"Yes. The badge has to be programmed to open this door. Only authorized staff can open it from the outside. But you gave me an idea."

I dashed to Ron's computer and started typing. Elvis followed me, snatching the phone receiver from its cradle.

He pressed the button a couple of times. "It's dead."

I raised my gaze to meet his. "Not a good development."

He set the receiver back down. "Definitely not. Your typical active shooter doesn't disconnect the phone system before he starts shooting."

"So, who does?"

"Someone a lot more organized. You may have been on to something a lot bigger with your computer snooping."

He peered over my shoulder. "What are you doing?"

"I just changed the access code to this room. As of right now, no one can use an access badge to get in here."

"Good thinking, but it won't give us much time. Someone with a big enough gun will be able to shoot their way in here if they are really determined."

"True." I ran to the security laptop and sat down.

"Now what are you doing?" Elvis asked, following me.

"I'm checking the cameras." I pulled up the video and saw two black-clad figures kneeling by the front door. One was securing a chain on the door handles while the other one was working over something in a backpack.

"Holy crap, Elvis. They're booby-trapping the front door. See those black and red wires? Jeez. Does that look like a bomb to you?"

"Unfortunately, yes. A sophisticated one, too."

I switched to the gym entrance and saw two other black-clad figures doing something similar on that door. I quickly scanned the other entrances—all six were being booby-trapped. Elvis watched over my shoulder.

He whistled. "It's a small army. I've counted twelve people already. This is *not* an active shooter scenario."

I stared at Elvis. "The Veiled Knights."

"Whoa. They're cyber mercenaries, not terrorists."

"The terrorists could be paying them."

"To do what?"

"I have a feeling we're about to find out."

I started to say something else when Elvis pulled me toward him and put a finger on my lips. He pulled me under the desk as someone crashed against the door. My heart jumped to my throat.

Someone outside the door yelled, "The badge isn't working. Go get something to blow the door."

There was some noise and then the same voice shouted, "Fine. Clock is ticking. I've got to get into this room in under ten minutes or we're dead."

The noise at the door silenced.

Elvis squeezed my hand. His face was deathly pale. "They must have tried the badge and it didn't work. They can't get in."

"Yet."

"Yes, yet."

I crawled out from beneath the keyboard and began typing in the system's admin account.

"You got a plan?" Elvis asked, following me.

"Sort of. I'm creating a back door to the main system. If we get out of here alive, we may need it. If they take control of the system, they're likely to change up the passwords and lock everyone out."

"True."

"This will give us an in."

My fingers were shaking as I typed. Elvis put a hand on my shoulder when I finished. "Good work. My turn."

He maneuvered through the system so quickly I wasn't sure what he had done.

"What did you do?" I asked.

"Notified the police. Planted a little bug. No time for more. The bug won't stop them, but I'm not certain how to best sabotage a system I don't even know. I'm not even sure it would be wise at this point. But it will prove to be a bit of a nuisance if someone takes over the system. We might be able to slow down their plan a bit via that back door of yours, providing we survive this."

I swallowed my panic. "Elvis, what are we going to do? We've got to get out of this room."

He looked around. "How? We're on the third floor and there are no windows. Even worse, there are adversaries on the other side of that door trying to figure out how to get in here. I'll be brutally honest and say things are not looking good for us."

I glanced around the room and then tore off my sweater. "Elvis, get naked."

His eyes widened. *"What?"*

"Take off your clothes now. Down to your underwear. That'll be enough to do it."

He backed up against the desk. "Lexi, I know you think we might die, but…"

I reached for him, putting my hands on his hips. "You are perfect."

I pulled up his sweater, yanking the shirt beneath it apart and sending buttons flying all across the room. "Strip. Now. No time for discussion."

I unzipped my plaid skirt and stepped out of it. Elvis still stood there, staring at me in complete shock.

"Elvis, hurry. Please, just take off your clothes."

He blinked and then kicked off his shoes. After a moment, he fumbled with his pants, pushing them down.

I stopped, staring at him. "Is that a reindeer on your underwear?"

His cheeks colored. "It's Christmas."

I squinted. "That's a really red nose."

He crossed his hands in front of the reindeer. "Look, Lexi, while I have thought about this, quite a lot actually, this isn't the way I imagined it would happen. Especially not within moments of death by terrorists, and especially not while in this underwear. Still, there's something you should know before we…"

I pulled off my sweater and the polo underneath, leaving me in nothing more than my bra, panties and green knee socks. "Elvis, please hurry."

His face turned bright red. "Wait. You're entitled to know before… Oh, hell, I'll just say it. I'm a virgin, okay? I'm pretty nervous right now for a multitude of reasons—not to mention the guys with guns out there. So while *theoretically* I know what to do, I'm just not sure how I'll perform under this kind of pressure."

I froze. "What?"

"I know it's rather surprising. The virgin part, I mean. Well, maybe it's not *that* surprising, but—"

"Elvis, I'm *not* propositioning you. I've got a plan."

His mouth fell open. "A plan?"

I strode over to the tall, thin vertical closet that held all the computer wires. I yanked open the door.

"We're going in here."

"Whoa." He pulled his pants back up and walked over to look. "There is no way we'll both fit in there."

"We will. But it will be tight. Really, *really* tight. Just eyeballing it, taking into account the width of your hips and mine, we can do it. But the closet is only twenty-five by twenty-two, which is why we have to strip down to almost nothing. It's our only option."

"Are you nuts? We won't fit. You have to account for the cables. You go in there alone. I'll stay out here and distract them if they come in."

"There'll be no distraction and we both know it. I did account for the cables. We'll fit. Please, you've got to trust me and my math. I won't go in without you, Elvis. I just won't. So, either we go in together or we stay out here together. The key word is *together*, okay?"

"Okay."

He pulled off his pants. Thankful, I grabbed them and stuffed them in my backpack, pushing it as far under the desk as it would go.

For a moment we stood face-to-face—me clad in my bra, undies and knee socks and Elvis in his reindeer underwear and socks. Normally, I'd be embarrassed but there wasn't time, and besides, this was my best friend.

I took his hand, pulling him to the closet. "Okay. I'm going in first. You come in next. Try to put your legs, arms and anything else you can in a space that isn't already occupied by my body. Got it?"

He nodded, a lock of brown hair falling over one eye. "Okay, got it."

I climbed in and then motioned for him to follow. He inhaled and then stepped inside. Instantly, he was pressed so tightly against me that I could barely breathe. My back smashed uncomfortably against a bunch of cables. Elvis shifted his position slightly so he straddled my right thigh, but he had no place to angle his hips except squarely against mine.

There was no ceiling to the closet. It was open to

the room, mostly for cooling purposes. That was good because it let light into the space, but bad because we couldn't make even the tiniest of noises or we would be heard.

Elvis's head was to the left of me, but my chin rested on his shoulder, my hair falling against his bare chest. He had lifted his arms and placed them on either side of my head, his fingers splayed out. Our torsos and chests were smashed together so hard that taking a breath was painful. His breath warmed my cheek and shoulder and I could feel every inch of him on me, including the part that now pressed hard against my inner thigh. My cheeks heated. He must've been feeling just as mortified, but I couldn't think about that now. We were doing what had to be done to survive.

Elvis managed to close the door. We were so squished I could feel it each time he tried to take a breath.

"You're right," he whispered. "We fit. Barely. There's no lock on the inside, but at least there's a small handle."

"We'll have to hold on to it as if our lives depend on it," I whispered back. "Especially since they do."

I wiggled my arm and inched it toward his. My fingers closed over his on the handle. "We've got this. No one will think to look in here."

His breath warmed the side of my neck.

"Lexi, this is a crazy idea."

"It's our *only* idea."

He managed a smile. "True. But it's going to be really embarrassing if the police find us asphyxiated and smashed in here together without our clothes on."

I wished I could pat his back reassuringly, but I couldn't move. "I'm not embarrassed."

"Well, you didn't just announce you were a virgin."

"That's nothing to be embarrassed about. I wasn't exactly experienced either…until recently."

We froze when we heard a noise. Gunfire. They were finally blasting the door open. I tensed as I heard a loud crash, the chatter of voices and footsteps walking toward us.

The terrorists were in.

My heart pounded. I was sure Elvis could feel it. My eyes met his. He smiled and mouthed, *We've got this.*

My fingers tightened on his as the footsteps got closer. A hundred thoughts raced through my head. Had I pushed the backpack far enough under the table? Was my rent paid through the month? Would Slash miss me? If I died, would my mother dress me in some pink, frilly dress for my funeral? Jeez, why hadn't I specified my final dress code in my will? Wait! Did I even *have* a will?

The footsteps stopped and the chair scraped across the floor. Whoever it was had decided to sit down at the computer terminal in the Server Room. I heard the tap of someone typing on the keyboard. My fingers squeezed Elvis's so hard I was surprised he didn't wince. I closed my eyes.

"What the hell is this?"

I recognized the voice. Willem Jouret.

A second accented voice I didn't recognize answered. "What the hell is what?"

"Someone has been fooling with the system again. Damn kids. They've been jacking it up. That's probably why the access code got all screwed up."

"Can you fix it?"

"Of course I can fix it. But it's going to take some time."

"We don't have a lot of time."

"I said I could do it. You worry about your part and let me worry about mine. Let me check the cables first."

Elvis's fingers tightened over mine as the footsteps approached the closet. I squeezed my eyes shut and wished I knew an appropriate prayer.

We were about to be toast.

SIXTEEN

Static crackled and a garbled voice spoke. The footsteps moved away from the closet.

"Yes, Computer Central is secure," Jouret said into what must have been a walkie-talkie. I heard popping noises and screaming. My horrified gaze met Elvis's.

The other voice on the walkie-talkie was barely audible over all the noise. "Damn, we've got early company. Be my eyes. What do you see?"

I heard more tapping and figured Jouret was checking the security cameras on the exterior. "They're already here. That was fast. I see at least three police cars out front with two figures already exiting the vehicles. I figure we've got about two minutes before we've got company at the front door."

"Then get your ass down here. We'll need everyone down here until we have the kids under control."

"Roger." The chair scraped across the floor and something hit the table with a crash. "Let me get my mask. Can't have anyone recognizing me. Come on, we've got to give them a hand."

Footsteps pounded and then silence.

I waited a full minute before I exhaled and pressed my lips against Elvis's ear. "They're gone."

We remained still for another minute until we were sure no one else was around. The cables were burning into my back. Elvis looked equally as uncomfortable with sweat beading on his chest. Finally he shifted his leg. It caused his hips to press even more tightly against mine, until I could feel every bump and curve of him nestled between my legs.

His face reddened. "Sorry," he whispered. "I was getting a cramp."

"It's okay. What should we do?"

"The security company must have gotten your message. I don't think the gunmen were expecting the police so quickly. This may be our chance to escape."

"Do we risk it?"

"We can't stay in here forever. If they're busy rounding up people and securing the physical perimeter, this may be our best chance."

"Okay."

Elvis began to wiggle against me so he could maneuver his way out. At one point his mouth was so close to mine, I could feel his breath on my lips. He stilled and I had the strangest feeling that he intended to kiss me.

Then the moment passed and he managed to shift his hips and fall out of the closet. I stepped out after him, shaking my limbs to get the circulation back.

"Hurry. Grab the backpack." He snatched his coat off the back of one of the chairs and then shoved it at me. "Put it on."

I shoved my arms into the coat, then pointed at the desk. "Elvis, look. They brought their own laptops." I pointed to the desk where a laptop had been opened, but not yet plugged in. Two more laptops encased in black, leather carry bags were lying on the ground. Elvis picked one up and slung it over his shoulder.

"What are you doing?"

"We're going to fight fire with fire."

My eyes widened. "What? Are you sure that's a good plan? When they see one missing, they'll know they've got renegades. They'll hunt us."

"Maybe. But this is our best lead as to what is going on here. I think the risk is worth it."

I considered. "Okay. Agreed."

I yanked my backpack out from under the desk. Elvis already stood by the door with the laptop bag over his shoulder.

"Watch your step," he whispered.

Debris and twisted metal had been scattered everywhere when they shot open the door. I wiggled my toes and glanced at his. Getting naked didn't seem like such a good idea now. I shivered and pulled his coat tighter around me.

He dared a quick peek into the hallway. "It's clear. Where to?"

"The Weather Station is a couple of rooms down. Let's go there and regroup."

"Seeing as how I have no better alternative, it sounds like a plan."

I had never been so glad *not* to be alone.

I took a quick look both ways and dashed down the hallway. Elvis was close on my heels. My heart was pounding so loud I was sure it could be heard three floors down. I slid sideways in my socks, skidding to a stop in front of the door. The room was dark, so I took that as a good sign. I pressed on the handle and the door swung open. We stepped into a blessedly empty room.

My heart still thudding, I clicked the door shut and locked it, turning to survey the Weather Lab.

"Nice setup," Elvis said softly.

I hadn't been in this classroom before. It looked a

lot like the other science labs with lab desks and stools. This lab also had several expensive-looking pieces of weather equipment. An electronic maximum-minimum temperature sensor sat on a side table across from an aneroid barometer. The walls were covered with white scrolls of paper with weather data, and someone had hung a handmade sling psychrometer near the window. The room was neat, with no open books or scattered papers, so I assumed there had been no class in session when the shooters came.

I crept to the window and peered out. I could see at least a half dozen police cars and assorted security personnel running around the perimeter. Their presence was comforting.

I jumped when a voice came on over the intercom system.

"Attention police and security personnel. Please be advised that the school is now secure. Do not, I repeat, do not try to access the building. Precautions, including explosive devices, have been taken to prevent your entry. We have over two hundred hostages and will kill two for every attempt made to enter the building. We are willing to negotiate for their lives. For now we have two simple demands. One, power should not be cut to the building. If electricity is cut, one student will be shot for every five seconds the power is down. Second, do not interfere with our cyber communications. If at any time our connection goes down, gets slow or is interfered with, students will be shot. Further demands will be forthcoming."

I exchanged a worried glance with Elvis. "What was that all about?"

"Don't know yet. The official response to an active

shooter scenario is an immediate breach by police. We learned that after Columbine. But apparently these guys want to make it clear this is a hostage situation and they are willing to negotiate. Totally different scenario."

"So no immediate help is forthcoming."

"I would say that's a safe bet."

"Jeez."

He took me by the arm. "Come on, Lexi. Let's go to the back of the room. There are shadows there and we'll be better hidden. We don't know when we might have company."

I followed him to the back of the room, shivering.

Elvis took the backpack from me. "You're cold."

"Scared witless actually. But at least I have your coat on. You must be freezing in your boxers and socks."

He shrugged. "Getting dressed wasn't a priority until now. Besides, my coat looks better on you."

"It smells like you." Wait, I needed to try that again. "I meant that in a good way."

"I figured. Glad to hear it." He dug into the backpack and tossed me my skirt, polo shirt, and green sweater.

I pulled everything on and then pulled out my shoes. Elvis stood looking ruefully at his shirt. I'd ripped off several of the buttons trying to get it off him, so it gaped open.

"I'm sorry, Elvis. I ruined your shirt."

"Hey, don't be sorry. I've never had a woman rip my clothes off before. I, um, kind of liked it. Under different circumstances, I might have even loved it."

Ooookay. Wasn't sure what to make of that comment, but I couldn't analyze it right now. Time to move on or we'd be discovered. I could stress out about it later, if we survived.

"Elvis, we have to find a hiding space in here in case they do another search."

He glanced around the room. "These storage cabinets over there are big enough." He began clearing out one of the lower cabinets. "We can both squeeze in here if we remove the equipment."

He began arranging equipment on top of the counter, making it look like it belonged there. I helped. When we were done, there was just enough space for the two of us to sit with the doors closed.

I examined our cramped surroundings. "This isn't much of a hiding space, but we have to work with what we've got."

Elvis nodded. "I need time to check out this laptop."

He booted it up and I tried to angle myself better so I could see what he was doing. The light from the screen seemed overly bright in the dark cabinet.

"It's password protected," I observed.

"As expected."

"But we don't have the software, or access to the software, to break it."

He shifted and rooted around in his pocket. He pulled out his car keys and held them up.

"You're going to start your car from here?"

"Glad to see terror has not robbed you of your humor." He flicked his thumb against a flash drive. "I've got what we need."

"Oh, please tell me you have decryption software on there."

"I have decryption software on here. Actually brought a variety in case you changed your mind and gave me a crack at that file."

"Elvis Zimmerman, you're amazing."

"Now you tell me." He grinned and plugged in the flash drive. "Okay, this is going to take some time."

"We seem to have a lot of it at the moment. At least I sincerely hope so."

He set up the software and it started working. Now we waited.

I wiggled my feet, feeling the adrenaline rush subside and my brain begin to work on something other than my immediate survival. "Jouret was seriously pissed I changed the access code to the room. Just wait until he finds your bug."

"Good. Pissed people make mistakes. We could use a little luck."

"Agreed. But it's not going to stop them."

"No. I didn't have time for anything that fancy." He tapped something on the keyboard. "But it'll rattle them, as did the police's early arrival. We've already put a couple of crimps in their plan."

I hugged my knees to my chin. "So, what do you think of their two initial demands? They can't possibly believe the police won't try to interfere with their communications. Given the way they've executed this operation so far, they aren't stupid. They'll know the NSA, CIA and everyone who is anyone in cybersecurity will be monitoring that connection six ways to Sunday."

"They'll encrypt, of course. I would venture a guess that your buddy, Mr. Jouret, has been busy crafting an impenetrable cyber fortress at the school to protect any electronic traffic. I suspect that's what's in the odd file on his desktop."

"Agreed. So, you think he's with the Veiled Knights?"

"He's South African. I don't see that as a coincidence."

"True. We'll have to figure out how that plays in.

Still, even if these guys encrypt, they must know the FBI, CIA, NSA, DHS and everyone else will have the best minds working on that encryption."

"It doesn't matter. They won't need the fortress to last forever. They just need it to stay up for a short period of time. I guarantee you they're on a tight timetable. They've made sure no one can get in from the outside, at least for a calculable amount of time."

"But they don't know about us inside."

"No, they don't, which gives us a tremendous advantage. If we can find out who these terrorists are and what the end game is, it might help us figure out what the Veiled Knights intend to get out of this."

"But how can the two of us take on an entire army of terrorists?"

"With our brains. If we can remain undetected, we've got a fighting chance."

I liked the quiet certainty in his voice. It made me feel safe and secure, at least as far as the situation warranted.

Elvis studied the laptop. "This is high-end equipment, which means their encryption software is likely to be good. It might take a bit longer than I'd expected. Good thing I brought the sophisticated stuff. I'm going to hit it with all I've got."

"That seems like an excellent plan."

I rotated my neck the best I could in our cramped quarters and tried to stretch out the kinks. "The police will know we're in here. They will run all the license plates in the parking lot. They'll know you're here, too, Elvis."

"Good. What about Slash? Does he know you're here?"

"Yes. In fact, I sent him a request earlier today to run

a trace on Jouret. It won't take him long to piece that together. He'll be all over that by now and, by extension, so will the police."

"Do you think he's out there now...in the parking lot somewhere?"

"I *know* he's there. He's probably setting up the command center and/or leading the encryption team. Either way, I'm pretty sure if we get out of this alive, he's going to kill me."

"Why?"

"He said trouble stalks me. He may be right. He specifically ordered me to stay out of restaurants, malls and public areas. In my defense, he didn't say anything about schools."

"I don't think he can hold this against you. You were working."

"I know. I guess he was right to worry about me. He's right about a lot of things." I pressed my ear to the cabinet and listened. "Elvis, I have an idea. There is a computer on the teacher's desk. I think it's time for me to take a look at what's going on via the back door."

He put a hand on my arm. "Wait. The terrorists are still likely to be doing sweeps. They may already be monitoring all online activity at the school and might be able to trace us directly to this classroom."

"I know, but these early moments may be our only chance to get a good look while they're still setting up stuff. I'm just going to take a quick peek. Nothing else."

He considered. "Okay. Then *we'll* both go."

"Why? You don't trust me?"

"I *do* trust you. More than anyone I have ever met. It's just...dangerous."

"Of course it's dangerous. We're trapped in a high

school by a bunch of crazed terrorists. Don't go all macho on me, okay?"

Before he could argue further, I opened the cabinet and fell out. I couldn't hear any movement from the hallway. I came up on all fours, groaning as my legs cramped from being squished in the cabinet. Pushing up to a crouch, I glanced around the room, noting the computer stations. There were three computers set up in a cluster beneath the window and one at the teacher's desk. I decided to take the teacher's. I crept over to the desk, staying low.

The computer was on and the screen saver was in play. I reached up and tapped the space bar when I heard a noise in the hallway.

I clicked the monitor off and scooted under the teacher's desk, hugging my knees to my chest. The door to the Weather Lab opened and footsteps stealthily approached my location. Elvis had been right. I should have waited.

I felt like throwing up. If whoever it was noticed me, I'd be toast. My legs started to shake and I squeezed my knees so hard my knuckles turned white. The footsteps stopped near the desk. Blood roared in my ears.

The footsteps moved on and black-clad legs came into view. The figure crouched down by the window and I saw it was a man with a dark ski mask. He had a long gun strapped to his body with a diagonal belt. He held another gun in one hand and wore a bulky vest. He was a mere two feet from me. If he turned counterclockwise a half turn he'd see me huddled there. I couldn't believe it. My life hung on a turn.

I didn't breathe or move for fear of catching his eye. Instead I closed my eyes and wished I knew an appropriate prayer.

A crash sounded, causing me to startle. I glanced up as the blinds over the window rattled and closed. Once they were down, the man turned away from the desk. He hadn't seen me. His footsteps slapped across the floor. The door to the classroom opened and then clicked shut.

I stayed crouched under the desk for a full minute, gulping deep breaths and hugging my knees to my chest, trying to stop my entire body from shuddering.

"Lexi?" Elvis whispered frantically.

"I'm okay." I took several more breaths and tried to steady my shaking hands. "Oh, crap. That was way too close for comfort."

I crawled out from beneath the desk and came to a crouch in front of the computer. My teeth were chattering. "One of the terrorists just closed the blinds, presumably to limit the view of the snipers and police. I managed to hide under the teacher's desk. I don't think he saw me."

"Thank God. Come back here."

"In a minute. I haven't had a chance to get a look at the system. I'm not wasting the trip."

I turned on the monitor and my fingers tapped the keyboard. It took me under thirty seconds to navigate to the back door I'd set up, slide into the system and take a look around.

"Hurry," Elvis whispered.

"I am hurrying, but I have to be careful."

I checked out a few things before crawling back to Elvis. My hands were still shaking. Badass, I was not.

I slid in across from Elvis and he gave me an awkward hug with the laptop squished between us.

"Jesus H. Christ. I have never been so scared in all of my life."

"What about in the closet an hour or so ago?"

He shook his head. "No, that wasn't as bad. At least we were together. This time, I didn't know what was happening to you."

"I'm alive. That's all that matters at this point."

"Truth to the ultimate degree."

I pressed a hand to my throat. "If he had turned even a micro inch to his left, he would have seen me. But he didn't and I'm still here. Holy cow."

He put his hand on my trembling one and squeezed. "Good. That's good. Breathe in. Breathe out. We're going to make it."

His steadiness comforted me. "Yes, you're right. We've got this."

"I just hope your trip was worth it. What did you see?"

"Well, I've got good news and bad news. Which do you want first?"

He exhaled. "The way things are going I'd rather have the bad up front."

"Okay. The bad news is they've already got internal monitoring software set up. Which means Jouret, if he remains the one working out of Computer Central, would peg us if we tried to do anything on any of the computers in the school. We're also isolated from the Internet connection, as expected. We won't be able to check the Internet to figure out what to do if surrounded by deranged terrorists in a high school."

"Bummer."

"My thoughts exactly. Needless to say, at this point there's no way we can contact the police so we can tell them what's going on in here."

"Do we even *know* what's going on?"

"Not really, but we will, right?"

"Right. What else?"

"Well, Jouret has been a busy boy. I noted several heavily encrypted communications going in and out. He's already talking with someone, but I don't think it's the police."

"Agreed."

"He's also changed all the passwords and locked everyone out internally. I can't say I didn't expect that."

"Me, neither. It makes our work more difficult, but not impossible."

"Especially since we have a back door. We just have to figure out how to access it without being noticed. Plus, nothing technical is ever impossible for you, Elvis."

"Appreciate the vote of confidence."

"You're welcome. Now for the good news."

"Well, the bad news wasn't as bad as I expected. But any good news is welcome given our current situation."

I managed a smile. "Well, the good news is that Jouret is the only person in the school logged in to the system right now."

"How is that good?"

"Because of the way he's logged in."

"Which is?"

"Through his own school account."

Elvis waited a beat. "There *is* more to this good news, right?"

"Of course. Here's the good news. He's logged in via his office as well as Computer Central."

A slow smile spread across his face. "I see where you're going with this. If we presume, which we should, that Jouret is working out of Computer Central, then it's logical to assume his office is empty. If we can get there, we can slip into the system right through his own account and see what he's up to without setting off any alarms."

"Yes. Except…there are two problems. One, I don't know where Jouret's office is. Second, we're in a school full of terrorists. We can't just roam around and ask someone where it is."

"Those are definitely problems."

The laptop dinged and I bumped my head on the top of the cabinet. I had become seriously jumpy.

Elvis opened it and checked. "Password bypassed. We're in. More luck coming our way. It wasn't nearly as hard as I expected to get in. Let's see what we have here."

I started to shift so I could see the screen when I heard a noise at the door. He quietly closed the laptop and put a finger on his lips. The cabinet went dark and we both stilled.

Then the door opened and I heard the soft chatter of voices in a language I didn't recognize.

Elvis leaned forward, pressing his mouth to my ear. *"Urdu,"* he breathed.

Urdu? I racked my brain to try and remember what country had Urdu as a national language. I stopped when I heard them start pulling things out of the cabinets.

Oh, God, I bet they were looking for the missing laptop. In a matter of moments, they would find it and peel it from Elvis's dead hands.

I couldn't see him, but I could hear his calm, steady breathing. He didn't seem overly panicked, just calmly waiting, as if he faced down crazed terrorists every day.

His quiet confidence comforted me. I held my breath and mathematically calculated how far away the searchers were based on their noise and movement. I tried to slow my breathing and think.

No question they'd be shocked to see us, and furious when they discovered the laptop. Unfortunately, no matter which way I considered it, the odds they would shoot first and ask questions later remained at ninety-nine point nine percent.

My eyes locked onto Elvis's.

It sounded like they were at the next cabinet over. If I calculated correctly, that meant my life would probably end in about ten seconds.

Nine, eight, seven, six, five, four...

I couldn't breathe. My heart pounded so hard I was certain whoever was standing less than two feet away could hear it. Elvis reached out and linked his fingers with mine.

Knock, knock.

I stiffened, glancing at Elvis. He frowned. The searchers exchanged hushed words directly in front of our cabinet and then their footsteps moved toward the door. More whispers, and then the door opened and closed with a slam. We listened for a several minutes without hearing anything before I whispered to Elvis.

"What the heck was that?"

"A knock."

"I know it was a knock," I hissed. "But what kind of terrorists knock?"

"No idea."

"You said they were speaking Urdu."

"Yes."

"Before I express my enormous surprise that you speak Urdu, please tell me in which country they speak the language."

"Countries." Elvis exhaled heavily. Despite his calm facade, he must have been as nervous as me. "Urdu is spoken mostly among the Muslim communities in Pakistan and India in the region of Hindustan. Both countries list Urdu as a national language, along with English and numerous other dialects. I don't speak Urdu by any stretch of the imagination, but Xavier and I worked in India for three months about a year and a half ago on a project for our company. I recognize the language and a few of the words."

"Pakistan and India?"

"Yes. There are numerous al Qaeda and Taliban operatives in both countries. We found Osama bin Laden in Pakistan."

"So which ones are they? Pakistani or Indian?"

Elvis shrugged. "No idea. It's not like I can ask for clarification."

"True. Now what?"

"Now, we move to one of the cabinets they've already searched."

"How about leaving this classroom entirely? I'd rather not be here when they come back."

"I wish we could, but I'm not sure that's a good idea. They might still be out in the hallway. We don't know where they are. At the very least, we have to assume they are monitoring the hallways with the security cameras. We've got better odds of survival at this point if we plant ourselves where they have already searched and make a new plan."

As reluctant as I was to stay, I didn't have a better idea at the moment. "Okay."

I carefully opened the cabinet and peered out. The room was dim. Since the blinds were closed, the room was shrouded in shadows.

Elvis fell out of the cabinet, groaning as he stretched

his cramped legs. We half-crawled and half-crept to the second cabinet in the row, moving carefully around the discarded items on the floor. After one more quick stretch, we climbed into the new cabinet, closing the door behind us.

Elvis immediately opened the laptop. "I'm not waiting any longer. We've got to see what's in here. Hope it was worth it."

He balanced the laptop on his knees angled the screen toward me so I could see what he was doing. He'd already accessed the hard drive and was looking around.

"Hey, look. It's that same file you saw on Jouret's computer."

"Okay, so now it's official. The Veiled Knights are somehow connected to this operation."

"Yes. So, I guess, given our present circumstances, it would be okay to have a crack at it and see what's in there."

"Crack away."

"Music to my ears. But coming from you, they are especially sweet."

I smiled and he started a new attack against the file. I watched with interest, offering suggestions here and there. Eventually, we came to a point where we could do nothing but wait and let the software do its work.

I must have fallen asleep because at some point, Elvis nudged me on the shoulder. "Lexi. We're in."

I blinked and rubbed my eyes, squinting at the glow of the screen. "Fantastic. How long was I out?"

"Nearly two hours. Don't worry, you didn't miss anything."

"Two hours? Really? Why didn't you wake me?"

"I was busy and no terrorists came back. I thought it best that one of us got some rest."

"Jeez, I'm sorry about that. I don't know what happened to me."

"You were exhausted, not to mention traumatized. You shut down. It's okay. I managed without you. The file buckled."

"Under your very precise ministrations."

He grinned. "Well, the software did most of the work. But I gave it a little help, of course."

"Of course." I smiled and tapped the screen. "Open that document first."

Elvis opened it. "It's in Urdu."

"You don't happen to have an Urdu translating software on that thumb drive."

"I'm afraid not."

"Drat. Okay, try that one."

He clicked on it. "It's a news article in English, thank God."

I leaned closer. "About what?"

"Politics in Pakistan."

"Angle it this way so I can read it, too."

We both read the article silently. When I was done, I leaned my head back against the cabinet.

"We're in big trouble, Elvis."

"Why?"

"See where the article is talking about these factions—the *Mehsuds* and the *Shahids*? Well, I may have had an up-close encounter with one of them."

"What?"

I quickly brought him up to date on my run-in with

Ansari Zogby and the bomb-making equipment the police found in the apartment he visited.

Elvis whistled softly. "Well, at least we know where
the bombs are now."

"Great. What are we going to do?"

He looked back at the article. "We have to figure out
their end game and work backward."

"How are we going to do that? I know squat about
warring factions in Pakistan. What does any of that have
to do with a high school in D.C.?"

"Let's try to break it down logically. According to this
article, there are two major Taliban factions at war with
the government in Pakistan. One faction, the *Mehsuds*,
have been the most powerful anti-government force in
the area. But when a drone strike killed their leader
back in 2009, there was a struggle over who would take
charge. A splinter group called *Shahid* split from the
Mehsuds and tried to take control of the group's activities and the money. There's been a lot of infighting. Now
there's real trouble because the Pakistani prime minister recently invited the *Mehsuds* to the table to negotiate
peace and possible representation in the government."

"What about the *Shahids*?"

"No. Just the *Mehsuds*. This has apparently upset the
Shahid. They are responsible for a string of bombings
across the capital city, killing several people. They've
also claimed responsibility for the assassination of a
prominent Pakistani politician who supported the peace
talks. They're threatening worse if the talks continue."

I nodded. "Yes, that's similar to what Slash told me.
But while all of that is horrible, what's the connection
to a high school in D.C.?"

"Not a clue. Let's see what else we can find."

Elvis angled the laptop back toward himself and clicked on another document. Blueprints filled the screen. He whistled.

"Blueprints for the school."

"I guess it would be too much to hope that they would identify the location of each teacher's office."

He rotated the view. "If only. These look like they came from the original builder. I imagine the police already have a copy of this."

"That's a given." I tapped on a spot on the blueprint. "We're here in the Weather Lab."

Elvis traced a finger on the air-conditioning and heating grids and the crawl spaces. "This is where the SWAT teams will look in terms of an entry. But given what I've seen of the expertise of the group so far, I would presume that they've thought of this, as well."

I blew out a breath. "You think they've got explosives there, too?"

"I wouldn't discount that possibility."

I pointed to another document. "Try that one."

He opened it and scanned it. "Another news article. This one focuses on U.S. involvement in Pakistan peace talks."

"The U.S. is involved?"

Elvis shook his head. "Actually, no. Well, at least according to this article, the State Department spokesman denies any involvement. It looks like there was a related Pakistani news article that surfaced saying the U.S. Senate subcommittee on Near Eastern and South and Central Asian Affairs had been secretly urging the Pakistani prime minster to shut out the *Shahids* because of their connections to al Qaeda."

I felt a headache start to throb behind my eyes. "This is all fascinating, but I'm not sure how it helps us narrow down what is going on. Do you think these terrorists are from the *Shahids*?"

"It seems the most logical assumption at this point."

"But why hold a school full of kids hostage in the U.S.? To what end?"

"I wish I knew. I think we have to wait until we hear the demands."

I leaned back, trying to stretch a part of my back that had started to hurt. "It's been hours since they broadcast their first demands. I don't think they're going to keep broadcasting demands by intercom. I think they would have issued more demands by now. They must be using the email system to communicate."

"We've got to get in. But first we figure out how to find and then get to Jouret's office."

"The sooner the better."

Elvis tapped his chin. "What about a school directory of some kind? I would assume classroom information and phone numbers would be available on the school's intranet, but do you think they might have also distributed a hard copy to the staff?"

"Maybe. It's a good idea, Elvis. I can take a look through the teacher's desk."

He shifted the laptop to me. "No way. I get to go this time. My idea, my trip."

"Okay. Fair enough. Hurry up."

"You don't have to tell me twice."

He climbed out of the cabinet and crept toward the teacher's desk. I closed the cabinet after he left and then waited. It was agonizing not being able to see him. Now I understood how he must have felt sitting in the cabinet not knowing what I was doing, waiting for me to return and hearing someone come into the room. The soft slide of the drawers opened and closed sounded and then the soft rustle of paper. It seemed like it was taking him forever. I was about to tell him to forget it and come back when the cabinet door opened and he slipped inside.

He held a thin paper booklet covered in a plastic folder. "A present for you, my lady."

"You give the best presents *ever*, Elvis."

"I strive for perfection."

I opened the booklet and flipped through. "Willem Jouret. Here it is. His office is Room 216. That's on the second floor, one floor down from us, two rooms from the stairwell on the right side of the hallway, according to the blueprints."

"Okay. So, how do we get there?"

One floor suddenly seemed light-years away. "I'm not sure. They'll certainly have the security cameras cycling through the corridors and stairwells. The real question is, at what intervals? We can't check because the security system is separate from the main system. Damn, what a pain. I didn't create a freaking back door to that system. Why in the heck didn't I do that?"

"Because you didn't have time." Elvis touched my hand. "Don't knock yourself. Seriously."

"Okay, you're right. However, it means getting to Jouret's office safely is going to be a crapshoot of the worst kind."

"We'll just have to chance it, if you're sure you want to do that."

What I *wanted* to do was to take a hot bath, eat a big juicy hamburger and snuggle under a warm blanket with Slash. I did *not* want to figure out a way to outwit a bunch of determined terrorists, especially when my nerves were shot and I was operating on too little sleep as it was.

I sighed. "Yes, it's what I want. We have to get to his office. It's our best shot at figuring out what's going on."

"I'm in full agreement despite the high probability of failure," he said. "I've also been thinking about ways to get messages to the outside without tripping the monitoring software. I've got some possibilities."

"That's good, Elvis. That's really good. I've got an idea, too, about how to get to Jouret's office. But I have a feeling you're not going to like it."

"Why?"

"We're going to have to split up."

One thing I really liked about Elvis was that he didn't jump to conclusions or think with emotion as a first instinct. He considered all angles, weighed the value and benefit of the proposal and made solid decisions based on intellect and reason.

"No."

I blinked. "No? What do you mean 'no'? You haven't even heard the plan yet."

"Just that. No. We're not splitting up."

"I haven't even given you my reasons yet."

"Don't want to hear them. We're *not* splitting up."

I put my hand on his arm. "Elvis, you have to listen to my reasons."

"No."

I drew back. We didn't have time for this.

I grabbed his face between my hands. "Whether or not you like it, you *are* going to listen to me, Elvis Zimmerman."

His mouth drew into a tight line. There was more

going on here, but I couldn't try to figure it out while numerous lives, including our own, were on the line.

"Right now we are the best hope for saving the lives of the students in this school. It's laughably clear that two geeks like us aren't going to be able to physically take on a small army of highly trained and heavily armed people. As much as I wish we had the Hulk's strength or Yoda's powers, we don't. That leaves us with our brainpower only. We've got pretty decent smarts between us. But on the practical side, I'm a student at this school, so if I get caught on my way to Jouret's office, I, at least, have a measure of plausible deniability to offer. I would be able to say with reliable conviction that I hid, got scared or whatever. You don't have a uniform, so they would shoot first and ask questions later. And if we both get caught at the same time, there is no backup plan, no way to help each other. We're doomed before we get started."

Elvis still didn't say anything.

I tried a different approach. "Elvis, you know I'm making sense. I know you do. I don't know why you're shutting me out. Please listen to me. I need you."

He finally spoke. "I'll figure something out. It's too risky to go running around out there separately. You're safer with me."

Panic gripped me. "You don't really believe that. You saw the size of those backpack bombs. We both know no one is getting out of here alive unless we can get the security forces inside to save those kids. Those terrorists aren't going to surrender."

"I just don't want anything to happen to you, okay?"

"I feel the same way about you. Seriously. Elvis, you're the best friend I've ever had. You understand me like no one else on the planet, not even Basia, and I never want anything to happen that could take you away from me. I know you're worried about me, but I need you to work with me now. Please, I can't do this without you. I just can't." The last word turned into a sob.

He sighed. "Lexi, don't cry. I'm sorry. It's just that if you got hurt…"

"We *will* get hurt—me, you and a lot more people—if we do nothing. We have to help these kids, Elvis. Together. And the best way to do that is to split up. Please, at least listen to my plan."

He finally nodded and I felt the knot in my stomach ease.

"You're right, Lexi. It's game time. I know what I need to do…what *we* need to do. We may have to operate separately, but we're still a team. As much as I hate the idea, I agree splitting up will give us a second chance to get to Jouret's office if one of us gets caught. Those kids are depending on us. What did you have in mind?"

I was so relieved to have Elvis back on board I nearly burst into tears. For a moment, I couldn't speak.

"Lexi?"

I blinked back the wetness from my eyes and tried to focus. "Um, let me reorganize my thoughts."

He gave my hand a soft squeeze. "Let me help, because I think I know where you're going with this. We need to calculate the safest and fastest way to Jouret's office. To do that we need to estimate the distance to the office from here, the speed at which we must go, how many locations we think the security camera is covering and the length the camera stays on each scene. We also need to factor in the frequency of roving patrols and the high probability that some of those patrols will not be scheduled. We also need to determine a way to communicate, whether by silence or an actual exchange, so if you are successful I can follow you at either the same interval or adjust mine accordingly, if you're not."

I managed a smile. "Exactly. You read my mind."

"Maybe it's like that with best friends."

"Maybe."

He smiled and then opened the laptop. "Okay. Let's get started."

SEVENTEEN

WE WERE TRAPPED in a high school with terrorists who had enough explosives to blow us to kingdom come and back, but relying on math to save our lives was still pretty fun. Elvis must have been thinking the same thing because he gave me a smile as he glanced up from the laptop.

"Do you think we should recalculate with a higher percentage of uncertainty in terms of the roving patrols?"

I shook my head. "No. We're good. I'm comfortable where we stand. It's as solid as we're going to get based on the high number of incalculable uncertainties. A twenty percentage success rate is the best we're going to get even if we assess it a hundred more times."

He sighed and closed the laptop. "You're right." He glanced at his watch. "Four minutes then. Are you ready?"

"As ready as I will ever be."

"You've got this, Lexi. No, *we've* got this. I'll be watching for the signal once you're in. I know you're going to make it."

"I will. You're sure you'll find me via the back door?"

"Of the entire plan, that's the part I'm the surest on."

"Good." I took a deep breath. "Okay. Goodbye, Elvis. It's time."

His grin faded. "Right. Look, before you go, I want you to know that I… I…"

"You what?"

"I… I'm behind you a hundred percent."

"Good to know." I started to crawl out of the cabinet and then stopped. There was something I wanted to ask him, and this might be my last chance. "Hey, Elvis, did you really think about having sex with me?"

"What?"

"Well, back in the computer room, before I made you strip, you said you'd thought a lot about 'it', which I presumed meant having sex…with me."

"Um, are you sure this is a good time to talk about it?"

It definitely wasn't. Even I knew that. "I just wondered."

"Well, I…" He looked down. "I can't do this right now."

"Okay. No worries. I know that ninety-six point eight percent of men think about whether they'd like to have sex with a woman within the first eleven seconds of meeting her. That's a biological fact, so I didn't take it personally one way or the other. I guess it doesn't matter anyway. It just surprised me. Forget I asked."

"Lexi—"

"Never mind. It was a dumb question. I hope I didn't embarrass you. I've got to go. Wish me luck one more time, Elvis."

He blew out a breath. "Good luck, Lexi. Be in that twenty percent success rate, okay?"

"Okay."

I crept out of the cabinet, took one last look at Elvis and closed the cabinet door. I crept toward the door. It was four fifty-six. We'd been under siege for more than three hours. I wondered if my parents and brothers knew I was here. I presumed Finn would have contacted them by now. I imagined that he, my parents and brothers were glued to the television along with most of America. They were all probably worried sick about me. Again.

But Slash... No, Slash wouldn't be in front of the television. He was almost certainly just on the other side of the school wall, ordering people around and trying to figure out how Jouret played into this and why I'd sent him the message about him this morning. He'd be unraveling that thread, which was a good thing.

He'd probably be more furious with me than the terrorists because I'd somehow got myself stuck in the middle of the very incident he'd been worried about. Maybe trouble did follow me like a stalker.

Even though we'd only been officially dating for a few days, I missed him. I missed his smile, his strong arms and even the way he teased me. He'd be moving heaven and earth to get to me, and knowing that warmed me inside. I hadn't ever had that kind of singular affection or attention, and it surprised me how much I'd started to like it. I'd never imagined I would.

My heart squeezed. How fair was it that I'd just entered into a relationship, and now there was a very real chance I might never see Slash again?

I paused by the classroom door, listening. Elvis and I had spent dangerous moments by this door, listening for footsteps to go by and creating a behavior-based graph. The pattern indicated activity in this hallway every eleven minutes. If we presumed that the security camera would not be active on this hallway while the patrol was passing through, it provided me a small window of time to get from the classroom to the stairway hopefully undetected. Of course, this all rested on the theory that the patrols were structured, not random, and that there would be no logical reason to patrol an area already covered by the security cameras. We had to trust that there was a method to the madness. As it couldn't be verified, we'd had to go with an educated guess, and now my life depended on our being right.

It was really dark in the classroom now and eerily quiet. I could see the occasional red and blue flashes from the police vehicles stationed outside, but otherwise, it was quiet. I swallowed the fear that lodged in my throat and glanced at my watch. The time was good. I should be in the clear.

I slowly eased the door open a crack and peered out to my right. The hallway was brightly lit and I had to squint a moment until my eyes adjusted. When I could finally see, all that came into view were a few books, papers and backpacks scattered across the floor. I shifted my position to the left and saw nothing that way either. I opened the door a bit wider and slipped out into the hallway.

I hugged the wall, heading for the stairway, feeling the bump of the locker combinations slide across my back as I moved as quickly and quietly as I could manage. I passed the first classroom, the second and was almost to the third when I heard heavy footsteps coming up from the stairwell.

Making an executive decision, I dashed for the third classroom and grasped the door handle. It was locked. Before I could turn around, I felt an arm snake around my neck and cover my mouth and nose, pulling me backward and into the second classroom I'd just passed. I flailed as whoever it was shoved me into the classroom and released me. I stumbled and then whirled around.

Brandon put out his hand. "Don't say anything."

EIGHTEEN

BRANDON EASED THE door shut just as the footsteps entered the corridor.

My eyes widened as he held a finger to his lips. I nodded and froze. The footsteps passed and then all fell quiet.

"What are you doing here?" I hissed when I felt sure it was safe.

He glared at me and then whispered back, "What am *I* doing? What are *you* doing sneaking down the hall? You're lucky I heard you."

"You heard me?"

"Well, yeah. The thump of your back along the lockers was a dead giveaway. Were you trying to be loud?"

"I was *not* being loud."

"You were, too. You're lucky I peeked to see who it was. I knew the guards didn't walk like that."

"Stop arguing, you guys." Piper stepped out from behind the teacher's desk.

I gaped at her. "What are *you* doing here? Who else is here?"

Piper shook her head. "No one else. We're the only three that eluded their net. Brandon, that was stupid. What if she's with them?"

"She's not with them, Pip."

I shook my head. "I am definitely *not* with them."

Piper crossed her arms. "There's something off about you, Lara Carson. I don't trust you."

"The both of you shut up and follow me," Brandon whispered, motioning us to the back of the classroom where we hid behind the lab desks and some chairs.

My heart still thundered. "Jeez, Brandon. You do realize you took about five years off my life with that grab-and-pull."

He ran his fingers through his hair. "Sorry. There was no time for a fancy meet and greet."

"I actually wanted to say I appreciate it. Thanks for saving me."

"You're welcome. Again."

My eyes widened. "It was you who knocked."

"Yep. We knew someone was hiding in the Weather Lab. We could hear you moving around. When I heard them go in there, I figured you might need a distraction."

"Wow. You don't know how close it was. But it was a really big risk."

Brandon grinned. "I'm fast and they didn't discover you, did they? Besides, this whole situation is one big risk. How did you elude the initial roundup?"

"I was in Computer Central. I heard them and changed the access code so I had time to hide. After a bit, I managed to get out of there and have been next door in the Weather Lab. What about you guys? How did you hide from them?"

Brandon glanced at Piper. "We, ah, were skipping. We were in the empty chem lab next to the cafeteria. We hid in the air-conditioning/heating ventilation in the lab when they came through hunting students and staff. I unscrewed the intake grill with this." He held up a Swiss army knife. "Thank God the staff doesn't know I carry it around or I'd be suspended. Again. But it goes everywhere with me. My grandpa gave it to me."

"Good thinking, Brandon. How did you guys get up here?"

"Heard them rounding up kids in the cafeteria and figured the chem lab was too close for comfort. We waited for a while and then made a run for it up here."

"Made a run for it? That wasn't very good planning."

"That's prime coming from someone who almost bought it in the hallway moments ago."

"Fair enough."

Piper put a hand on Brandon's shoulder. "Look, we're all scared. But we're alive and safe, so far at least."

I nodded. "You were lucky and so was I. Apparently I'm going to have to revisit my calculations on guard rotations."

Piper looked at me as if I'd lost my mind. "Where were you going?"

"I'll tell you if you first update me on everything you know about the situation."

Brandon sighed. "Well, it's not a student with a grudge shooting up the place. There are dozens of soldier types and they are all heavily armed. They're speaking a foreign language and seem well organized. Terrorists of some kind, I think. They've put bombs everywhere. We saw one in the stairwell when we ran up here."

"That's not good."

Piper twisted her green sweater between her fingers. "This was all planned in advance. Very organized. They already had a list of everyone who was in school today. They read the list aloud in the cafeteria and checked them off as people were accounted for, even the teachers. We heard all of it. That's how we knew you were still on the loose somewhere. There were only three students unaccounted for—the three of us. I don't think they're looking too hard for us, though. We're just three scared kids. After all, what could we do against an army?"

"What about Headmistress Swanson?"

"They have her, and Ms. Eder, too."

I considered. "Visitors?"

"Only one—a parent who was in the office to pick up her daughter for a dentist's appointment. She's in the cafeteria, too, or at least she was. It's been hours since we've been down there."

"Okay." I digested the information for a minute. That meant the terrorists didn't know about Elvis. Ms. Eder hadn't signed him in, thank goodness. I briefly considered telling the kids about Elvis, and then decided against it. If we were captured, it would work in Elvis's favor to have fewer people know.

"There's more," Piper continued. "They locked us out of the school's network. Changed all the passwords and limited our access. All the phones are dead. We are completely isolated."

I shook my head. "Not completely. I created a back door into the system before I got out of Computer Central. We can't do anything but look at this point because they've got internal monitoring software in play, but it works in our favor."

Piper frowned. "How did you gain access to Computer Central? You need a special badge to get in there."

"I… I lifted it from the office."

Brandon leaned forward and I could see the white of his eyes gleaming in the dark. "Well, that was awesome thinking under pressure. You rock it, Lara."

"I have my moments."

Piper looked at me. "So where *were* you going just now?"

I didn't want to involve them, but now I had no choice. They needed to know, at least in a peripheral way, in case something happened to me. "To Mr. Jouret's office. He's in on this."

Piper gasped. "He's *what*?"

"He's running the tech end of this operation for the terrorists."

"No way. You've got to be kidding me." I could hear the shock in Brandon's voice. "He's our teacher, for God's sake."

"He's also working for these guys. Trust me. He was the one who came into the computer room to take control of things while I was hiding in there."

"Where did you hide?"

"I squeezed into the cable closet."

"How did you fit?"

"Very carefully."

Brandon began to pace. "Look, I want to believe you, but are you sure about Jouret?"

"I'm positive."

Piper gasped. "That's just not possible. They have to be making him do it."

"They weren't. You have to trust me on this. He's a full participant."

"But why? And how would he get away with it?"

I shrugged. "Presumably he's working on the assumption that no one in the school knows. I'd guess he'd work it so he'd be released as part of a prisoner exchange or something. I heard him say he was wearing a mask.

No one would know if I hadn't been hiding there and heard him."

Brandon snorted. "I always knew the guy was a jerk."

Brandon and Piper fell silent and I knew they were considering what I'd said. I had to tell them more.

"You guys asked me where I was going. I was heading to Jouret's office because I think it's empty. He's most likely still in Computer Central managing the system from there, but his account is still logged in via his office terminal. If I can get in there, I can see exactly what he's up to without having to waste time on decryption or triggering any of the internal monitors they've set up."

Brandon whistled. "Brilliant. We'll help you get there."

Piper leapt to her feet. "Are you crazy, Brandon? Go back out there? There are guys with guns out there." There was a waver in her voice.

Her palpable terror reminded me just how young they were. As much as I needed them, I couldn't risk them.

"She's right, Brandon. I should go alone."

"No way." Brandon was adamant. "If you can get into the system through Jouret, we can get you to the security system. You *need* us to do this."

"Wrong. You can't get me into the security system. It's not integrated with either the school system or the phone system. As it stands now, there is no way to access it even if we manage to get in undetected through Jouret's account."

Both kids went silent and I realized my mistake too late.

"Just how do you know so much about the system, Lara?" Piper's voice was quiet and for the first time I heard the Irish in her speech. "You're new here…just a few days. You mysteriously gain access to Computer

Central and now you've an expert on the school's system?"

Sometimes the best defense was offense. "So what? Aren't you?"

She crossed her arms against her chest. "It's too much for a new student."

"Look, I don't care how or what she knows, Piper." Brandon had a hint of impatience in his voice. "This isn't the time for that. We either trust her, or we don't. I'm on the side of trusting her. Right now, she needs our help."

Piper pressed her lips together and stared at me.

He turned to me. "Lara, I'm going to tell you straight-up. Piper and I built an invisible bridge between all three systems—the phone, the security and the computer system. We connected them because it helped us move around the system faster and unnoticed. No one knows about it except for us. So, I'm telling you again, you *need* us. If we can access the system via Jouret's account, we can use the bridge to get straight to the security system and see what they see. We might even be able to manipulate some of the data to our advantage. But most importantly, we'll have options."

My heart soared. I'd never been so freaking happy in my entire life for the brilliant hacking skills of a couple of kids. I almost hugged them before I remembered the whole reason I was at the school in the first place was to dissuade them from such activities. I'd have to worry about that later, *if* we survived.

"That's prime, Brandon. Really, *really* prime. Where's the bridge? How can I find it?"

Piper blew out a breath, her voice heavy. "Brandon is right. You won't be able to find it easily without our help. We designed it that way on purpose. We'll have to go with you and help you find it."

"No. It's too dangerous. Besides three is a crowd."

Brandon lifted a hand in protest. "Trust me. We are *way* better poised to do this than you. You haven't been here as long as we have."

"It's my back door. I know what to do."

"It's our bridge."

We were at an impasse. I tried to dissuade them. "Look, be sensible. We can't all three go down the hall-way and expect to make it to Jouret's office undetected. We'll be as loud and obvious as a herd of elephants."

Brandon would not give up. "Then we'll go separately. It increases the odds that at least one of us should make it. Even only if one of us makes it, we're all good enough to take care of the basics. Now that you know about our bridge, you'll find it if you look hard enough, right? It might take time, but you're that good, aren't you, Lara?"

I felt my resolve weaken and realized I was feeling just like Elvis had—protective. Thinking of him made me smile *and* worry that all of this discussion was tak-ing way too long.

"Yes, I'm good. In turn, I presume you're both capa-ble enough to find my back door, if I give you a start-ing point."

The two exchanged a glance. "Yes."

My mind raced through scenarios and possibilities for ways I could lessen the danger, but I couldn't think of anything. The brutal truth was I *did* need them and it *was* a dangerous situation. If we didn't find a way to get the police in, it was highly likely we'd all be roasted if the bombs detonated. Statistically, the three of us head-ing out, at different times with different routes, had a better chance of making it to Jouret's office than just one. Plus there was Elvis, who was waiting for the signal that I had made it.

Four people.

Four chances.

The odds for success had been raised exponentially.

A decision had to be made. I didn't have any more time to dawdle.

"Okay, you're in. But only if we do it my way."

It took me less than five minutes to bring them up to speed with my plan. I included a brief description of my back door and they told me more or less how to find the bridge. It wouldn't be easy if only one of us made it, but it wouldn't be impossible either. Just like that, we were armed with the knowledge we needed. Now all we had to do was to make it to Jouret's office in one piece.

Piper started pacing in the back of the room. "How can we be sure Mr. Jouret is not in his office?"

"We can't. It's just a logical best guess based on the fact that he doesn't have access to the security system from his terminal. He'd have to be in Computer Central to do that, and I'm ninety-nine percent certain he'll be wanting to monitor the security cameras."

Brandon stood and stretched his legs. "Lara is right. He's *got* to be there. It just makes sense."

Piper stopped. "Okay. Then let's do it."

I glanced at my watch. "I estimated the patrols to be at intervals of eleven minutes. Clearly that was a miscalculation. Based on my original estimate, I should have had five more minutes to get to the stairwell and down the stairs. If I adjust the times accordingly, we only have a window of seven minutes. We have to wait for the next patrol to pass. Let's listen and then I'll go first."

Brandon spoke up. "No, I'll go first, and I do not say this out of a misguided need to be macho either."

I could barely see his silhouette in the dark classroom, but he stepped up next to me and pressed something into my hand. My hand closed around it.

"The Swiss Army knife?"

He took it back. "Yes. In case Jouret's office is locked. I can pick the lock in about fifteen seconds. I've done it before. Well, not on Jouret's office exactly, but let's just say I know what I'm doing."

I sincerely didn't want to know which school offices he'd been picking the locks on. "Okay. You're first. I'll follow seven minutes later, and Piper, you bring up the rear."

"I'll be here alone?" There was a tremble in her voice.

I heard more than saw Brandon move toward her. "Only for seven minutes, Pip. You can do this."

He murmured something else to her, but I'd moved away to listen at the door for the patrol and couldn't hear what it was. I kept my eye on my watch. About four minutes later, I heard footsteps. Brandon and Piper joined me at the door. I put my hand on Brandon's arm. We listened as they passed and then gave him a thumbs-up. Piper's breath caught and he gave her a one-armed hug.

I opened the door a crack and we squinted at the light as we peeked out, checking the corridor both ways. The light illuminated Brandon's face and it struck me how young he was. I sincerely hoped I knew what I was doing. He gave me a grin and sprinted down the hallway toward the stairwell. He made it in just a few seconds and disappeared into the stairwell. I carefully closed the door and we waited, listening for any signs that an alarm had been raised.

NINETEEN

A MINUTE, THEN TWO, passed and we didn't hear anything. My heart was beating pretty fast. Piper remained so still I began to get worried.

"It's okay," I whispered awkwardly. "He's going to be fine."

"Who are you really?" she whispered. "I know you're not just a student. Are you the police or something?"

"No. I'm not the police. But you're right. I'm not a student either. There is no time to explain now. You'll just have to trust me."

"I do trust you or I wouldn't have agreed to do this. You've a special skill with the keyboard. I was jealous of you."

My eyes widened. Someone was jealous...of me? Lexi Carmichael, the klutzy geek girl? Unfathomable.

"Me? Why?"

"You are really good at the keyboard, you're blonde, and...well, Brandon admires you."

"I've had a lot of practice at the keyboard."

"It's more than that. You're intuitive. That's pretty rare."

I wondered how she could know that or recognize it as intuitive. But I didn't have time to ask her because I heard a noise in the hallway. I held up a hand and she stilled immediately. Footsteps. Faster and more deliberate than the previous ones. We waited until they passed and there was no noise.

I bent my head close to Piper and whispered, "That was faster than seven minutes."

She nodded and I listened, before lifting a hand. "I'm going now. I may have an even smaller window than Brandon. You'll have to listen for the guards and decide when your best window for escape comes, okay? You can do this."

"I know I can. Lara, thank you. I don't know who you are exactly, but I'm glad you're on my side."

"The name is actually Lexi, and I'm definitely on your side. Oh, and I'm not blonde either. Anyway, good luck, Piper."

Her hand squeezed my shoulder. Steeling myself, I opened the door a crack. I felt the blood rush to my ears as I surveyed the hallway.

Empty.

I glanced over my shoulder, seeing the fear in her eyes, and wondered if it was reflected in mine. Couldn't worry about that now. I slipped out into the corridor. Piper clicked the door shut behind me. Unlike the previous trip when I flattened myself against the wall, this time I took a cue from Brandon and dashed straight for the stairwell.

I kept expecting to get shot in the back or someone to raise a cry of alarm, but I reached the stairwell unscathed. I skidded to a stop at the door and pulled it open. I slipped inside, taking a moment to listen for any noise. Glancing up I saw the security camera mounted on the wall and was thankful the red dot was not activated. Hopefully that meant it wasn't filming me right now.

I crept down the stairs. My heart was slamming

against my chest by the time I reached the second floor. The stairwell door was heavy and I couldn't hear a thing on the other side, so I had no idea if anyone was there or not. Regardless, I could waste no more time, so I carefully cracked it open. A glance down the hallway indicated it was deserted. It looked like a war zone with papers, books, pens, pencils and backpacks strewn all over the place. I didn't see Brandon either, which I decided to take as good news.

Piper had told me that Jouret's office was the second office on the right-hand side of the hall. I slipped into the second-floor hallway and dashed the distance, coming to a quick stop and pressing down on the handle of the door.

It was locked.

I stood there exposed, not knowing what to do, when the door abruptly opened. Brandon grabbed a fistful of my shirt, yanking me into the room. I stumbled forward as he clicked the door shut behind me.

"Damn, that was fast. I almost didn't open it. Why did you follow so quickly?"

I doubled over, trying to catch my breath and calm my racing heart. "The guards changed up their pattern. It seems they're increasing the frequency of the patrols. Maybe something is going on outside."

"Does Piper know?"

"She knows."

I straightened. The room seemed overly bright, perhaps because I had just spent so many hours in the dark. There were no windows and the room was about as large as my bedroom.

"Did you turn on the lights?" I spoke in a whisper, but even that seemed abnormally loud in the empty office.

Brandon shook his head and answered me in a hushed voice. "No. They were already on."

"Okay, good. We don't want to change up anything. The guards will expect a light to be on, so it stays on."

"Got it."

I glanced about the office. There were two bookshelves, half-full, with several tomes on cybersecurity arranged in a neat display. Two visitor chairs sat in front of a standard teacher desk. Jouret's desk was clean except for two in-boxes with a few papers inside manila folders, an empty coffee mug and his computer monitor. On the right corner of the desk stood a large statue of a South African totem pole. I picked it up and examined it. It weighed a freaking ton.

"Come over here, Lara. I want to show you something. You were right. Jouret is still logged in here."

I set the statue down and joined him behind the desk. "Don't touch anything on the keyboard. Leave that to me."

"I'm not touching anything."

I bent over the monitor, tapped a key and got a feel for Jouret's personal layout. Two more taps of the keyboard I was in through the back door and into the system, completely undetected. Now I could see everything. Even better, his emails would not be encrypted to me, because the system thought I was him.

It was that damn easy. He'd been either supremely arrogant or exceptionally sloppy.

I glanced through his mail account. "Hmmm… Jouret has been a busy boy. Nine messages since the takeover. Interesting."

I sat down in the chair. Time to get serious. I had just started typing when Brandon leaned over my shoulder.

"Where the hell are you going?" He tapped the screen. "Finish checking his mail. See who he is talking to."

I glanced up. "I will, Brandon. But I have to do something else first. Go wait by the door for Piper. If my calculations are correct, she should be here in about three to four minutes. I don't have time to explain my method right now."

He hesitated, but then moved from behind the desk. I slipped into my back door, depositing a single clue for Elvis to find. I imagined his relief when he saw it. We'd made it this far. We *could* do this.

I headed back to the mail server and began methodically reading the message train. I became so engrossed I jumped when Brandon spoke.

"Piper's not here yet. What do you think happened to her?"

I glanced at my watch. She *was* late. If she wasn't here by now, it meant she'd either decided to wait for another interval or she'd been caught.

I tried to keep the worry out of my voice. "I don't know. Maybe she decided to wait another round. The patrols were mixing it up. She's a smart girl. I'm sure she has her reasons."

He started pacing in front of the door. "Have you found anything interesting yet?"

"Absolutely. I'm starting to get a better idea of what might be going on here. First of all, Jouret is taking orders. He's not the boss of this operation. He's being told what to do by someone imaginatively calling himself X, who is sending messages to Jouret's account via what is certainly a bogus account in Turkey. No way he's stationed there, but the police will have to spend time tracking it down anyway. The messages are heavily encrypted. It's going to take the police's encryption team a hell of lot of time trying to decode these."

"Lucky for us that we're on the inside."

"That's no kidding."

He stopped, ran his fingers through his hair. "So, what's this X guy saying?"

"Well, he told Jouret to post the demands publicly to a specific site."

"What site?"

"Give me a sec." I clicked on the link and then let out a breath. "Well, that's rich. The FBI's website."

"What?"

"Yeah, X is playing them good. Given the media attention and numerous hits the demands are certain to generate, the FBI likely has its hands full trying to keep the website from crashing. But they won't close the hack because it is an open channel of communication. The police and the FBI will keep it open for that very reason. But this makes all communication internationally available and very visible."

"Unbelievable. What are the demands?"

"The first two are the ones we already know. Keep the Internet connection open and the power on without interference or else they start executing students."

"Okay, what else?"

"Nothing else. Just that they're willing to negotiate students' lives for forthcoming demands. That's it. Weird. No other forthcoming demands. Yet."

"That's it? It's been several hours."

"Well, they're definitely up to something behind the scenes. About two hours ago, Jouret sent identical private messages to The Honorable James Herman and The Honorable Naomi Walters from his account. Ring any bells?"

"There's a girl here at school I know named Jennifer Walters. I think her mom is a senator. It could be her. Not sure about the Herman connection."

My mind started racing. "U.S. senators. This could be significant."

"What did he say in the email to them?"

"He asked them for proprietary information on something called Operation Dove. Ever heard of that?"

"Not a thing. Then again, I've got a C right now in U.S. Government."

"I've got nothing either. These emails are odd. But listen to this. Jouret said he'd release the student whose parent got back to them first with the information."

"Blackmail? All of this insanity for information?"

"I know. Weird. But that's what it's looking like so far. From what I can see, neither senator has replied yet. Give me more time to read."

At that exact moment there was a noise at the door.

"Piper," Brandon uttered. He rushed to the door, yanking it open.

Willem Jouret stood there looking at us in astonishment.

TWENTY

I HAVE TO give credit to Brandon's quick thinking. Before my brain could even process that Jouret stood there, Brandon had already pulled him into the office and taken a swing. Jouret shouted, but it was reduced to more of a yelp when Brandon's fist made first contact with his jaw. Coming to my senses, I leapt over the desk and jumped on Jouret's back, trying to pin his arms to his side. Brandon crashed into us, and the three of us went tumbling to the floor in a mass of arms and legs.

Fists were flying in every direction, and I took several hard jarring hits to the cheek, side and ribs.

In the confusion, I saw Jouret fumbling with something at his waistband of his pants.

"He's got a gun, Brandon!"

Brandon was pummeling him in such a crazed frenzy I wasn't sure he'd heard me.

I clawed at Jouret's arm and he backhanded me hard. I fell sideways and tasted blood. Panicked, I threw my body against his hand, trapping it against his stomach and hoping that he wouldn't be able to angle it up and shoot me in the gut. Jouret used his other hand to yank me into Brandon. Luckily, I managed to hook a finger on the gun so when I fell sideways, the gun slid out of his hand and went skidding across the floor.

Howling in anger and frustration, Jouret sat up and

gave Brandon a vicious head butt. A sickening crack sounded and Brandon crumpled to the floor.

I launched myself stomach-first across the floor, skidding across the tiles with my hand stretched out for the gun.

"Don't even think about it," Jouret said. He caught my ankles and landed with a bone-jarring thud on my lower back and legs. I fought, but he used his weight to trap me beneath him and crawled over my body to the gun. I squirmed and thrashed, but he outweighed me by a hundred pounds and he was using every one of them to his advantage.

I was completely crushed beneath him by the time he reached the gun and roughly rolled me over onto my back, straddling me at the waist and pinning my arms by my sides. He stared down at me with a split lip. Blood dripped from his nose, down his mouth and chin and onto my chest. Someone, probably Brandon, had also clocked him a good one in the right eye and it had already started to swell. His breathing was harsh, but he stared at me with murder in his eyes.

"Who the hell are you?"

His accent was so thick, I hardly understood him. He looked like some kind of monster, his face smeared with blood. I figured I probably looked as bad as he did. Maybe worse. Blood filled my mouth and my cheek and lips throbbed. "I'm just one of your students."

He slapped me on my sore cheek. "Try again. Why are you in my office?"

I tried to catch my breath and stop the ceiling from spinning. Tears leaked from my eyes. "It was a safe hiding place. There are terrorists out there, in case you didn't know."

I braced myself for another hit, but instead he stud-ied me. "You kids attacked me. You didn't ask for my help, so that means you already knew something about me. You suspected I was with them." It took him about two seconds to figure it out. "Shit. My account. I'm still logged in. How much do you know about what's going on here?"

I didn't have a chance to answer because I saw a blur of motion and heard a hard *thud*. Jouret abruptly slumped sideways to the floor and lay still. I blinked several times until Brandon came into view. He was holding the hid-eous totem pole statue.

Without a word, he stretched out a hand and I took it. He pulled me to my feet and I immediately retrieved Jouret's gun from the floor. Every part of my body screamed in pain. A quick glance at Jouret indicated he was out for the count.

"Thanks." I turned to Brandon. "Are you okay?"

He looked awful, with a knot the size of Texas on his forehead. His eyes were glassy, his shirt was in tat-ters and he had a nasty bruise that took up most of his left cheek.

"I'm alive. How hurt are you?"

I gingerly touched my cheekbone and swollen lip and felt the wetness of blood. My side ached and my legs were shaky. But I, too, was alive. I was beyond thank-ful for it.

"I'll live. Do you know how to use a gun?"

"I've been hunting a couple of times with my dad."

"Then that makes you eminently more qualified to use it than me." I handed him the gun.

A noise sounded at the door and we froze, our gazes

locking. It hadn't been a knock, but it wasn't a banging either.

"It could be the terrorists," Brandon hissed. "Maybe they heard us fighting."

"Only if a patrol was passing by, which one shouldn't have been," I hissed back, wiping the blood from my mouth. "But wouldn't they just unlock the door?"

"It could be Piper."

"It could. But look what happened last time we opened the door." I glanced again at the door. "We have to check. If it's her, we can't just leave her in the hall. The security camera will be making its rounds. Move back behind the door and hold the gun out in a threatening manner."

I took a deep breath and opened the door a crack. Piper and Elvis fell inside. Before I could say a word, Brandon jumped on Elvis and pressed the gun against his neck.

"Stop!" Piper and I gasped at the same time.

I put a hand on Brandon's arm. "Whoa. It's okay, Brandon. He's with me."

I saw the wild look in Brandon's eyes. Terror and the urge to survive did strange things to people. Brandon was clearly on overload. I began to tremble. What if he accidentally discharged the gun?

I fought for calmness when I wanted to scream. "Brandon, please. It's safe. He's with me. His name is Elvis and he's my friend. Please put the gun down."

After what seemed like an interminably long moment, Brandon pointed the gun away from Elvis's neck.

I gave an audible sigh of relief and threw my arms around Elvis. He had the stolen laptop looped across his shoulder and it dug into my hip as I pressed my face into his shoulder and took a moment to be grateful we were both alive. I was shaking so hard, my teeth were chattering.

When I looked up, Brandon gave me an accusing look. "Who is he? Why the hell didn't you tell me there was someone else running around the school on our side?"

"I had my reasons, but ultimately it was for your safety and his. It's a long story." I looked at Elvis. "You got my message."

Elvis kept his arm around me. "Yes. Lexi, are you okay? Who are these kids? What happened?"

"We had a surprise visitor." I pointed to Jouret on the floor.

Elvis touched my cheek and bloody lips with his fingertips. "He hurt you."

"Thanks to Brandon, I'll live."

Piper covered her mouth in horror. "So, Jouret *was* here in his office. He hurt you both. Oh, my God. We were wrong. He wasn't in Computer Central."

I shook my head and it hurt. "No. Jouret wasn't here at first. He surprised us. We answered the door because Brandon thought he was you."

Elvis tightened his arm around me. "What did he do?"

"He tried to kill us. Basically, Brandon and I fought for our lives. How did you and Piper meet up?"

Elvis glanced at Piper. "In the stairwell. We scared the living daylights out of each other, but luckily we came to the quick conclusion we were on the same side. Especially when we discovered we were both headed to Jouret's office on your instructions, Lexi."

Brandon looked between Elvis and me. "Who's Lexi?"

I sighed. "Brandon, my name is not Lara Carson. It's Lexi Carmichael. This is Elvis Zimmerman. I'm not really a student and he's not either."

"*What*? You're a cop? A cop who doesn't know how to use a gun?"

"I'm not a cop. I work in cyberintelligence."

Brandon's eyes widened. "Wait. You're a spy? Doesn't spy training include weapons instruction?"

"Forget about the freaking gun. I'm not a spy either. Look, my background is irrelevant at the moment."

"I totally disagree. Who are you and who is he? Did you guys know this was going to happen?"

"Absolutely not."

Elvis knelt down next to Jouret. "Sorry to break up this fascinating discussion, but we definitely need to move to Plan B."

I threw up my hands. "What Plan B? We're not even finished with Plan A. We need to think and reorganize. Plus, seeing as how I almost got killed a few minutes ago, I'm finding it a bit hard to collect my thoughts at the moment. I know Jouret's presence here throws a major crimp in our plan, but can't we just gag and tie him up until we can get our thoughts together?"

"There's no need to tie him up, Lexi." Elvis straightened, brushed off his pants. "He's dead."

TWENTY-ONE

WHEN I WAS *really* in high school, long before I had learned the important difference between hacking and cracking, I sometimes dreamt about the day when I would rule the world with my computer. I could go *where* I wanted, *when* I wanted, with no fear of retribution or capture. In all of those dreams, I sat safely behind a computer and worked my magic. At no time did my dreams involve actual physical contact or interaction with people, including terrorists who wielded bombs and guns. My world domination did not involve physical pain, threat of immediate death, torture of any kind or severe emotional distress.

Unfortunately, right now, my dreams were sheer fantasy. I had to deal in reality. So, while I sat contemplating the horrors of my real life in Mr. Jouret's chair, Brandon was throwing up in the corner. Piper patted his back and murmured comforting words. He was a kid and he'd just killed a man, albeit it with my help, but I couldn't dredge up a single word to help him. I knew firsthand how it felt—the shock and horror—but at this moment, I didn't have it in me to summon the emotional strength to try and console him. I wanted to cry. I wanted to run away. I wanted to scream. Every part of my body hurt and I was at the end of my rope.

Jouret lay dead on the floor just meters from my feet.

I'd just participated in the death of a teacher, even if it was in self-defense. We were still trapped in a high school filled with bombs and deranged terrorists.

What in the hell had I been thinking? Sure, Lexi, go back to high school. You'll have a lock on it this time around. You're a mature, capable and confident woman. You've got this.

Jeez.

I couldn't believe it was possible, but high school was *definitely* worse the second time around.

Elvis kept his hand on my shoulder, talking to me and trying to anchor me to reality. I couldn't focus on his words so I had no idea what he was saying. My brain, in an attempt at self-preservation, had shut down. Finally, he turned my chair toward him and snapped his fingers.

"Lexi. Are you okay?"

I thought of my mom and dad, my brothers, Finn and Slash. I imagined the terrified kids and staff in the cafeteria and X, who was probably waiting for an update from Jouret. Everyone was counting on me, but especially Elvis. Elvis had always been there for me. Now I needed to be there for him.

For everyone.

Time to pull myself together.

I wiped a hand across my eyes. "I'm okay, Elvis. I just needed a minute."

He searched my face, a lock of brown hair falling over one of his eyes. "I understand. You look terrible. That must have been one heck of a fight." He let go of my shoulders and pressed a warm bottle of water into my hands. "Here, drink this."

I glanced up in surprise. "Where did you get it?"

"Inside Jouret's desk. Go ahead. Take a drink."

I unscrewed the top and took several long sips. Elvis took a tissue and wet it with a couple of drops of the water and dabbed at my mouth and cheeks.

"He got you good. Bastard."

"We got him better."

He gave me a wry look. "One of the things I like best about you—a serious competitive edge."

It made me smile a little, but my lip hurt for it. I handed him the water. "You take a drink, too, Elvis. How long has it been since we had some water?"

"Too long."

He took a few gulps and then tossed Piper the bottle. She caught it, took a drink and handed it to Brandon.

Elvis returned to me. "So, are you really good?"

"Good isn't the word that leaps to mind, but I'll survive. My head hurts, but let's do this anyway."

"Okay." He picked up a pencil and a piece of paper. "Let's examine the data we have accumulated. What do we know so far?"

I quickly brought him up to speed on what I'd discovered on Jouret's computer. He listened without interrupting once, taking a few notes. When I finished he paced back and forth.

"Okay, that fits with what I've been thinking. I have a theory, Lexi. I think we may have been onto something when we were reading about the situation in Pakistan. The more I think about it, the more I think these terrorists might be either *Shahid*-approved or a splinter of the group."

"But for what purpose? And why are they in the U.S.?

This is a Pakistani government matter. The U.S. isn't even involved, at least according to the State Department."

"But think about it. What if we *were* involved? Secretly."

I considered. If the U.S. were involved in secret negotiations with the Pakistani government in an effort to bring the warring factions together, it could cause dissension among those who were either not invited to the table or were threatened by peace.

"Operation Dove. My God. That could be it. Those two senators, Herman and Walters, I wonder if they are on some kind of intelligence committee."

Elvis paused. "That's a very strong possibility. That would certainly be the way to go if the terrorists want information to either disrupt or disband the negotiations."

I stroked my chin, mulled over that possibility. "Right. Because what's the fastest way to bring an end to secret negotiations?"

"Make them public."

"Exactly."

Elvis ran his fingers through his hair. He looked utterly exhausted with beard stubble on his chin and bloodshot eyes. I was sure I looked a thousand times worse. I desperately wished for a couple of ibuprofen and some water. I needed a clearer focus and the pain was interfering with that.

I patted my sore lip. It was swollen and felt funny. I ignored it. "Okay. That makes sense on the terrorist side. But what's in it for Jouret? He's from South Africa and from what I can see has no dog in this fight. So, how do the Veiled Knights factor into this, if at all?"

Elvis shook his head. "I don't know. But I think the

bottom line has to be money. It's *always* about money for mercenaries like Broodryk. Look, I'm not sure how much more time we have to discuss this. They are going to be looking for Jouret soon. If he's their only tech guy on the team in the school here, they're going to be in big trouble."

My brain went on overdrive, sorting, considering and weighing the options and dangers. Elvis must have thought I'd zoned because he leaned over me again. "Lexi, are you okay?"

"Yes." I blinked and nodded. "I know what we have to do, Elvis. I think I have Plan B. It's super risky, but it may work."

"Spill."

"Well, first we need to get Jouret out of here. Drag his body to the stairwell. Make it look like he fell down the stairs or something. I think we're all in agreement they can't find him in here. We need to be able to work in here on his computer. Jouret didn't realize he was still logged in here until he saw me. Maybe the others haven't either. It's our only chance."

Piper and Brandon were now listening from across the room, staring at me as if I'd come from another planet. Maybe I had, but maybe an alien brain was what we needed right now. I waved them closer so I could keep my voice down.

Elvis knelt next to me. "I don't think the terrorists would buy the idea that Jouret slipped going down the stairs."

"Probably not. But it doesn't matter. What matters is that we can't leave the body in here and we can't hide him in a place where they couldn't find it easily. They'd tear the school apart looking for him and they might find us. We only need them to find the body somewhere other than here."

Elvis frowned. "They're going to go crazy looking for whoever did it and possibly retaliate."

"Possibly. No doubt that once they find his body, they'll do another sweep of the school. But they have no reason to do more than a cursory look here. That's why you will stay here and hide."

Elvis looked around the office. "Here? Where?"

I pointed to the heating and air-conditioning grill hidden partially behind one of the bookshelves. "There. It was a good hiding place for Brandon and Piper in the chem lab. It should work here, too."

I saw a flicker in Brandon's eyes. There was life after all behind the zombie facade that had come over him after killing Jouret.

I held out a hand to him. "Give me the knife."

Instead, Brandon walked past me. He knelt down in front of the grate, pushed the bookshelf out slightly. He removed his knife, then unscrewed the grill. He stuck his head inside. "Plenty of room to hide."

"Good." I rubbed my forehead, trying to subdue the pounding headache. "You'll hide in there and wait until the terrorists finish what will presumably be a second sweep of the school. At some point they're going to have to accept it was a freak accident or realize they don't have the time or resources to hunt down whoever did it. I think they're on a schedule of some kind. Then as soon as it's safe, you guys get back out here and get to work. Hopefully no one will realize Jouret's account is still active from his office. Brandon or Piper, it will be your job to get Elvis into the security system side of things. Elvis, these two created a secret bridge between the three systems. No one will know about it. With the bridge, Elvis should be able to establish careful albeit limited communication with the police."

Elvis didn't speak, but I knew by the way he was looking at me, his mind was racing ahead with mine, trying to figure out where I was going with this.

Brandon lurched to his feet. "Fine, except where exactly will *you* be during all of this?"

I tried to sound confident. "I'm going to be the one getting rid of the body."

TWENTY-TWO

PIPER GASPED. "WHAT? You're going to get rid of the body? That's crazy. They'll kill you."

"Yes, they might, if they catch me. But I have to risk it."

Brandon frowned. "Why does it have to be you? Why not him?" He jerked his head toward Elvis.

"For two reasons. First, Elvis can't go because he's not on any list of students, staff or visitors. He's not even supposed to be here, which makes him highly suspect. They may think he's from the police, kill him and then start executing students. We can't risk that. Second, Elvis is a pro at systems. I may be good, but I assure you, Elvis is on a higher level than most of the police cyber team out there. Add to the fact that we've actually got him on the *inside* of the system, and we have a fighting chance. But only if we protect him."

Elvis closed his eyes. He agreed with me, even if he didn't want to. The expression on his face was killing me, so I looked away and forced myself to continue.

Brandon straightened. "Forget it. I killed Jouret. I'll dump the body."

"No!" Piper clutched his arm.

I wished I could wave a magic wand and make it all better, but I couldn't, so I forged ahead. "First of all, *we* killed him, and it would have been him or us. It's called self-defense and/or self-preservation. Take your pick.

Secondly, I need to ask an important question. Our lives may depend on the answer, so I need the truth. Brandon and Piper, which of you actually wrote the initial code for the bridge?"

They both looked at me with mouths agape.

Brandon spoke first. "What kind of question is that?"

"Just answer it. Which one of you is the author?"

Piper looked at me in puzzlement. "Why does it matter? We both created it. We both know how to work the bridge."

"I know. But in this particular situation, we have to expect that the unexpected might happen. Elvis might need to make a split-second decision and will require instantaneous assistance. Trust me, every second will matter, so I need to know who was the original author. The code will be intuitive to that person. I know both of you understand what I mean."

The two of them exchanged a glance, and then Brandon swept his hand out toward Piper. "She's the original brains behind the bridge."

Piper put a hand on his arm. "That's not true. Brandon is an excellent coder. I couldn't have done it without him."

I sighed. "I don't doubt that. But it does mean that you, Brandon, win the lottery. You'll help me drag the body to the stairwell. And…and I'm sorry. Neither one of us can come back here directly. Once we dump the body, we have to go elsewhere. We can't risk leading the terrorists back here to Jouret's office…to Piper and Elvis. When the terrorists come here—and they will—I want them to do nothing more than a superficial search of this place. After all, his office is locked and secured. But they'd do a much more thorough search if they caught either of us purposefully returning here."

Piper gasped at the implication. "No."

Brandon closed his eyes. "Damn, this is turning out to be my lucky day."

"That doesn't mean we can't make it back here. We'll both try, but it's imperative that we wait until well after the sweep. The code on the door will be three short knocks, a pause and two more knocks. Elvis, Piper, don't open the door unless you hear the code. Okay?"

"No." Horror reflected in Piper's eyes. "I won't do it. It's insane. I don't agree."

I felt like the Wicked Witch of the West, but I had to be strong. "We don't have time to form a committee or vote, Piper. This is not a democracy. Time is not working in our favor. I believe these terrorists intend to blow this place. Go down with the ship. They have no intention of surrendering. We *have* to circumvent that—to save dozens of lives. To do that, we have to figure out a way to let the security forces in. You have to trust me when I say that Elvis is a master. He is our best chance of getting out alive. Brandon and I will try to make our way back, okay? But it's the only way."

She started crying and Brandon put an arm around her shoulder. "Hey, Pip, it's okay. Lara… Lexi is right. I've got to do this and so do you."

I ignored the pain in my side and face and glanced at my watch. "Where's Jouret's gun?"

Elvis walked over the desk, picked up the gun, opened the chamber and checked the bullets. He closed it with a slam against his palm and tucked it into his waistband. "It's mine now."

I watched him in surprise. "You know how to use a gun?"

"I've only had two classes, but it will have to do."

"You're...taking classes?"

"Well, knowing how to use a weapon has seemed a necessary life skill lately, so I've been bringing myself up to speed. Better late than never, I guess."

I tried to remember what I'd been saying. "Ah, okay. Piper, you and Elvis need to get into the vent. We'll slide the bookshelf in front of it. When they are gone, you need to show Elvis how to access the bridge. Brandon and I will hide elsewhere until we feel it's safe to try to get back here. Okay?"

Piper put her face in her hands, but Brandon nudged her hands away and lifted her chin. "Do it, Pip. For me. Okay?"

She nodded, tears spilling from her eyes. During the entire conversation, Elvis said nothing but never took his eyes off me. I swallowed hard and continued.

"Just remember Elvis will be our critical link to the outside. His safety is vital. Piper, help him. Trust his methods and do what he says when he says it."

Brandon shoved his hands in his jeans. "Stick it to these guys, Pip. I mean it. Brains over bombs. Be my girl. I'll do my best to stay alive."

Piper started sobbing. Since I couldn't confirm he would come out of this alive, or that I would either, I didn't say anything that might have comforted her.

Piper threw her arms around Brandon and he held her tight. I turned away, giving them a small illusion of privacy.

Feeling like I'd just sentenced someone to death—and maybe I had—I bent over Jouret's body and steeled myself to grab his arms. I stopped when I felt a hand on my shoulder. I looked up. Elvis stood there, his eyes filled with determination and something else.

I straightened. "Elvis, please don't try to talk me out of this."

"I'm not."

"You're not?"

He frowned. "Do you want me to?"

"No. It's just...you haven't said much."

"I was thinking, processing and looking for holes. I thought you knew that."

"I figured."

"Then you know my silence means I believe your plan is solid, despite its hasty conception. If I thought it were reckless or without merit, I'd stop you, no question."

"But earlier in the cabinet..."

He sighed. "Okay, look, I admit my knee-jerk, guy re-action is to protest. Do I want to protect you? Of course, I do. I'd like to tell you that everything will be fine. But we've just been over this, so what's the point? However, for the record, I really, really hate this plan. I hate being separated from you and losing control of this situation. But it's the right call, Lexi, because this isn't about you, me, us, our egos, our feelings or anything else. There are hundreds of scared kids out there who are depending on us. I know what I have to do and so do you. As much as I hate it, it's our best chance and I know it. Okay?"

I let out a breath. He *got* it. Just like that, he *got* it. I had never been so grateful to have him here at this very moment in time.

"Thank you, Elvis. I'm sorry that coming here put your life in such danger, but on a purely selfish note, I'm really, *really* glad you're here."

"I'm glad I'm with you, too. I mean that. I'm not going to fail."

"I never thought you would."

"Good. Just remember we're a team—a damn formidable one. Once I'm in the security system, we've got a fighting chance. No matter what tricks these guys may have up their electronic sleeves, I'm in my element once I'm in. Just hang in there. Hide and stay alive. Okay? I've got the rest of this for us."

A lump formed in my throat. "Okay."

He touched my good cheek. "We're going to save those kids and each other."

I appreciated the conviction behind his words. "Yes, we will."

He pulled me toward him and I hugged him, resting my chin on his shoulder, listening to his steady breath.

"Lexi, thanks for being the best friend I've ever had aside from Xavier. Being an identical twin doesn't always make it easy to find friends outside of each other."

"I understand, and right back at you. I've been pretty lucky in the friend department, too."

Brandon walked past us, heading to the vent. "It's showtime, guys."

He looked awful with a purple knot on his forehead, caked blood on his mouth and nostrils and a wide bruise on his jaw that stretched across his cheek. But he was functioning and he deserved a lot of credit for that.

Elvis nodded, gave me a last hug and with a final look over his shoulder at me, climbed into the vent. Piper, with tears still streaming down her face, climbed in after him. Brandon pushed the grill shut without fastening it. Together we slid the bookshelf in front of the vent.

"The bookshelf isn't that heavy," Brandon instructed

them. "When you are ready to come out, one good push should slide the bookshelf outward enough to give you room to slide out. Just don't push too hard and knock it over. That's likely to get you unwelcome company."

"Got it," Elvis replied. "We'll do our part. You just do yours. Good luck."

Brandon picked up Jouret's feet and motioned for me to take his arms. "Thanks. We're definitely going to need it."

For a kid, he was handling everything a lot better than I expected. Brandon Steppe had some serious grit. I grabbed Jouret's arms. We dragged the body to the door and listened. I thought about Elvis, just steps away, and was reassured by his words.

I've always got your back.

He always had. Somehow I knew that would be an absolute certainty in my life.

I closed my eyes, trying to calm my racing heart and searching for the mental techniques I'd learned in yoga. Focus on the here and now. All other matters had to be stored in the back of my brain. Breathe in, breathe out. Imagine yourself floating weightless on a cloud…

I opened my eyes and saw Brandon staring at me.

"What's wrong?" I whispered.

"I just realized you look really familiar. Have you ever been on television?"

"Jeez."

I heard the noise first. I held up a hand, shushing him. The footsteps were steady and regular. No running or rushing in panic. No alarm had been sounded…yet. The footsteps passed and faded into silence.

I looked at Brandon and whispered, "You ready?"

He exhaled a breath. "Do I have a choice? Let's get this show on the road."

TWENTY-THREE

AFTER THE FOOTSTEPS passed, I cracked open the door, did a double check to ensure the corridor was empty and then pulled it open wider for us to drag the body out. Brandon went first, pulling the legs. Terror gave me a strength I didn't know I had. I followed at a half run, holding his arms and trying my best to keep up. Brandon was far stronger and faster, so my side with Jouret's head kept bouncing across the floor like a basketball and making me sick to my stomach. We somehow made it into the stairwell in what seemed like record time. The muscles in my shoulders were screaming, and I had trouble catching my breath from the throbbing pain in my ribs. A quick glance at the security camera indicated no blinking red light, which ideally meant it was not filming our body disposal.

There was no time to waste.

Push him, I mouthed to Brandon.

I slid my hands under his shoulders to get a better grip when disaster struck. Jouret's belt buckle hooked onto the laces of my right shoe. Before I could warn him, Brandon heaved the body. I went with it and tumbled down the stairs, landing with a jarring thud on my right shoulder. Jouret's body landed mostly on top of me. My teeth snapped together and stars danced in front of my eyes. I heard a gasp of horror and looked up at Brandon, who stood frozen in shock.

There was noise on the other side of the first-floor stairwell door. Someone was coming to investigate. I pushed at the body and tried to wiggle my foot out of my shoe, but Jouret was damn heavy. Worried, I looked up at Brandon.

"Go," I hissed. "Now."

He looked at me for a long horrified moment before turning and dashing to the second-floor door and disappearing into the corridor. I pushed hard at Jouret's body once more just as the door to the first-floor stairwell opened. Gasping, I looked into the surprised eyes of a ski-masked guy with a machine gun.

He almost dropped the gun he was so shocked. Unfortunately, he quickly recovered, shouting for help and aiming the gun at my head. I closed my eyes and waited for the blast. I'm pretty sure that I had never been more terrified in my entire life.

After a moment, I cracked one eye open. He hadn't shot me. Yet.

Instantly the entire stairwell filled with armed thugs, shouting and waving weapons at me. One of them rolled Jouret off me. I scooted back against the wall, hugging my knees to my chest. The guy checked Jouret's pulse and apparently determined he was dead.

When he made his announcement, the chatter in the stairwell got louder and more strident. The guy who'd found me dragged me roughly to my feet, pressing his gun against my neck.

A man strode into the stairwell and everyone fell quiet. He was dressed all in black like the others, with a vest and an assortment of guns and weapons either connected to his belt or vest. He was, however, the only one not wearing a ski mask.

I recognized him instantly. He looked very much like his younger brother.

Mazhar Zogby.

I didn't have to fake terror or fear. I covered my face and burst into tears.

He stood directly in front of me. "Who are you? What's your name?"

He didn't even have a trace of an accent. I remembered he'd been fourteen when he came to the States.

"L-Lara Carson."

He studied my uniform. "You're a student here?"

"Yes."

He glanced down at Jouret's body. "Why did you kill him?"

"I didn't."

"Then who did?" He reached out and roughly grasped my chin, turning my face from side to side.

"N-no one. We fell down. I… I was trying to get away from him. He was my teacher…b-but he said he was taking me to the cafeteria anyway. He seemed really mad that I had hidden. He was acting strange. He wouldn't help me."

I started crying again, mostly because I hoped he wouldn't shoot a crying girl, but also because at this point, Zogby's fingers were digging into my sore cheek and it hurt like crazy. To my relief, he finally released my face with a grunt of disgust.

"I don't believe you. You're nothing more than a girl. I'll ask you again. Who did this?" Anger was palpable in his expression.

"N-no one. I swear. I didn't want to go to the cafeteria. I told him, but he wouldn't listen. I was really scared, so I pushed him and he slipped on the stairs. He fell and I went with him. I hit my shoulder and face on the stairs." I shuddered and looked at Jouret. "He hit his head and then he just lay there on top of me."

Zogby swore, first in English and then, I presume, in Urdu. He swore for what seemed a really long time, then he began pacing in the tiny space in the stairwell while we all watched him, no one daring to say a word.

At some point, he strode up to me, then grabbed me by the shoulders and shook me hard.

"Where are the others?"

"What others?"

"There are two other kids missing. Where are they?"

I shook my head. "I have no idea."

His eyes narrowed to slits. "Where have you been hiding all this time?"

I decided to stick as closely to the truth as possible. "The Weather Lab."

He frowned. "There were no classes scheduled in that classroom when we arrived. Why were you not in your assigned classroom?"

"I was skipping."

He shoved me away and gave a hoarse laugh. "Skipping? All of this because you were skipping a class? Unbelievable."

Zogby abruptly turned and slammed his fist against the wall. I jumped and then shrank against the handrail, wondering if he'd hit me next.

After a few agonizing moments of tensing myself for his fist, Zogby barked an order. The stairwell immediately emptied. A pair of guards went up to the third floor and disappeared, while another pair headed for the second floor.

The fresh sweep had started.

I hugged my trembling body, hoping with every fiber of my being that Elvis, Brandon and Piper were safely hidden and would remain that way.

It was just the two of us alone in the stairwell. Zogby stood there and stared at me with his hands on his hips. There was murder in his eyes and I had no idea what he would do. Trying to shut down the list of horrific possibilities that were now racing through my brain, I dropped my gaze to his vest and the assortment of weapons and gadgets that hung there. It didn't ease my concern. Unfortunately, all the things in his current possession could kill me if he resorted to torture rather than snap my neck with his hands.

When he moved, I actually cowered. He grabbed me by the upper arm, jerking me toward him. I winced as a shaft of pain shot through my ribs and sore knee.

"Let's go, Lara Carson, and see if you really are who you say you are."

I was relieved he didn't intend to kill me on the spot, yet scared witless at what might happen next. I tried to keep up with him but pain shot through me with every step, so I limped along. He half-dragged me to the cafeteria.

I didn't make it easy. My legs were shaking so badly, I almost fell twice. He had to pretty much hold me up. Two guards who stood duty outside the doors looked at me curiously as Zogby pulled me forward.

They exchanged short words and then Zogby pushed me inside the cafeteria. I straightened and looked around, trying to take in everything at once. The terrorists had meticulously organized the cafeteria. They had pushed tables and chairs to the side of the room, using them to barricade the extra exits. The students sat in the middle of the cafeteria on the floor. Bile rose in my throat. An outer ring of kids had been wired with explosive vests. I could see the red lights on their vests blinking. One of the kids with a vest raised his head to look at me.

Wally.

My mouth fell open and he blinked in astonishment when he saw me. I gave him a halfhearted smile as I glanced around the rest of the cafeteria. The adults sat at two round tables to the side of the students near the front of the cafeteria, apparently cuffed with their arms behind their backs. My gaze locked with Bonnie's and she seemed both shocked and worried to see me.

I tamped down my terror and took in the scene as carefully as I could, counting on my photographic memory to help me remember everything. I knew—perhaps better than most—that sometimes salvation is in the details.

Zogby led me to a table covered with papers, a laptop similar to the one that Elvis and I had stolen and a couple of water bottles. The sight of the water reminded me how thirsty I was. I suddenly had trouble swallowing.

Zogby sat down at the table, shuffled through some papers and then chose one. He looked up at me and then down at the paper. He made a mark on it and stood. I sincerely hoped the mark meant I had been located instead of singled out for execution.

I stood waiting. Zogby still seemed very unhappy with me. He circled me like a predator waiting to strike. I tensed when he stood behind me. He could shoot me, hit me, or hurt me and I wouldn't even know it was coming. My palms started to sweat and my legs quivered, but I tried to stay calm. I closed my eyes and thought of Elvis,

Brandon and Piper and hoped they were surviving the sweep. We desperately needed a bit of luck to go our way.

Maybe that's what Zogby was waiting for. Waiting to see if his men rounded up anyone else. Then he would torture us, perhaps in front of each other, to see if we would spill whatever secrets he thought we had.

If I got out of here alive, I promised myself I would never *ever* watch any movie involving bombing, torture or terrorists. I'd had enough of real-time visuals for a lifetime. It would be all puppies, kittens and sunshine after this.

Zogby circled to the front of me and opened his mouth as if to ask me a question when another man ran in the cafeteria. He motioned frantically for Zogby to approach. My stomach twisted hard. Oh, God. Had they found the others or had they killed someone else?

With a final glare at me, he strode over to the other man. The two spoke in a heated fashion before Zogby approached the teachers' table.

"Which one of you is Frank Fitzgerald?"

"I am."

"Are you are a computer teacher at the school?"

"Yes."

"Good. Come with me."

Zogby said something and one of the guards unfastened his handcuffs. Mr. Fitzgerald stood, shaking out his hands, a grimace of pain on his face.

Zogby yanked his arm. "Let's go. Now."

Frank looked terrified. "Wh-where am I going?"

Bonnie stood up, almost falling over. "Wait. Where are you taking him?"

"Sit *down*, Headmistress," Zogby said, his voice cold. "This is none of your concern…yet."

He jerked his head at me, then a guard ran over and pushed me into the circle of students, forcing me to the floor directly behind Wally. My knee hit the cafeteria floor hard, but I was beyond thankful to still be alive. I sat up, scooting closer to Wally, who sat with his back to me.

"Wally, are you okay?" I whispered.

He nodded slightly without turning around, apparently too afraid to talk. I could see the back of the black explosive vest and felt a swift rush of disgust at people who would do this to kids. I wished I could tear it off him and throw it far away.

"Hey, you're going to be fine. Just hang in there, okay?"

A girl sitting nearby glared at me, then hissed at me to shut up. I sighed while I searched the cafeteria. All exits to the cafeteria except the one leading in and out of the main hallway had been blocked off and booby-trapped. I counted four guards in the cafeteria, not counting Zogby, and the two stationed outside the door. Six. That meant a lot of the security guys were either roving around, on the roof or planetarium or stationed in other parts of the school. I fervently hoped our plan was still intact and Elvis, Piper and Brandon were still alive. Any other thought was too awful to contemplate. I had to think positively and hold it together.

Time seemed to crawl, especially when I had nothing to do but wait. I spent most of that time memorizing everything I could in the cafeteria, including the faces of students, the patterns and habits of the guards and the frequency with which the kids were allowed to go to the bathroom.

The guards handed out water and took groups of three

students to the cafeteria bathroom every fifteen minutes. I sipped my water, wanting to ration it, but I was so
thirsty it was gone before I could stop myself. I watched
the cafeteria clock, and when Zogby returned with Mr.
Fitzgerald I knew he'd been gone exactly fifty-six minutes. Fifty-six minutes and I hadn't heard any shots or
seen anyone else dragged into the cafeteria. That had to
be good news, right?

Please, please, let them be safe.

Zogby led Mr. Fitzgerald toward the teachers' table
and pulled a chair away from the group. He then motioned for Mr. Fitzgerald to sit while he scowled and
paced back in front of him, clearly agitated. He looked
ready to snap.

He suddenly stopped and pointed at Bonnie. "Stand
up."

Bonnie came to her feet, swaying slightly, off balance
with her arms bound behind her.

"What does he teach here?" he asked, pointing to
Mr. Fitzgerald.

"Computer science."

"He is useless. You are not getting your money's
worth."

Mr. Fitzgerald held up his hands. "Hey, I'm not worth-
less. Look, I don't know Phantomonics. I told you, I'm
not that familiar with the program. Kids use it these
days to download bootleg music and videos. It's an illegal program popular among some teens. Why would
I have reason to know it? That kind of programming is
definitely not part of the curriculum here."

My mind raced at his words. Phantomonics? How did
a bootleg hacking program like Phantomonics get on the
school's system? I hadn't seen it when I'd been in the sys-

tem a few days earlier and I definitely would have noticed it then. I certainly hadn't seen it a while ago while in Jouret's office, although I hadn't really looked. So why in the world were the terrorists asking Mr. Fitzgerald to try and circumvent it?

The answer hit me hard.

Elvis.

Elvis had planted it. He had said he'd put a bug in the system when the terrorists first arrived. I'd forgotten all about it until now. Now that their tech guy was dead, they had to find someone else to fix it. It made sense they'd go to a teacher except…except Elvis was a freaking genius. Somehow, in that mad, crazy moment, he'd thought ahead. He'd planted a bug figuring an adult—like the terrorists or the cyber mercenaries themselves—would have a hard time dealing with a kid-centric hacking program like Phantomonics. It wouldn't stop a decent programmer, but it *would* slow them down.

But the terrorists didn't know anything about Phantomonics and apparently the cyber mercenaries were too busy at the moment to deal with it. So, in the absence of Jouret, Zogby had taken Mr. Fitzgerald to Computer Central to figure it out. As Elvis had correctly foreseen, Mr. Fitzgerald was indeed unfamiliar with the program—not to mention extremely nervous—so he hadn't been able to address the problem. I'm not sure Jouret would have been able to figure it out either, at least not quickly.

Zogby was speaking softly to Mr. Fitzgerald, but I couldn't hear it. Mr. Fitzgerald was clearly agitated. His tie hung loosely around his neck and his dress shirt was stained with sweat.

"Seriously, I might be able to figure it out, but you

didn't give me enough time. Please give me another chance. These things aren't instantaneous." His voice wavered.

"You had fifty minutes."

"Fifty minutes is nothing when dealing with an unknown program. I need more time."

"I'm afraid your time is up."

Without another word, Zogby pulled out a gun and shot Mr. Fitzgerald in the forehead.

Just like that.

TWENTY-FOUR

THE FORCE OF the shot knocked the chair and Mr. Fitzgerald backward. Blood and gore spattered over Bonnie's suit. Zogby must have used a silencer because the shot itself was nothing more than a whine, but the thud of the chair and his body hitting the cafeteria floor seemed abnormally loud.

The students started shrieking in terror as two of the guards ran toward us, waving their guns and shouting at us to be quiet. The screams stopped, but kids still sobbed and moaned. I sat frozen in stunned revulsion, taken aback by the sudden, horrific brutality. My stomach lurched and I had to swallow back the bile. Most of the teachers were openly crying. Wally wept, too. I could hear his sniffles and hiccups in front of me.

Zogby turned the gun on Bonnie. Despite her obvious terror, she raised her chin and met Zogby's gaze evenly.

"Come here, Headmistress."

She didn't move. "What do you want?"

"I *want* you to bring me the smartest student in this school. One who is preferably familiar with Phantomonics. Your teacher said this is a program that kids are familiar with, so bring me one who can deal with it. Think carefully before you choose, because your life depends on it."

She didn't move, so one of the guards grabbed her and dragged her toward us. He stopped, gripping her by her upper arm. His hold must have been tight because she winced and had tears in her eyes.

She looked over the group of students and then her eyes fell on me. I tried to give her a small nod and a reassuring look, but her eyes skipped over me before she turned back to face Zogby.

"I'm not choosing anyone. They're just children."

"Well, that leaves us with a problem, doesn't it? I would choose you, Headmistress, or one of your teachers, but apparently they are lacking in qualifications."

"I…don't know which student can address that problem. I'm not marking any of them for execution."

He lifted the pistol, pointing it at her. "Well, if we don't have a volunteer, I guess you're the next to go."

I leapt to my feet. "No. Stop it. I'll do it. I'm familiar with Phantomonics."

Zogby blinked, startled, and then walked over to me. "You again?"

"Yes. I know the program."

"Well, aren't you quite the clever girl?"

"I'm into computers. It's why I'm at this school."

Zogby turned the gun on me. "You are curious to me. You fight with Willem, killing him in an accident, and now you happen to know this Phantomonics. Coincidence?"

"You asked for a volunteer, so I'm volunteering. I know the program. That's all."

He frowned. "Did you put that program on the computer?"

"No. How could I? You locked everyone out of the system."

"How do you know that?"

"I… I didn't know what was going on. I was scared

and I wanted to figure out a way to get out. But all the passwords were changed."

He wagged the gun at me. "I don't trust you."

"Then I guess we're at a stalemate."

He stood, thinking. I could almost imagine him weighing the pros and cons of using me.

Finally he spoke. "You do realize the penalty for failure, right? You saw what happened to your teacher when he wasn't able to unlock the program."

I swallowed hard. "Yes. Just please don't hurt anyone else."

He turned to Bonnie, his eyes narrowing. "All right, Headmistress. Can she do it? Is she smart enough to handle this? I suggest you answer with care."

Bonnie didn't answer. Zogby walked over and placed the barrel against her forehead. "I'll ask you one more time. Can she do it?"

"Tell him, Ms. Swanson," I said softly. "It's okay. You know I can do it."

Bonnie closed her eyes. "Yes. She's one of my brightest students. She can do it."

It was so quiet in the cafeteria that I could hear myself breathing. After what seemed like the longest moment in the universe, Zogby lowered the gun. I let out a huge rush of breath. Then disaster struck again.

"No, wait. She's not the smartest student in the school. I am."

My mouth opened in shock as Wally struggled to his feet, the vest too large and cumbersome for his small form.

"I've downloaded over one hundred thousand songs and videos with Phantomonics. I know this school's system front and back. I could navigate the system blind-folded. I'll do it instead of her. Leave her alone."

I looked at him in shock, a million thoughts running through my head, the most prominent being that as a result of his valiant attempt to play the hero, he was about to get himself killed.

I scrambled to think of something to negate his comment. "You are *so* not better than me," I sputtered. "I've downloaded a half million files. You're still taking baby steps compared to me. I know this system way better than you."

Wally glared at me. "You wish. I'm a certified Phantomonics pro, not to mention an ace hacker. And don't you dare call me a baby."

Zogby stepped between us. "You'll *both* come. Let's go."

I glared at Wally and he frowned at me as we fell into line behind Zogby. My heart beat faster as we left the cafeteria and headed for the stairwell. Computer Central was a good place for me to be right now for a number of reasons. First, even if I couldn't do anything, I would have a front row seat to all cyber activities. Second, I might have a chance to help Elvis by covering for any of his movements. In fact, the only downside to all of this was that I wasn't sure how I'd manage Wally. Lives were already dangling by a super-thin thread and I didn't like an unexpected variable like Wally being thrown into the mix. Of course, this all hinged on whether I could handle the bug Elvis had planted and that I didn't get shot first.

Zogby led us into Computer Central. I glanced at the vertical closet where Elvis and I had hidden. Some black-clad guy with a ski mask sat in front of the monitor typing. He glanced up when we entered. Zogby said something to him in Urdu and the guy shook his head, vacating the chair.

"Sit down," Zogby ordered us.

Without waiting for instructions, I slipped into the main chair, beating Wally by a half a second. He sat in the chair beside me, scowling.

"I'm so much better than you," he snarled. "You know it."

I ignored him, checking the computer setup. Next to the computer, the terrorists, or perhaps Jouret, had arranged one of the laptops similar to the one Elvis and I had stolen. The laptop was running, but a screen saver was on, so I couldn't determine its purpose. I cocked my head a bit to see which cable was connected to it, and was puzzled to see it was the phone cable. Jouret had likely overridden all external controls to the phone and security systems, leaving the terrorists in full control of all systems. No surprise there.

But what was the purpose of the laptop?

Zogby said nothing, just stood behind us, watching.

"Um, can I start?" I finally asked.

"Not yet. I'm waiting for someone."

A beep sounded and Zogby leaned over me, pressing a button on the laptop. A face filled the screen. Although covered in a dark ski mask, it was a masculine one. The eyes held my attention. Light blue with thick, white eyelashes. I was taken aback by the sheer coldness in them. Wally shivered beside me and I figured he got the same message that this guy was seriously bad news.

"Who is that?" the man on the screen asked.

His words were short, clipped and impatient. Not quite British, not quite Dutch.

South African.

Holy cow. If I had to guess, I would say I was face-to-face with Johannes Broodryk or someone else in the Veiled Knight's organization. My bet, however, was on Broodryk, because as a wizard, he would definitely want control and that meant his hands on the keyboard.

Zogby leaned forward so his face was visible to the visitor. "Apparently she's the brightest student in the school in terms of computer science, at least according to the headmistress."

"A girl?"

Zogby shrugged. "She was also the one we found with Willem. According to her, he found her wandering the halls and was bringing her to us in the cafeteria. When she realized what he was doing, she fought him and they fell down the stairs. Willem hit his head or broke his neck. That's her story."

Ice Eyes focused on me. I felt like his eyes were burning a hole all the way to my spine. He measured, evaluated and considered.

"What's your name?" he finally asked.

"Lara Carson."

"How old are you?"

"Eighteen."

"How did you evade the initial roundup?"

"I… I was skipping class."

"How did Mr. Jouret find you?"

"I came out of the Weather Lab because I was thirsty and I had to go to the bathroom." I hoped I sounded like a scared student. At this point it wasn't that much of a stretch.

Ice Eyes continued to stare at me. People typically blink an average of once every five seconds. I was certain he'd gone at least two minutes. His eyes would haunt me for years, *if* I got out of this alive.

Finally he spoke. "Are you really the smartest student in the school?"

"In terms of computers, yes."

Wally coughed beside me, but I ignored him.

I couldn't see Ice Eyes's mouth, but I think he smiled. Coldly. "Good. I admire both confidence and cleverness. Apparently you fought off a man twice your size. I'm intrigued, although quite irritated with you, Lara."

I said nothing.

He finally spoke. "Are you familiar with Phantomonics?"

"Yes."

"Do you wish to live?"

"Yes."

"Excellent. I will test your intelligence. You will either pass or fail. If you fail... Well, you do know what happened to your teacher, Mr. Fitzgerald, don't you?"

TWENTY-FIVE

THE IMAGE OF Mr. Fitzgerald's head exploding made my stomach churn. "Yes."

"Then you will unlock this Phantomonics program and turn it off. I'm finding it a nuisance. Can you do that?"

"I have to look at it first. But I think so."

"That is not a good enough answer."

"Then, yes, I can unlock it."

"That's better. Just as long as you do *exactly* what I say."

"Okay."

"Excellent. No heroics. I will be monitoring your every move, every keystroke. A smart girl like you understands I can do that, right?"

"Yes."

"The man behind you will kill you if you make the slightest mistake or I sense deception of any kind. No questions asked, no second chances. Are we clear?"

I glanced over my shoulder at the guy who had just vacated the chair. He tapped his gun and smiled.

I looked back at Ice Eyes. "I'm clear."

"Good. Who is that sitting next to you?"

Zogby angled the monitor toward Wally. "He's her helper. Another student who says he knows the program."

Wally gave a halfhearted wave. "Hi, my name is

Wally. I'm good at Phantomonics, too. Possibly better than her."

I resisted the urge to smack him on the head.

Thankfully, Ice Eyes dismissed Wally without a word. He turned his white laser stare on me again.

"Get rid of Phantomonics, Lara. Not one keystroke more. Unlock it, delete it and stop. You have fifteen minutes. If you are as good as you think, it shouldn't take you much longer than that. If it does we'll drag your bodies to the cafeteria for show. I figure peer pressure of that level should motivate another student more capable if you prove incompetent."

Wally made some sort of strangling noise, but I stayed calm. Somehow I knew it was important I didn't let my glance waver even once. I could not let him sense weakness or he'd use it to his advantage.

"I won't fail."

"We shall see."

Wally shivered, glancing at me in apprehension.

Ice Eyes nodded, apparently satisfied. "Remember, Lara, I'll be watching. Don't disappoint me."

His face disappeared from the screen and I exhaled. I looked over my shoulder and saw that Zogby, too, had vanished. The guard had moved to the desk with the security and phone laptops. The way the desk was angled toward the door, or what was left of it, he could watch both it and us. Right now, he stared at something on the laptop.

"He's monitoring the security cameras," I whispered to Wally.

"Can he hear us?"

"Not unless we speak up." I pointed discreetly at the laptop where Ice Eyes had just been. "Same with him. If

we whisper, he shouldn't be able to hear us. They probably don't care if we talk just as long as we don't try to
leave or cause any problems."

Wally looked over his shoulder. "Are they going to
kill us?"

"Not if we can do what they want. They need us right
now, so that works in our favor."

"If I survive this, I'm never going to Skype again. Mr.
Ski Mask Psycho gives me the willies."

"I call him Ice Eyes."

"What?"

"Mr. Ski Mask Psycho. I call him Ice Eyes."

Wally shuddered. "He does have weird eyes. Almost
no pigment."

"Agreed. Look, Wally, I need to unlock this program.
I've got to concentrate and I only have fifteen minutes.
Be quiet for a bit, okay?"

I leaned forward, my fingers poised over the keyboard. I had full access to the system, but I was also
being heavily scrutinized. Where to start? How to do
this?

Before I could type a single stroke, Wally put a hand
over mine. "Wait. Let me do it. This is my life at stake,
too."

I paused, closed my eyes. "Jeez. Don't distract me.
Let me take a first shot. If I fail, it's all yours, okay?"

"If you fail, we're both dead. You heard him."

"If I'm floundering, I'll turn it over to you with time
to spare."

"How do you know how much time I'll need?"

I wanted to scream at him to be quiet, but I knew he
was scared. So was I. I dug deep for patience. "I'll know.

I'm good for this, Wally. Just sit tight. But do it quietly. I need to think without distractions."

He lowered his voice even further. "Do you really think he knows what you're doing? If he can't unlock something as basic as Phantomonics, he probably doesn't have a clue about computers. Can't you just send a clandestine message for help or something?"

"Wally, will you shut up? Please." The guard glanced over at us, so I whispered, "Look, I believe unequivocally that this guy is a master. You have to trust me how I know this. He's definitely good enough to unlock something as basic as Phantomonics and watch every keystroke I make. Think about it. If he's not familiar with the program, it will take him time to figure it out. Time he apparently doesn't have. He must be on a timeline, which is where we come in. So, shut up and let me work."

"Are you sure you know what you're doing?"

"I'm sure. But I need to think."

"Fine. I can help, just so you know."

"I know. For now, be very quiet. I need to stay focused."

He zipped his fingers across his lips.

I sighed and started typing. I had to get into the zone to keep my nerves from undercutting me. The last thing I needed was Wally breathing down my back, trying to provide some kind of useless instruction. I knew exactly how to unlock the program, but I couldn't do it instantaneously. I had to take sufficient time to make it clear I was good, but not so good I threw suspicion on myself.

Crap. I had to think back. How much had I known at eighteen? How would I have approached this hack? Everything depended on how I handled myself right now. If my suspicions were right, a cyber wizard was watch-

ing me. That meant every step had to be just right or he'd
know I was faking or holding back.

I began to type. I could feel the minutes tick past and
a bead of sweat slid down my temple. My hands were
shaky.

Wally leaned over, practically sitting on top of me,
watching my every move. I ignored him as I tried to
think what steps I would take if I didn't already know
the answer. I had to be thorough and logical to make sure
my method made sense to Ice Eyes. He needed to understand exactly what I was doing and why. I had to make
it believable to him or I was dead…and so was Wally.

I purposely made a mistake and heard Wally hiss.
"That was stupid."

"Shut up."

"Go back two steps."

"Leave me alone, Wally. I'm thinking. How much
time do I have?"

Wally glanced at his watch. "Six minutes."

"I'm going to do this."

"Let me take over. You're too far behind."

"I know what I'm doing." I did a couple more maneu-
vers and Wally whistled. "Wow. I didn't see that coming."

"How much time?"

"Three minutes."

I took a few more steps and unlocked the program.
With a single keystroke, I deleted it. I sat back in my
chair, folding my hands in my lap. I had no earthly idea
whether or not Ice Eyes would buy any of it.

Wally whopped and slapped me on the back. "I don't
believe it. You did it, Lara. That was amazing. I have
a newfound appreciation for your mind. If you want

to go out sometime, maybe I could change your mind about guys."

I pointed to his vest and then the chair. "Sit down before I blow you up myself. I mean it."

The screen flickered and Ice Eyes came into view. "Well done, Lara."

"Thank you."

"You are very, very good."

I decided not to acknowledge that. I felt like he was searching for something and the less I said, the better.

After a bit, he spoke again. "Well, congratulations. You passed. For now."

Wally heaved a big sigh of relief.

I hated the fact that I had helped Ice Eyes in any way, but it had been necessary to gain at least a small measure of trust in order to stay alive and in my front row seat.

"I have a new assignment for you, Lara. Are you ready?"

"I guess."

"I want you to upload the following message on the FBI website, following these exact instructions."

"Okay."

He forwarded the message and instructions, and then his face disappeared from the monitor. I carefully read the directions and uploaded the material exactly as instructed, reading the message while I did it.

"Why doesn't he just upload it himself?" Wally whispered.

"How would I know? I guess he's busy. Do you want to ask him?"

Wally gulped. "No."

"Then let's see what we're uploading."

Wally read over my shoulder.

One teacher is now dead. If you pull a stunt like the Phantomonics one again, we will kill three more. You have been warned.

Wally looked at me. "The police put Phantomonics on the system? How did they get in? But even more importantly, if they could, why didn't they put something more significant on?"

I couldn't tell Wally who did it and why, so I ignored the question and kept reading.

We will release one student at exactly twenty hundred hours via the south side gymnasium door. The student to be released is Martin Herman. His release is in appreciation for Senator Herman's timely cooperation. If any attempt is made to enter via the gymnasium or interfere with his release, I will shoot 15 students and staff in retaliation. More demands will be shortly forthcoming.

Wally drew in a sharp breath. "They're actually going to release a student?"

I read the message again, then sat back. "Apparently, yes. One down and three hundred more to go."

TWENTY-SIX

WALLY CROSSED HIS ARMS. "You do realize this is totally, one hundred percent un-fricking-fair."

I shifted in the chair. "What's unfair?"

"He's going free."

"Better him than no one."

Wally sighed. "Yeah, but did it have to be Mack? Figures he'd be the only one of us to survive."

"Mack? Wait. Mack is Martin Herman? You've got to be kidding."

"I wouldn't kid about something so crappy as that."

I sat back in the chair. "Mack's father is a senator?"

"Yep."

"Any idea what senate committee he might be on?"

"Not a clue. Usually I try to have as little to do with Mack as possible."

"It could be important. I think Ice Eyes is trying to blackmail the senators for information."

Wally looked at me with wide eyes. "Information? About what?"

I looked over my shoulder, kept my voice at a low whisper. "I'm not sure. I think it might be a peace process in Pakistan that the U.S. might be involved in. It's called Operation Dove."

"What? You've got to be kidding? Why would they hold a high school in the U.S. hostage in order to promote a peace process in Pakistan?"

"Because this group doesn't want to promote it. They want to sabotage it."

"What does that have to do with our school?"

"Well, Excalibur Academy happens to teach two of the children of well-known senators, whom I would presume are on an important U.S. foreign policy committee."

Wally twisted his face in a disgusted expression. "Extortion? Blackmail with kids as the bargaining chip? That is *so* rank."

"You won't find me disagreeing with that. But I imagine it would be extremely effective."

His mouth twisted into a scowl. "So, these terrorists are going to kill us for information? That's the sum price of my existence? What does Ice Eyes get out of it? Are these terrorists paying him?"

"Probably. But it's a huge risk for him. It would have to be a heck of a lot of money. An operation this size had to be exceptionally well planned and organized. It had to cost a ton of money. The added cyber component to this operation would have made it super pricey. I don't know for certain how big terrorist budgets are these days, but given the scope of this operation, I have a feeling there isn't enough money in it to make it worth his while."

"So why is he doing it, then?"

"It has to be the opportunity to make more money. A lot. He's a mercenary. But how he intends to get it, I'm not sure yet."

My mind raced, sorting through the emails I'd read in Jouret's account while in his office. Jouret's email to the two senators had said to reply directly to his email account. I was certain I'd not seen a reply of any kind from Senator Herman. I still didn't see one now, so what the heck was Ice Eyes talking about? How had Senator Herman cooperated?

The FBI cyber command team was probably going nuts now that word of the release was live. I wondered what Slash was doing and what he would think if he knew it had been me who uploaded the message to the FBI's website.

I glanced up at the security camera and watched the light blink red. We were the view of the moment. I looked over my shoulder at the guard by the door and he raised his eyes from the screen and met mine.

Oh, yeah, he was definitely keeping tabs on us. But at least he wasn't close enough to hear us if we kept our voices down, and Ice Eyes couldn't hear us unless we spoke up.

I looked back at the camera. I'd timed the rotation earlier in the cafeteria. From what I could tell, the camera cycled through all nine views in and outside of the school, holding the picture for sixty seconds. Nine minutes for an entire cycle. I thought of Elvis and prayed he and Piper were alive. If they had survived the second sweep and Piper had showed him the bridge, it was highly likely Elvis had already tapped in to the system and made contact with the police's cyber team. He might even be watching me at this very moment.

Ice Eyes suddenly appeared on the computer monitor. My hands jerked on the keyboard. I was beginning to hate the way he came and went like a freaking ghost.

"I have confirmed the upload. Nice work, Lara. I appreciate the fact that you require so little instruction. Stand by."

Like I had a choice. I leaned forward, scouring the desktop, wishing I could click on a half dozen items while knowing I couldn't. Jouret's mail was open, which is how I could see he didn't have a reply from Senator Herman, or anyone else for that matter, but other than that, little else was visible to me.

Wally touched my arm, causing me to jump.

"Jeez, Wally. What do you want?"

"I want to ask you something."

"Ask away."

"Look, I respect your sexual preferences and all, but if we ever get out of this alive, will you go out with me? I mean, just for a drink or something. I need some practice with girls. Besides, I think being in imminent danger has brought us closer emotionally, not to mention physically."

I sighed. "You're not even old enough to drink."

"Technically, neither are you. But I can make us a couple of excellent fake IDs. No one would be the wiser."

"Jeez, Wally, don't tell me things like that."

"Is that a yes?"

"No!"

"No? Really? How can you say no? I'm wearing an explosive device, perhaps in the final moments of my pathetic life, and you are going to let me die knowing nothing but rejection from women, even lesbians?"

"I'm *not* rejecting you."

"You just said no. In what universe is that not a rejection?"

"It's really complicated. It's not a rejection in the technical sense. It's just an I-can't-go-out-with-you-for-a-number-of-important-reasons rejection. Okay?"

We were saved from further discussion when another guard entered Computer Central. He spoke rapidly to our guy then slipped out. I checked the clock. Five minutes until Mack's release. My fingers itched to go into the security system. I wished I could see what was happening.

Ice Eyes was busy on the system. The cursor moved around and he was clicking on different things. He was checking the mail, as well. He seemed to be waiting for a message from someone.

I presumed by now the terrorists had Mack by the gym door. No matter which way I looked at it, his release was good for the police and for us, despite the fact that Mack was a first-class jerk. The police could debrief him and get a lot of useful information. He might even tell them about me. If he told them that I'd been taken to Computer Central, it might change the way they approached the situation. Well, at least how Slash played things. It also meant the police would know about the bombs, the vests, how many terrorists were present, their mood and many other things. More information made for informed decisions. Informed decisions were a plus in our current situation. If all went going according to our plan, and if Elvis were still alive, he should be able to feed them some additional information from the inside, which would be critical.

If he were still alive.

I couldn't bear to contemplate the alternative.

I had to focus, get my head in the game. I was exhausted, hungry and very thirsty despite the bottle of water I had drunk in the cafeteria. I glanced over my shoulder. Our guard was intently watching his monitor. He had an important job right now monitoring the security cameras during the exchange, so I knew he'd be far less focused on us. That gave me an idea.

I leaned over toward Wally and whispered in his ear. "Wally, do you know Morse Code?"

"Hey, I may be a geek, but it doesn't mean I have *that* much time on my hands."

I sighed. "I don't know it either. What about sign language?"

"Not really. Well, I know the alphabet. More or less."

I perked up. "Is that more or less?"

He shrugged. "Both. It's not like I use sign language every day. In fact, I've never used it. I'm not even sure I remember all of the signs for the letters, but I can try."

"That will have to do."

"For what?"

"Never mind. Just teach me what you know, okay?"

Learning sign language was good for me. Wally and I kept our hands in our laps and made our motions as small as possible. It took my mind off the fact that an exchange was taking place during which we might all be blown sky-high if something went wrong. It also gave Wally something to do and calmed him down, which benefited me, as well.

"Do you think Mack is free by now?" Wally asked me after teaching me the letter *L*.

I glanced at the clock and then over my shoulder at our guard. He'd been steadily giving reports via the walkie-talkie for the past fifteen minutes. If I spoke Urdu I might have known what was going on.

I turned back to Wally. "I think so. It shouldn't take that long to open the door and push him out. If that's the way they are doing it."

"I don't think the police will try to storm the place if they're releasing hostages, right?"

"Agreed. They wouldn't want to jeopardize that."

"Good. It's not like I want to be fried chicken any-time soon."

My eyes fell to his vest. The red light was still blinking.

"Don't think about it, Lara. I don't. It helps."

I raised my gaze to his face and he gave me a weak smile. "Look, if it's my time, it's my time anyway. No sense worrying about it when we can't do anything."

"You're *not* going to die. At least not today."

"I certainly hope not. So are you going to tell me why you're all hot to learn sign language?"

"No."

"I knew you were going to say that. It's your favorite word."

"Then don't ask next time. Come on. Let's keep going. How do you make an *M* in sign language?"

We had gotten all the way to the letter *U* when Ice Eyes suddenly appeared as a small box in one corner of the screen. I quickly folded my hands together in my lap.

"Are you ready for your next assignment, Lara?"

"Yes."

"Good. I want you to send the following email. Wait a moment, it should appear in your in-box momentarily."

I heard a ding and saw the email. A quick glance indicated it was from a different account than he had sent the earlier one. He was hopping around sending the police cyber team all over the world chasing after phantom accounts.

Damn him.

"I got it," I said.

"Open it and make sure the content is there."

I opened it up and started reading. Wally rested his chin on my shoulder to read as well.

Dear Senator Walters:
As you can see we have released Senator Herman's son. He provided the information we needed despite the

FBI's warnings. I will give you one final chance to provide information on Operation Dove in exchange for the release of your daughter. You have exactly one hour to respond to this email. If you do not answer, your daughter will be executed at exactly twenty-two hundred hours. If you do answer, be aware that we will be closely comparing your information to that of Senator Herman's. If the information does not agree or if I am suspicious of it in any way, we will execute her. Be advised that I know more than you might think and have eyes and ears in many locations. Be very sure that the information you send me is accurate. You have one chance only.

I felt sick. "The content is there."

"I couldn't hear you."

I raised my voice. "It's there."

"Cut and paste it into an email in your account. Mark it urgent and send it to the following address." He rattled off a personal email for Senator Walters.

I did exactly as he said and he disappeared from the screen without another word.

"What the hell was that all about?" Wally whispered.

I closed my eyes. "It's all about the money. He's blackmailing them."

"Well, duh. I got that. Looks like he's exchanging the kids for the information. Just like what you said. Apparently he's got half of what he wanted."

I shook my head. "That's the problem, Wally. I don't think Senator Herman gave him anything."

TWENTY-SEVEN

WALLY LOOKED AT me with an incredulous expression. "What are you talking about? He just released Mack. How is that not giving him anything? Senator Herman must have given him something." His voice got louder.

I glanced over my shoulder and saw the guard staring at us. "Keep your voice down, Wally."

"Sorry."

We stayed silent for a few minutes. When Wally thought the guard had lost interest, he leaned over whispering, "Why did Ice Eyes send that email to Senator Walters if Senator Herman didn't send any information?"

"He's tricking her."

"I'm so not following you."

I lowered my whisper so far that Wally had to lean his head on my shoulder to hear me. "I think Ice Eyes let Mack go for a purpose. He made a big public announcement about it, thanking the Herman family for their cooperation. But as far as I can see, the Herman family didn't cooperate at all. The FBI never would have let Senator Herman or Senator Walters give in to demands from the terrorists. But by releasing Mack, Ice Eyes made it seem as if the Herman family *did* cooperate, just without FBI permission. Senator Herman can protest six ways to Sunday that he didn't do it, but he's now a suspect with the FBI, the police *and* Senator Walters. Ice Eyes is effectively driving a wedge between all the parties involved. At the same time, he's privately appealing to a mother's desperation to save her daughter."

"Oh, my God. Would Senator Walters do it? Send the information to save her daughter?"

"Would you, if it were your kid?"

Wally swallowed hard. "So, what happens to us if Senator Walters sends in that information? Is it game over?"

"I don't know. I think there's some component to all of this that I'm missing." I glanced up at the security camera and saw the red light was blinking. "Stop talking. We're on camera."

Wally looked up at the camera and then down at his hands. "I'm so hungry."

"Me, too. But I'd rather have something to drink."

"God, I'm dying for a drink of water, no pun intended. Let's ask the guard. I'll do it."

I nodded, so Wally lurched to his feet. I looked at the red light on the security camera and then blinked. I wasn't one hundred percent sure, but I thought I'd seen the red light blink twice before it blacked out. Either I was becoming delusional or it was possible Elvis had sent me a message. Or maybe it was just wishful thinking. I did hope with all my heart he was there watching over me.

Safe and alive.

I heard Wally talking behind me. "Hey, dude, we're really thirsty. We need to drink. Water. We want to have something to drink." I turned around and observed that the guard had the rifle aimed at Wally's head.

"Sit down."

"Sure, sure." Wally held up his hands and backed up. "Look, we're just thirsty. Please. Just a bottle of water."

The guard grunted and sat down, fumbling with the contents of a black duffel bag. He tossed Wally a bottle of water. Wally caught it with one hand.

"Thanks, dude. Appreciate it."

He brought the bottle back to his seat and handed it to me. "Ladies first."

"That's very chivalrous of you."

"Of course. I'm a gentleman."

I smiled and twisted off the cap, taking a gloriously long gulp of the water. I had to stop myself and hand it over to Wally. He took a long drink. After that we had only about a third of the water left. I wet my lips and looked away. It would be better to ration it.

"Now what?" Wally asked. "I hate all this sitting around and waiting to get blown up."

I looked at the guard again, but he didn't seem to care if Wally and I whispered as long as we weren't bothering him.

"I have an idea. Wally, let's play fantasy for a minute."

His mouth dropped open. "Oh, thank God and all the stars above. It's really happened. Do you have any idea how long I've waited for a girl to say that to me?"

"Not *that* kind of fantasy. Jeez. A military fantasy."

"Oh, figures."

"Do you play any of those online shooting games? You know like Honor Bound or Strike Force Delta Six?"

"Exactly how does that figure in with our current dire situation?"

"Just humor me."

"Fine. Truthfully I don't play them much. My parents don't allow it, so I have to do it on the sly, which cuts into time spent on said games."

"Okay, just follow me. If you wanted to blow something up in one of those games, how would you do it?"

He considered for a moment. "Bombs, of course. Hand grenades, if I were on the run."

"Let's stick with the bombs. Say you have multiple bombs. How would you set them off?"

"Remote control, of course."

"What about a timer?"

"Well, a remote could start a timer. I'd definitely want a remote as opposed to kneeling in front of said bomb and programming it to go off. I'm not a fan of timers. There are just too many chances for something to go wrong. Frankly I'd prefer a remote button that would result in an instantaneous boom, since it lets me be more in control of the exact timing. Countdowns are only good for drama in the movies."

I tapped a finger on my chin. "Good. Okay, so, let's say you have a remote. How exactly would you set off your bomb using this remote?"

"Are we getting technical here?"

"Yes. You any good at engineering?"

"I'm decent. I like to put stuff together."

"Excellent. Play bomb maker for me."

He looked at me for a long moment and then down at his vest. "You're thinking of the vests, aren't you?"

"Yes," I admitted.

"How to disarm them?"

"Maybe."

He blew out a breath. "Okay then, quit playing and get real. I can handle it."

"You sure about that?"

"Of course, I'm sure."

"All right then. I don't see a timer device on these

vests. So, my guess is that they are being controlled by a single remote. That also means they're probably wired to blow at the same time. This would make sense since it would provide the leader with an instantaneous ability to set all things off, which would likely to be important to him, especially if he were under duress."

"Makes sense."

"So, we agree the most likely assumption here is the leader would have a quick-trigger remote designed to set off all the bombs at once?"

"Yes." Wally held up a hand. "But there's a caveat. If I were the leader and wanted to live through said explosion, I'd make sure my remote had a fairly decent range. However…"

"However, what?"

He frowned. "Our situation is unique. There are too many vests and we're in too confined an area."

I nudged his arm. "Which means?"

He exhaled a deep breath. "Which means these guys intend to go down with the ship. Blow themselves and us to the moon. Range isn't a factor here."

Elvis and I had already come to the same conclusion, but it helped to know someone else did, too. "Okay. Let's operate on the assumption that range is out. Now, given these parameters, how would you create the remote?"

"You're really focusing on the remote. Why?"

"I hope it will be the weak link."

He stared at a spot above my shoulder, thinking. "That's pretty clever thinking. So, how would I create it? Smartphone. Yeah, I'd create my own app. Fast, easy and secure and known just to me."

"True, but a smartphone requires Wi-Fi to work."

"Right. I forgot. A cell phone won't work here in the school building."

"So, how else?"

"Well, there is laser triggering. You know, point at the target and click."

My brain raced, considered. "Yes, that's a possibility. Laser triggering. Except it would take a lot of time to set off each vest one at a time. Not a good plan if things went bad quickly. I'm still leaning toward the scenario that will blow everything sky-high all at once. That would make more sense. I mean, think about it. Why do they have the kids with vests flanking the others in a circle?"

"Because it's easy to keep an eye on us?"

"No. Because it's a maximum arrangement designed for one big kaboom. When the vests explode, they'll take all the kids with them all at one time…maximum destruction."

Wally gave an audible gulp.

I put a hand on his arm, trying to reassure him. "Sorry. I was just theorizing aloud…trying to think like one of them. That's *not* what's going to happen. We're going to stop them."

"How can you be so sure?"

"Because we're smart and they're bullies. This time we are going to win."

"I wish I had your confidence."

"I'm happy to share. Now, speaking of being smart… would a laser trigger require the bomb to be in visual range?"

"Yes, I'd think so. Most laser triggers have a limited range."

I considered. "But you're here, Wally. The leader didn't think twice about you leaving his sight. I think that implies he doesn't care about range or visual. He's just going to push the button on the remote and kaboom."

Wally looked down at the vest. "I wish I could take it off, but they said it would explode."

I patted his shoulder. "They probably just said that to scare you. Still, we aren't going to risk it. Don't worry. We'll do even better. We'll render it inoperable. We'll get through this. Hang tough."

"You do realize if I explode you'll go with me."

"You're *not* going to explode. Let's stop worrying about what the terrorists want to happen and use our energy and brains for what *we* want to happen. Worrying will get us nowhere."

"True."

"So, help me out, Wally. The terrorists need a vehicle for the remote. How would they make it?"

Wally fell silent thinking. After a moment, he spoke. "If I couldn't use Wi-Fi, it would have to be something else that utilizes a frequency."

I closed my eyes and searched my memory. I went through a visual catalogue of everything I'd seen in the school, on the terrorists and on Zogby himself. I made myself go slow to make sure I didn't miss anything.

Then, just like that, I had it.

I snapped my fingers. "His belt."

"A belt? Whose belt?"

"The leader's belt. The guy who brought us here to Computer Central. He's the same guy who is running the deal in the cafeteria. I think it's safe to assume he's running the show here at the school, right?"

Wally looked perplexed. "Sure seems like it. But what does his belt have to do with anything?"

"As the leader, he'd be the one to explode the bombs."

"That seems the most logical."

"Well, I noticed he has an odd device clipped to his belt. It looks like a garage door opener."

"A garage door opener?"

"Yes." I started to get excited. "Actually, it makes perfect sense. Wally, how do you open your garage door from your car?"

"I don't have a car."

"Theoretically speaking."

"Oh. Well, you press a button and it opens. Not following you."

"Why does the door open?"

He snapped his fingers. "Because the remote talks to the door via a code transmission that utilizes a radio frequency."

"Exactly. A frequency. A radio frequency."

Wally's eyes widened. "Wait. Are you saying they rigged the remote using a radio frequency via a garage door opener? Wow, that's pretty ingenious."

"Simple, cheap and effective. But that's really good news for us."

"Why?"

"Because all garage doors in the U.S. use a standard radio frequency. The codes are different, but the frequency is standard."

"How is that good for us?"

"Because, if we can jam the frequency, the remote won't work…"

His eyes lit up. "…and the vests and bombs won't explode."

"Exactly."

His momentary excitement faded. "Well, in theory

that rocks, but how are we going to build a jammer under the watchful eyes of our guard and Ice Eyes?"

"We don't have to. Someone else will. If I can get them a message."

"Just who is someone else and how would you get them a message?"

I smiled. "Just trust me, okay?"

He stared at me for a long moment and then sighed. "It's crazy, but I do."

TWENTY-EIGHT

I HAD STARTED watching the security camera very carefully, hoping for a signal of some kind. I'm not sure how many cycles had passed before I saw it again. A double blip on the red light. It was so quick I thought I might have missed it. But I didn't. I had definitely seen it.

I whispered to Wally. "Distract the guard for a few seconds."

"How?"

"I don't know. Tell him you have to go to the bathroom or something. Just keep his eyes off the security camera for as long as you can. Every second will count."

"Okay. Here goes." Wally stood up. "Um, excuse me. I have to pee. Can we have a bathroom break?"

Leaving my hands in my lap but in view of the camera, I started to spell out words in sign language letter by letter. I couldn't be sure Elvis was watching or if he were even alive, but it was the best I could do on short notice.

Wally talked fast behind me. "Whoa, hey. Peace, love and tranquility. Lower the gun. I just got to go, that's all. I haven't gone for hours. I don't want to make a mess in here."

I'd only spelled two words and part of the third when the guard barked at Wally to sit down and hold it or he'd shoot him.

Wally sat down and the guard resumed his spot in front of the laptop. "Did that help?"

"Yeah, thanks."

"What were you doing?"

"Sending a message."

"How?"

"Sign language."

"I guess I shouldn't ask how and to whom you sent this message, right?"

"Right." The computer dinged and I leaned forward. "Crap."

It was an email from the personal account of Naomi Walters.

Wally leaned over so far he practically fell in my lap. "Oh, God. Please tell me that isn't what I think it is."

Ice Eyes must have been waiting for the message because he immediately clicked it open. I scanned the message along with him. It was detailed information on U.S. involvement—which had been publicly denied—in the Pakistani peace process with members of the warring factions in their country.

Wally's eyes were so wide they almost popped out of his head. "Oh, my freaking goodness. This isn't good, right?"

I didn't have time to answer because Ice Eyes's face appeared on the screen. "Lara, send the following message from your account. Thank Senator Walters for her cooperation and tell her we are reviewing her information. Then upload the subsequent message to the FBI website that Senator Walter's daughter, Jennifer, will be released via the gymnasium door in five minutes at exactly twenty-two twelve."

I did as I was told. My hands trembled as I pushed the send button.

Ice Eyes verified I had sent it and then nodded.

"Good. Now access Excalibur Academy's parent emergency email list from Willem's account."

I clicked on the address book and found the list.

"I've got it."

"Excellent. I just sent you something else. You should be receiving it momentarily."

The computer dinged and I saw a message sent from another account, this one from Brazil. I opened and read it silently.

You will receive this message only once. The first parent to respond to this request and wires $500,000 in bitcoins to any of the following websites will have their child released. After that, the price goes up. It will be $600,000 for the second child, $700,000 for the third child and so on. Only ten children will be released through this system, so if you want your child to be one of the lucky few, we suggest you act quickly. Your window of opportunity closes in ninety minutes.

He listed more than a dozen websites at the end.

"Lara, copy the message exactly as it is and paste it into a new email. Then send it to the parent list. I'll be back in a minute."

He disappeared from the screen.

Wally whistled. "Why does he keep insisting on using the school account to send his messages? And what the heck is a bitcoin?"

"He keeps using the school system because he's spent a hell of a lot of time protecting it and making it virtually impenetrable. It's a freaking fortress." I clenched my fists in my lap. "But the bitcoin news is bad. I knew it had to be money. I just didn't expect this."

"Why? What is a bitcoin?"

"Money. It's all about money. Bitcoins are a digital currency. Some people call it crypto-currency because the creation and transfer of bitcoins uses cryptology. They can be bought and sold electronically for many different currencies and are near impossible to trace."

"Whoa. I'm a geek and even I can't understand that. What are you talking about?"

"Don't bother me right now, Wally. I'll explain it better to you later. We can't send this message. It stops here."

"What?" Wally hissed. "Are you out of your mind? Stop him? Have you forgotten the guy with the gun over there?"

I ignored him. The time had come for me to act. My mind raced on overdrive.

I had to prevent this email from going out. I'd just seen the end game for Ice Eyes, so now I knew for certain *what* he wanted and *how* he intended to get it. Bitcoins was an ingenious method. Once the email went out, he could vanish and monitor his bitcoin websites from whatever spot he wanted. When he got all the money he wanted, he could alert the terrorists to either release the kids whose parents had paid or instruct them to blow us all to pieces in a final grandiose act of publicity for their cause. He'd have no more use for Wally or me. From this point forward, we'd be disposable. We were actually vulnerable now, but because we were in place and had been conveniently pliant until this point, he'd probably decided to use us for one last task.

I felt sick.

But how could I stop a cyber madman watching my every keystroke and a whacko with a gun mere steps behind me monitoring my physical movements? If I refused to send the message, Wally and I would be executed on the spot. Then the guard would send the email. If I did something more complicated like openly sabotage the system, I'd be shot and Ice Eyes would use another system to send out the email. It was a bit riskier for him, but not impossible at this stage of the game. So how to stop him now, without him knowing how or what I'd done?

Think, Carmichael, think.

Ninety minutes.

I had ninety minutes and then game over.

Then, just like that, I had it. A plan. It was breathtakingly simple, and far from guaranteed to work, but it was worth a shot. I was out of time for anything else.

I brushed my hand across the desk and knocked a pencil on the floor. I leaned over to get it, taking a quick look at all the wires and cables underneath.

The guard barked at me and I retrieved the pencil and held it up. "Sorry. Dropped this."

He glared at me and then went back to monitoring the security laptop.

"What are you doing?" Wally whispered as I shifted around in my chair.

"Saving our necks. I hope."

After a minute, I copied Ice Eyes's message into a new email and then pushed Send. I immediately got an error message.

Wally looked at me. "What the hell just happened?"

"The network is down."

"At the exact moment you sent the email?"

"Actually a little before."

His eyes widened. "You did that?"

I touched his arm. "Keep your voice down."

Wally wiggled agitatedly in his chair. "Oh, God. He's going to be royally pissed. He'll know you did it."

"He won't be able to prove it."

"But what the heck does it solve? He can just send it himself from a bogus account."

"Sure, he can. He could have done that at any time during this operation. But it's risky. He's spent considerable time and effort preparing and protecting this network. Creating a new, bogus account will take time he doesn't have. He has to be really, really careful, even from a bogus account. I guarantee you that every decent mind in the cybersecurity field is all over this one. Wizards can be traced by other wizards and caught, trust me. It's a big risk. Plus he can't be sure how many parents will open an unfamiliar email and click on an embedded link. This way he's more assured of a timely parental response."

The phone on the desk rang. The sound was so jarring and unexpected I jumped.

The guard seemed surprised, too. After a moment, he picked up the receiver. He listened and then handed the phone to me.

"What did you do, Lara?" It was Ice Eyes.

"Nothing. I just tried to send the message like you requested but it bounced back." I tried to sound innocent, if that were even possible.

"No one tampered from the system on the outside. So whatever just happened, happened internally. You did something."

"No, I didn't."

"Get up from the chair, Lara."

I stood and the guard sat. Ice Eyes gave him some instructions to troubleshoot the network problem.

It didn't work.

"Check to make sure she didn't disconnect the network cable." Ice Eyes sounded irritated.

The guard leaned over the desk and looked at the wall plugs. He unplugged the network cable and then plugged it back in. "The network cable is plugged in."

He checked the connection, but no luck. "The network is still down."

"I'll ask you again, what did you do, Lara?"

"Me? Nothing. How could I? You can see my every keystroke."

Ice Eyes fell silent and the guard grunted and returned to his desk. I sat down, my legs shaky.

"Oh, my God," Wally whispered heatedly. "He sounded really pissed."

I lowered my voice. "Ice Eyes is blackmailing the parents for money in bitcoins. It's a legitimate electronic currency, but next to impossible to trace. Merchants and businesses around the world who want to exchange in bitcoins join the system by providing their information the same as they would to process a credit card transaction. The transactions are public—that's required by international law—but bitcoins have a significantly lower transaction fee. The U.S. is widely considered to be one of the most bitcoin-friendly countries in the world, and the system is growing rapidly."

"So, this is about money?"

"In part. Ice Eyes is charging the parents for a service, so to say. In this case, they pay him via a website of his choosing and he releases their children for a scalable cash payment. The first parent to pay the fee pays the least, and the last pays the most. While the transactions will be initially traceable, I guarantee you, he'll be long gone with the bitcoins, cashed in for a currency of his choosing long before the authorities can find him."

Wally's mouth opened. "Wow. That totally sucks."

"Yes, it does."

He shook his head. "I still don't get it, though. If the exchange takes place via a website, why can't the police just shut down all the websites?"

"Come on, Wally. You already know the answer to that. First of all, it takes a court order to do that. The government can't just run around shutting down websites willy-nilly. There's an actual process involved. Secondly, look at the URLs he chose for the websites. They are in twelve different countries. There is no way the U.S. government, even on a good day, could shut down *one* of those, let alone *twelve* in ninety minutes."

He rubbed his eyes. "So, we are royally screwed? He'll take the money and run while the terrorists make their statement by blowing this school sky-high?"

"We're not screwed yet. I did what I could. I think there's someone else out there who has my back and also knows what's going on. I just hope he takes it from here."

"You *think* there is someone else out there? You aren't certain?"

I wasn't going to lie to him. Not at this stage of the game. "No, I'm not certain."

"Oh, my God. We're going to die. We're going to die."

I put a hand on his arm. "Calm down, Wally. It won't help to completely lose it right now."

I glanced up at the security camera, willing the red light to come on. I'd missed the last round as I'd been busy with Ice Eyes, but I wanted to check it this time around. If I saw the double blink, I would try to send to another message about the garage door remote.

I briefly entertained the possibility that I'd become completely delusional. Seeing double blips on a security camera might just be wishful thinking. Elvis might be dead, captured and/or incapacitated. But I couldn't operate like that. I just couldn't.

It was far easier and more comforting to imagine that Elvis was monitoring both the security camera and Jouret's account. If so, he'd already know about the bitcoins and that I'd somehow sabotaged the network. He'd also know the end game and understand what I'd done, though I didn't know what he'd do next. I didn't even know what *I'd* do next.

Whatever happened next was a mystery even to me, despite the high probability that it involved my death.

Ice Eyes came on the monitor. He was smiling.

"Ah, there you are. I just wanted to inform you your services are no longer needed, Lexi Carmichael. You are hereby terminated."

TWENTY-NINE

I FROZE. HE KNEW my name. How long had he known? How had he found out?

Wally gave me a puzzled look, but I stayed motionless. My mind raced with a dozen thoughts and none of them made any sense.

Wally frowned. "Lexi Carmichael? Who's that? What's he talking about? What exactly does he mean by *terminated*?"

Ice Eyes seemed amused at my lack of a response. "Don't look so shocked, my dear. You are good, but I am better. I must admit I am quite curious as to what you are doing undercover at a high school. Ah, the plots we weave."

I still couldn't answer. *Wouldn't* answer.

When he saw I wasn't going to respond, he shrugged, clearly disappointed. "Well, I'm afraid all of your plotting has come to naught."

I finally found my voice. "I wouldn't get too cocky, Broodryk."

I saw the flash of surprise in his eyes. It felt good.

"Ah, so you know my name, too."

With a flourish, he pulled off his ski mask. "Well, in that case, no need for this if we are to be truly acquainted." The pale skin, white hair and eyebrows and complete lack of skin pigment confirmed his albinism. "It appears I *have* underestimated you."

"Don't feel bad. It happens a lot."

Wally leapt to his feet, covering his eyes. "Wait. Oh, my God, no. He showed us his face. Do you know what this means? In the movies when the bad guy shows his face, it's doomsday for those who see it. We can identify him. We even know his name even if I don't know how. He's definitely going to kill us now."

"He was going to kill us anyway. Sit down, Wally. It's okay. Please."

To my relief, Wally promptly collapsed down in his chair without another word. He kept breathing really fast, however, and I hoped he wouldn't hyperventilate himself into unconsciousness. Or maybe that would be better. Who knew?

I returned my focus to Ice Eyes.

He was grinning, full of himself. "I must say you've been an able substitute, my dear. *Too* able, which inspired some digging. I was able to unmask you relatively easily, Lexi, if I may call you that."

"No, you may not. Also, in my defense, the cover was supposed to fool some creative high school students, not a deranged cyber mercenary."

He chuckled. "Ah, I have so many questions for you. I might have even enjoyed your company. Unfortunately, I regret time constraints force me to conclude our business arrangement. A pity, really."

"I'm in no arrangement with you."

I felt a tap on my shoulder and turned around in my chair. It was the guard. He motioned with his gun for Wally and me to stand up. His eyes were cold, distant. I knew what was coming next.

Wally did, too. While I stayed seated, he leapt to his feet agitated, raising his hands. "No, no, no. Oh, God, no. You can't kill us. You just can't. We helped you. *She* helped you. She took down Phantomonics. Who is Lexi Carmichael? Why isn't anyone telling me anything?" He began to wail and wave his arms around.

While the guard's attention was on Wally, I unhooked the keyboard. I gripped it in both hands as I stood and turned, bringing the keyboard with me. Using all my strength, I swung it as hard as I could, hitting the guard's gun arm. He yelped as the gun flew out of his hand and skidded with a bounce under the desk.

To my utter astonishment, Wally launched himself at the guard with a primal scream, flailing his fists and biting the guard like a rabid dog. The guard raised his fists and began fighting back. I snatched a loose cord and came in behind the guard as he grappled with Wally. I flipped the cord over his head and pulled it tight around his neck.

I'm five-foot-eleven and he was about an inch shorter than me, which gave me a bit of an advantage. But he was also a male, physically stronger and most likely trained in paramilitary skills. Plus, he definitely outweighed a skinny girl like me. So I just pulled the cord as tight as I could and held on for dear life.

It seems strange, but it didn't occur to me that I was deliberately trying to end the life of a person. The world of ethics and intellectual debate had ended. Life at this moment had been reduced to a primal state. Kill or be killed. I didn't want to die. I didn't want Wally to die either. So, at this point, it was either him or us.

Ice Eyes shouted something from the monitor, but I couldn't make out the words. The world around me seemed to decelerate, as if every movement I made was happening in some weird slow motion.

As soon as I had started choking him, the guard stopped hitting Wally and reached up to try and pull the cord from his neck. When I pulled tighter, he staggered backward, leveraging the full weight of his body into me and smashing us back into the wall. My head and back banged hard against it, but I held on to the cord for dear life, trying to stay behind him and keep my body safe from his sharp elbows. Wally resumed his attack, although I had my doubts as to the effectiveness of his punches.

I had no idea how long it took for a choking person to lose consciousness, but it seemed never ending. I pulled the cord so tight I couldn't feel my fingers anymore, but I was tiring and I think the guard knew it. In a last movement of desperation, he managed to score a kick to Wally's face, sending him flying backward and crashing into the desk. Wally's head hit the corner of the desk and he lay on the floor clutching his hair and moaning.

The guard then collapsed to his knees, using the weight of his body to fall forward and bring me with him. I struggled to keep my grip on the cord, but I slipped. He rolled sideways, freeing himself. He sprang to a crouch, glaring at me with a bloody nose and mouth. I guessed Wally had scored a couple of good hits after all.

He muttered something in a foreign language. I was pretty sure it wasn't affectionate. His fingers curled into fists as he launched at me with a yell. I stepped sideways, but in the small room he easily grabbed a fistful of my polo, throwing me to the floor with him. In less than a second he was sitting on top of me, his hands around my neck, squeezing. Now it was my turn to choke. I bucked, squirmed and struggled, but he had me in a tight vise. A strange black crowded my vision and my lungs screamed for air. I could feel the wetness of tears leaking from my eyes as my strength ebbed.

Suddenly I heard a loud crack. The pressure around my neck loosened. I rolled sideways, gasping for air. I couldn't see straight and wheezed a few times. I gulped in breaths trying not to throw up as the tears rolled down my cheeks. I felt someone kneel beside me and gently push the hair from my face, tucking it behind my ear.

"Lexi. Are you...okay?"

I blinked and looked up. Elvis knelt next to me, holding my hand. "Oh, God. I... I didn't know if I'd make it in time. But you're alive. You're okay."

My brain didn't seem to be functioning. I couldn't figure out why and how he'd gotten here. "Elvis?"

He pulled me up and into his arms, squeezing me hard. I held on to him for dear life, resting my head on his shoulder, tears sliding down my cheeks. He touched my back, shoulders and hair as if he couldn't believe I was actually alive.

"I thought I was too late. It happened so fast. But you're alive. Oh, God, I made it in time."

"Elvis?" I couldn't seem to think straight. "What... How did you get here?"

"I ran. Just ran. I saw what was happening on the security monitor. I shot him in the head. I used a makeshift silencer—Piper's jacket—so no one would hear the shot. I worried about accuracy, shooting through it, but I was more worried someone would hear." He took a breath. "I'm babbling. You're alive, but we have to go. Even with the jacket, someone still might have heard the shot. They're coming."

He tried to pull me to the door. My legs wouldn't

hold and I swayed, almost falling down again. Elvis held me firmly.

Oh, God. Elvis was alive and he had been monitoring the security camera. I'd *known* it. But how had he gotten here from Jouret's office? Had he simply dashed down the stairwell and through the hallway without a thought to his own safety, just to save me? Nothing made sense. Why couldn't I think properly?

My throat hurt. I touched the tender skin on my neck.

"Hurry, Lexi," Elvis urged. "We've got to go. Eight minutes to breach time."

My mind struggled to keep up. "Breach?"

He pulled me toward the door, but I resisted. "No. Wait. Wally. We can't go without him."

I glanced over and saw Wally still lying on the floor, moaning and holding his head. He must have hit it hard. Blood was all over his hands and matted in his hair. I pulled away from Elvis, staggering toward him. "Wally, are you okay?"

Elvis got behind Wally. "Help me pull him up."

We lifted him to a standing position and I grabbed an arm and steadied him although I was barely standing myself.

"He's still got an explosive vest on." Elvis frowned.

"He's got to come with us."

Thankfully, Elvis didn't argue. Somehow we began half-carrying, half-dragging Wally into the hallway.

"Where are we going?" My breath was coming in huffs. My ribs hurt, my head felt ready to split open and my neck throbbed.

"Two doors down. It's showtime."

I could hear pounding footsteps. Ice Eyes had likely contacted Zogby by now. Elvis opened the door to the classroom and we staggered inside. It looked like an English lab—most likely some sort of Middle Ages Literature—with book covers and quotes hanging all over the wall.

A poster of William Shakespeare hung next to the door, with the caption, *"It is not in the stars to hold our destiny, but in ourselves."*

Elvis began pushing a heavy file cabinet in front of the door. "Both of you, get to the back of the room and make yourself as small targets as possible."

I ignored him and started helping him push the file cabinet. Elvis knew better than to try and argue with me when I was determined, so he didn't waste his breath.

Wally stood watching us, swaying unsteadily on his feet.

I pointed to the teacher's desk in the corner. "Wally, sit on the floor before you fall down. Just stay away from the windows and door, okay?"

He looked dazed. I figured he'd suffered a bad concussion if not something worse. All the blood from his head troubled me, but I had no time for an inspection now. Thankfully, he tottered toward the desk, sliding down it and into a mostly sitting position. Once there, he cradled the back of his head in his hands and moaned.

I tried not to panic when I heard shouting in the hallway.

"So, what's the plan?" I asked Elvis as we gave a final push to the cabinet. "What breach are you talking about? Is that good or bad news? Where are Piper and Brandon? Did you get my sign language message? What do the police know? Did you see that Ice Eyes is blackmailing the students' parents for bitcoins?"

Elvis leaned back against the cabinet, panting. "That's

a lot of questions, and I don't have any time to answer a single one of them."

I heard more loud noises in the hallway.

Elvis rubbed his eyes. He looked exhausted. "The guards must have discovered what happened. They'll be here any moment, checking in the nearby classrooms for you. They've got us pinned down. Go check on the kid, Lexi. Please."

He was using that as an excuse to get me away from the door, but I staggered forward several steps anyway and knelt beside Wally. Every muscle in my body hurt and my ribs were throbbing so hard, I was pretty sure at least one was fractured or broken.

Something banged hard against our classroom door. The file cabinet shook from the effort.

Wally began to moan louder. "They're coming to get us. We're going to die."

"No, we're not. Hold on, bud."

I straightened and returned to Elvis, standing next to him.

"I've got this," he snapped. "Get away from the door, damn it."

"No. *We've* got this. I'm your partner, remember?"

"Except you almost got killed a minute ago. That exempts you from all partnership responsibilities."

I put a hand on his shoulder. "It's not like you to be illogical, especially since the odds of us dying in the next five minutes are statistically significant. I'm *not* cowering in a corner. If I'm going to go down, I'm going to do it next to you, Elvis. Okay?"

He took a moment to give me a smile and then reached over to squeeze my hand. "It's not illogical. I'm actually taking a cue from you. We need to split up, give them more than one target. We've got to stall for time to stay alive. Here, take the gun." He held it out. "Get over there by the teacher's desk next to the kid and hide. Shoot only if someone attacks you. There are only three bullets, so choose wisely."

"You've had two lessons. You do it."

"No, take it, please, and use it to protect yourself."

There was something in his eyes I couldn't define. Swallowing hard, I took the gun. "Fine. Where will you be?"

"Over there." He pointed to the back of the room.

I heard gunfire and jumped. "Oh, God. We're about to be Swiss cheese."

"They're firing at the door handle. I locked it. We just need to hang on a bit longer, Lexi. Stall as much as you can. Help is on the way, okay?"

I had no idea what help he was talking about, but I limped across the room and crouched beside the teacher's desk. Wally still sat braced there, his eyes closed.

"You still alive, Wally?" I whispered.

He cracked an eye. "Barely. I'm just bummed I'm going to die a virgin. It's a cold, cruel world."

"Sex? That's all you can think of at a time like this? What's with men? Look, no dying just yet. Stay tough, okay?"

I checked to make sure the safety on the gun was off and held my hand out, bracing my elbow with my other hand. My arms were shaking so badly I didn't think I'd be able to shoot straight.

Three shots.

That's all I got, if I wasn't killed first.

The door opened and people began pushing at the filing cabinet. Elvis ducked behind one of the cabinets at the back of the classroom and crouched down.

I forgot all about my firing stance when someone sprayed five shots across the classroom, the bullets thudding into the walls. I fell on top of Wally, pushing him to the floor as plaster and wooden chunks of the desk fell on us.

Someone yelled something in Urdu and the shooting stopped. I didn't dare move.

Then a voice shouted out, "Lexi Carmichael? Come out and I won't kill you."

THIRTY

Zogby. He knew who I was, too, most certainly thanks to Ice Eyes. I didn't answer, but I could feel Wally squirm beneath me.

There was some more chatter in Urdu, but someone hushed them. I held my breath as Zogby spoke.

"Yes, I know who you are. You're not a student. You're a computer expert pretending to be a student at this school. What exactly you are doing is unclear, but I know enough. In fact, I know quite a bit about you… and your family. Come out, Lexi, and we'll end this peacefully."

I didn't feel a peaceful vibe from him at all. Actually, I felt sick. He'd referenced my family. What was that supposed to mean?

I hadn't answered, so Zogby said, "Ms. Carmichael, will you come out for this?"

I heard a squeal and then a soft voice said, "L-Lexi?"

I closed my eyes the second I recognized the voice. Bonnie Swanson.

"I'm going to kill the headmistress unless you emerge peacefully," Zogby said. "Step out with your hands above your head. I will count to three and then I'll shoot her once in the forehead, exactly as I did to Mr. Fitzgerald. Don't think I won't do it. After that, I'll parade a succession of students in here, shooting each one of them until you come out peacefully. Do you understand me?"

I couldn't figure out why they didn't keep shooting up the place and kill me. Then I realized they didn't want to draw the attention of the police just yet. They had shot just a few times with silencers, so the police might not detect it. However, if the police heard a lot of shooting, it was highly probable they would come storming in, figuring the hostage situation had gone bad. It was also possible Zogby presumed I had the guard's gun, which I didn't. But I *did* have Jouret's gun. Regardless, it meant that they were worried I would make a lot of noise and trigger a police invasion earlier than they wanted. Apparently they didn't want anything to interfere with their grand finale.

Zogby spoke. "One."

I wasn't going to let Zogby shoot Bonnie even if it meant giving up my own life. I slid the gun into Wally's hand, putting my mouth to his ear and whispering, "You've got the gun now. Three bullets. Protect yourself, okay?"

Wally nodded and I was beyond grateful he didn't try to protest or argue.

"Two."

I slid off Wally and sat up. "Okay, Zogby. I'm coming out."

I staggered to standing, put my hands up and braced for a shot. None came. Zogby had the gun pressed to Bonnie's forehead. Her blue eyes were filled with tears, her face grimy and her blouse torn and stained. Despite her terror, she looked surprised when she saw me. I probably looked unrecognizable—nothing short of a walking zombie—with a bruised and battered face, ripped clothes and blood from Wally and myself smeared all over my arms and face.

To my relief, Zogby lowered the gun. He strode toward me. "How in the hell do you know my name?"

"Oops. Guess I shouldn't have said that." Elvis had said we needed to stall, so that's what I'd try to do...if I didn't get shot first.

"Just who are you?"

"I thought you already knew my life story."

"Enlighten me."

"It's pretty boring. I'm just an ordinary, old-fashioned American girl."

His eyes narrowed. "Why did you kill Hadim?"

I felt my stomach twist. *Hadim.* That was his name. It felt surreal and surprisingly painful to give a name to a man I'd just tried to choke to death.

I lowered my hands. "He tried to kill me. Call it self-preservation."

"You are unarmed. Where is his gun?"

"In the computer room. Under the desk. If you don't believe me, you can check."

Zogby turned around and barked an order. One of the guys in the doorway disappeared.

"What about that kid who was with you?"

I shrugged. "As soon as we started fighting, he ran in the other direction. I don't blame him. He's probably hiding somewhere in the school."

Zogby issued another order and several more guards disappeared. He returned his attention to me.

"For one girl, you've caused a lot of problems."

"Wow. You sound just like my mother."

He didn't appear amused. Instead he strode over to

me and pressed the gun to my head. Strangely I felt no terror.

Bonnie started to cry. "No. Please don't hurt her. Please."

Bonnie didn't sound like a headmistress anymore. She certainly didn't look thirty years old. I guess facing death stripped a person to their most vulnerable state.

I was having more of an out-of-body experience, as if I were watching the situation happen to someone else. Somehow I'd come to terms with the knowledge I'd done everything I could. Hopefully it had been enough to save Elvis and the kids. At this point, their fate was no longer in my hands. Perhaps there was peace to be found in that.

"Wait."

Half a dozen guns cocked as Elvis stood from his spot behind the cabinet and walked toward me. "You're not nearly as smart as you think, Zogby. You're about to fail on a spectacularly international level."

Zogby looked as if his eyes were going to pop out of his head. "Where did you come from?"

Elvis stopped beside me, taking my hand and giving it a squeeze. While I wanted to throttle him for exposing himself, I felt a rush of immense gratitude that I wouldn't die alone. I squeezed his hand back.

"I'm just another person who slipped through your net. We all know what you're doing. The *Shahids*, Operation Dove, the bitcoins."

Zogby looked incredulous. "Are you a…student?"

"You made a colossal mistake choosing this school and making children your pawns. Children have the international right of noncombatant immunity. By involving them, you taint your cause in the crudest, most disingenuous way. This entire operation has backfired on you. Instead of exposing the U.S.'s clandestine participation in Operation Dove and sabotaging the process as you'd intended, you have handily provided the U.S. government with a springboard—which now includes full international support—to become actively involved in the Pakistani peace process."

Zogby opened his mouth and then shut it without saying anything. His eyes were even wider than they were moments before.

I unlinked hands with Elvis and clapped. "Wow. I *so* could not have said that better."

Elvis gave me a small grin. His hair fell over one of his eyes in a gesture so familiar my heart skipped a beat. "Well, it's good to know you're impressed. We'll have to talk more politics sometime."

Zogby's eyes narrowed. "How do you know of the Pakistani negotiations?"

Elvis faced him calmly. "We found the files on the laptop and we're aware that your plan to extort information from two U.S. senators on Operation Dove has failed."

"It hasn't failed. We have the information."

"Perhaps, but it doesn't matter now. You made two crucial mistakes. Method matters and children matter. Maybe you see it differently, but in the West, using children as hostages to promote a political cause is morally repugnant. You've just rallied the entire nation, our allies and probably even people who don't even like us, to oppose you."

Zogby sneered. "I don't care what the West thinks. I care only that my people know the truth."

"Oh, your *people* definitely know the truth now.

You've made it perfectly clear to everyone why the Pakistani government didn't invite you to the table."

Furious, Zogby raised the gun at Elvis.

I shrieked "No!" just as Wally jumped up from behind the desk, firing three shots in rapid succession at Zogby.

Zogby screamed and then went down as all chaos broke loose.

Elvis and I dropped to the floor as at least two guards fired at Wally. One missed and shattered a classroom window.

Suddenly someone began firing at the guards from out in the hallway. There was more yelling as the guards turned their guns away from us and started peppering the hallway with gunfire at unknown assailants.

The shouting, smoke and horrible sound of gunfire made my ears ring. I rolled toward the teacher's desk, covering my head with my hands as Elvis launched forward, grabbing Bonnie by the arm, pulling her toward him. He dragged her behind a cabinet just as another guard stepped into the classroom and started spraying automatic gunfire around the room. The rest of the classroom windows shattered and chunks of plaster and paint fell from the wall, showering me with white powder.

I tensed for more gunfire when the guard abruptly went down. Someone had shot him.

Hooray! It looked like the good guys were finally in the house.

It was about freaking time.

I pushed to my knees, cutting my palms on broken glass and plaster chunks, and crawled behind the desk.

"Wally!" He was lying on his side, unmoving. Panicked, I rolled him over, relieved when I heard him moan.

"Jesus H. Christ!" I shouted, the terror that had gripped

my throat when I thought he was dead changing to anger. "What in the hell were you doing? I said to protect yourself, not play Rambo."

"Ouch… I've been shot."

There was so much blood everywhere—on me and on him—I had no idea where he'd been hit.

"Where? Where does it hurt, Wally?"

"Everywhere. Right side especially. My shoulder."

I pushed off some wood shards from the desk and inspected his shoulder. The wound was bleeding, but not gushing, which was good. I pulled off my sweater and then my polo shirt, and pressed the soft cotton against the wound, the goose bumps rising on my back and arms.

I looked up and saw Elvis and Bonnie had joined us. Elvis ushered Bonnie behind the desk and knelt beside me.

"He's been shot in the shoulder," I said to Elvis. "Can you help me lift him?"

Elvis lifted him up off the floor, and I started to tie my shirt around his shoulder when I felt the cold press of metal in my neck.

"Get up, bitch."

I recognized the voice. Zogby. He was still alive.

I rose slowly.

Elvis lowered Wally back to the floor and held out his hands. "Look, it's over, Zogby. Finished. Let her go."

"Shut up. It's done when I say it's done."

He shifted his grip so he had his arm wrapped around my neck, my body shielding his. The gun pressed against my right temple. Wally had scored at least one shot on Zogby. I could feel the warmth of his blood slipping against the bare skin of my back. He tightened his grip around my neck when I noticed the device in his left hand just below my chin.

Oh, God. The bomb remote.

I had no idea if Elvis had gotten my message about the garage door and if he'd even understood it, let alone told the police to build a jammer. My presumptions seemed beyond foolish now. After all, I'd made an educated guess based on a freaking video game.

If I were wrong, we were all about to go up in flames.

Zogby tightened his choke hold and I gasped for breath. I could vaguely hear him saying something to Elvis.

"...we are willing to give our lives in pursuit of what we think is right."

Elvis, bless his heart, was actually arguing with him. In fact, I'd never heard him talk so much in all the time I'd known him.

"It's Foreign Policy 101, dude. Children are *not* acceptable collateral damage."

He was desperately trying to keep Zogby talking or goad him into turning the gun on him instead of me. Sporadic gunfire and screaming still came from the hallway. I had no idea what was going on or who was winning.

My whole world had narrowed to this single moment in time with Elvis standing in front of an armed madman, trying to sacrifice himself in my place with nothing more than words at his disposal.

He kept talking. "Killing innocents is an indefensible practice in practically every language, culture and religion. Sometimes the killing of children may be accidental or unintended, but it is *never* right. *Never.* Worse, this was not accidental or unintended. You targeted this school on purpose. You intended to use innocents from the very beginning for nothing more than political gain."

I closed my eyes. I wanted to scream at Elvis to be quiet, that I would rather die than watch him get shot first, but I knew he wouldn't stop no matter what I said. He started to say something else when a voice rang out.

"Drop the gun. Now."

THIRTY-ONE

WE ALL FROZE.

Zogby turned carefully, keeping me as a human shield. I recognized the voice and then I saw him.

Slash!

He stood framed in the doorway in a crouch, two guys behind him. All of them were dressed in heavy vests and helmets, and each had a gun with special scopes pointed at Zogby and me. I didn't have to look to know there was a high probability of three red dots on Zogby's forehead at this very moment.

I tried to catch Slash's eye, but he didn't even look at me. His focus was utterly on Zogby.

"Well, gentlemen, I'm glad you're all here," Zogby said. "Because it's time to say goodbye."

"He's got a detonator," I shouted.

It was too late.

Zogby's thumb pushed on the device under my chin. I felt him stiffen and then his head exploded, showering me with blood and carnage before his body crumpled to the ground.

I stood there frozen in shock and covered in a dripping mess of gore.

"Cara!"

The three men rushed across the room at once. One kicked the gun far away from the body while the other rolled Zogby over. I couldn't look at his body. The room filled with security forces, but Slash only had eyes for me.

I threw myself into his arms and despite the gore, he held me tight. He was kissing my hair and murmuring something to me in Italian when my legs collapsed. He didn't let me fall, but held me tightly against him.

"Zogby…the bombs…" I gasped.

"They didn't go off. It's going to be okay. You're okay. What did they do to you? Where is your shirt?"

My mental capacity was limited for the moment while I processed what had just happened. "I'm fine. I'm okay. That was a really good shot. A bit close for comfort, but I'm impressed by your accuracy at such close range."

"Never. Never again put me through that hell, *cara*."

He squeezed me so hard I couldn't breathe. I managed to pull back, then cupped his face in my hands.

"I'm so sorry, Slash. I had no idea the terrorists would come here. Are you sure you still want to be my boyfriend after this?"

He laughed hoarsely, hugging me again. "Don't you *ever* think about leaving me."

An agent called to Slash. He gave me a quick kiss. "Be right back."

While Slash was talking to the agent, Elvis came over, shrugging out of his tattered shirt, slipping it on me. "Take this. You're freezing."

I realized I'd been standing there in my bra the whole time, having given my shirt to stop the bleeding on Wally's shoulder.

"That was way too close for comfort." Elvis's fingers shook as he tried to button the shirt on me. Unfortunately, as I'd ripped off most of the buttons at the start of our ordeal, there were only two to fasten.

I put my hand across his, stopping him as he fumbled to fasten the first one. "Why didn't you stay hidden, Elvis? They might not have found you."

He raised his gaze to meet mine. "Why did you give the gun to Wally?"

"I wasn't going to let Zogby shoot Bonnie."

"Well, I wasn't going to let Zogby shoot you."

We shared a brief smile as Slash returned. "Move to the back of the room. All of you. We have a live situation here."

"Wait. I've got to check on Wally."

Slash looked puzzled. "Who's Wally?"

"A student. He's been shot and is lying behind the teacher's desk. He shot Zogby and saved us. He's got my shirt."

Slash went to the desk and knelt down. He picked up Wally and carried him in his arms toward the back of the room.

"He's been shot. Twice. Luckily, the explosive vest saved his life and stopped one of the bullets from entering his heart. It's his lucky day."

I looked down at Wally. "You're right. I guess it's all in the perspective."

While two agents crouched in the doorway, guns facing out, Slash motioned for Elvis and Bonnie to go to the back of the room. "The school is not secure yet. It's not safe to try and get you out. We need to barricade you in for the moment. You'll have to stay here until we get the all clear to move you."

Elvis dragged a cabinet away from the wall and Slash set Wally down behind it—a makeshift barricade. We all joined Wally behind the cabinet. Slash knelt on one

knee next to me and wiped something off my cheek. I
didn't ask what it was.

"How did you know we were in here?"

Slash answered but kept his eyes on the door, his gun
at the ready. "Heat imaging. We didn't see you specifically, but we saw a small group in this room and decided
to make it our first priority once we breached."

"Lucky me."

His jaw tightened and I realized just how worried he'd
been. "Nothing else is going to happen to you. Stay here.
I'm going to call a medic about the kid."

Slash rose and pulled out a cell phone. He walked
a few steps away and began speaking in soft tones to
someone on the other end. After a minute, he returned.

I leaned against him, resting my head on his shoulder.
He put one arm around me, helping to keep me warm
and stable.

"Are you sure you aren't hurt, *cara*?"

"I'm okay. Really. I'm alive and very grateful for that."

Sirens screamed in the background and the sounds of
sporadic gunfire still punctured the air.

"We've got a medic and an explosives expert on the
way to our position. Pockets of resistance still remain,
which is why it's not safe to move yet. We definitely can't
move the kid from the school until the vest is removed.
But we can treat him here."

I glanced at Wally, who lay oddly still. Bonnie, who
was trembling uncontrollably, sat next to him, still pressing my school polo shirt against the wound in his shoulder.

My brain suddenly snapped into thinking mode.

"Slash, the vests. Zogby tried to blow them. He had
the remote. I felt him push it, but it didn't work."

"We got your message."

I blinked in surprise. "I was right?"

Elvis nodded. "You were. They *were* using the garage door frequency as a remote, just as you suspected. Thank God, Piper knew sign language. When she translated the words, I immediately figured out what you were trying to say and passed on your suspicions to the police."

"I can't believe it. I just guessed."

Elvis gave me a thumbs-up. "You get an A-plus on that test."

Slash kissed the top of my head. "*Si*, it was a very good guess. We went with it and jammed that frequency, along with a few others, just in case. Your guess saved them, *cara*."

I shook my head. "No, *I* didn't save them. *We* did. This was a total group effort."

My cheek rested against his neck and I could feel his pulse racing. "Never again will I allow you to be in such danger. I won't permit it."

Wally groaned and I leaned forward, wincing from the effort. He was conscious, but still in pain. He grimaced when I squeezed his hand.

"You still hanging in there?" I asked.

He opened his eyes. "Did the good guys win?"

"Absolutely. Thanks to you, Rambo."

"Am I going to explode?"

"Not today."

"Oh, thank God. Does this mean you're going to go out with me now?"

Slash peered down at Wally. "Did you just hit on my girlfriend?"

He squinted up at Slash. "Girlfriend? What? Wait. *That's* your boyfriend? I thought you were gay."

Slash looked at me and raised an eyebrow.

I shrugged. "It's a long story. I'm not gay, Wally."

Wally smiled weakly at Slash. "Oh, great. Uh, *sir*, just so we are perfectly clear, I wasn't hitting on her. Seriously. No hitting whatsoever. Tapping is a better word. Yes, maybe a little tap, a teensy-weensy one, but definitely not a full-fledged hit. All in good fun. Ha, ha. Right, Lara?"

I rolled my eyes. "It's Lexi. Lexi Carmichael. That's my real name."

"You have a fake name *and* a fake sexual preference? Hey, do your parents know you're dating a guy who has a gun?"

I sighed. "Jeez."

I glanced over at Slash. "Hey, how did you guys get into the school without tripping the alarms and explosives on the doors?"

Slash pointed to Elvis.

Elvis shrugged. "I took it straight from the movies, Lexi. I recorded a quiet view of one of the exits and then uploaded it and played it in a loop on the security camera when that view came up on the rotation. The guard in Computer Central never knew the difference."

I glanced between the two men. "So, you connected with Slash on the outside?"

Elvis nodded. "He was all over my initial contact. He knew I was in here with you, so it was almost as if he was waiting for me. He was damn good."

Slash lifted a hand. "I *was* waiting for you and I'm familiar with the legendary Zimmerman techniques, which is why we worked together seamlessly. You didn't disappoint."

Elvis turned his gaze on me. "In the meantime, Slash

had the police drill a hole in a wall at that exit. They
threaded a miniature camera through the hole and got
a good look at the bomb. Experts figured out how to
disarm it, so Brandon snuck down the hall and did it."

My mouth fell open. "What? Brandon? All by himself? Holy cow. Is he okay? How's Piper?"

"I'm not sure about Brandon, but Piper should be
okay," Elvis assured me. "At least she was safe in the
office when I ran out. The guards missed us in the first
sweep after you left. No one thought to check the vent behind the bookshelf. Once they were gone, Piper showed
me how to access the bridge to the security system. After
that, it was a walk in the park for me to tap in to the security cameras. Brandon showed up about an hour later,
safe and sound and told us what had happened to you. I
searched everywhere on the cameras for you. You can
imagine my surprise when I finally found you front and
center in Computer Central."

I managed a small smile. "I *knew* it. You saw me
there. You sent a message with the double blip."

"Yes. I wasn't sure you'd see it or get it. It was a big
risk. I didn't dare do anything flashier since you were
being monitored."

My heart lifted. "I *knew* if you'd survived the sweep,
you'd be on that camera. I was watching for a signal of
some kind. That was really prime, Elvis."

"Well, I knew you'd be watching, too, which is exactly
why I did it. But there is one thing I don't understand.
How did you disable the network? I was watching every
keystroke, just like that psycho, and I didn't see you do
a thing. But I know you did."

I grinned. "You bet I did. I bent the network cable
with my feet. Simple as that. I anticipated said psycho—

that would be Johannes Broodryk, by the way—would ask the guard to check that the network cable was still plugged in, but hoped he wouldn't have the guard inspect the length of the entire cable. He didn't. It was laughably easy."

Elvis's mouth dropped open. "Seriously? You bent a freaking cable with your feet? That's it?"

"Well, it wasn't *that* easy. I had to use all my foot strength to do it. But, essentially, yes, that's it."

Slash laughed. "Brilliant. Risky, but truly brilliant."

"Actually, going back to high school made me think of it. Jouret was talking about deception analysis in his class. I needed to do something simple to fool Broodryk, to make him think I was doing something complex when in reality, I wasn't."

Elvis grinned. "That's really thinking outside the box."

"I wasn't going to let him blackmail those parents. I knew the terrorists had no intention of making good on the student releases. It was end game once he had the bitcoins."

"I agree," Elvis said. "You did the right thing, Lexi. I was trying to think of something myself, but you beat me to it. You do realize you took on an international cyber wizard and bested him by bending a cable with your feet. I'm in awe."

Slash ruffled my hair. "That's my girl. You're extraordinary."

"All of you guys are extraordinary," Bonnie said, her face looking pale, but her voice was strong. "Hiring X-Corp was the best thing I ever did for this school."

Elvis smiled. "Guess we make a good team."

I smiled back at my best friend. "We always have."

THIRTY-TWO

I<small>T TOOK THIRTY</small> minutes or so before the police had secured the school. I walked—well, limped—out of the school, holding on to Slash's arm. Elvis and Bonnie were behind us and we all trailed the gurney that held Wally. The medic had arrived and injected him with some kind of painkiller and he'd promptly passed out. Shortly thereafter, a bomb technician had removed the vest.

Slash kept his arm around me as we walked. Elvis helped Bonnie, who was wobbly on her feet from exhaustion and severe stress. Slash guided us toward the impressive row of ambulances that had lined up along one side of the school. I'd gone just a few steps when I heard someone call my name. I looked around and saw a guy pushing his way through the crowd, flashing a badge.

"Lexi!"

"Beau!"

I slipped away from Slash and wobbled toward my middle brother. He enveloped me in a big hug.

"Jesus, Lexi, I thought computer security was supposed to be a quiet job. I'm the policeman in the family. I'm supposed to be the one at risk, not you. Just so you know, that incident made us all about ten years older. Dad may be developing a heart condition from this."

"Jeez. Believe me, becoming a hostage was *not* my idea."

He pulled back and searched my face. "I'm glad you're

okay. How badly are you injured? What happened and how did you get mixed up in it?"

"It's a long story, Beau. But I'm good. Really. Despite my appearance, I don't have any life-threatening injuries. Are Mom, Dad and Rock holding up okay?" Rock was our older brother.

Beau shoved his fingers through his hair. "We've all been worried sick. I had to pull every favor owed to me, but I managed to get into the Command Center. I kept Mom, Dad and Rock abreast of the situation in real time."

"That was good of you, Beau."

He touched my cheek. "Don't make it a habit. You look like hell."

"You always say that."

He laughed. "True. But today you look worse than usual."

"It's been a heck of a hard day."

Slash came up beside me, putting his arm around me again. Beau looked between us.

I cleared my throat. "Uh, Slash, meet Beau. Beau is my brother and a policeman in the Robbery Division in Baltimore."

"I met your brother in the Command Center."

Beau nodded. "Yeah, he was instrumental in getting me in. I owe him big."

"You owe me nothing."

"Well, then, thanks."

The two gave each other something between a high five and a handshake. It looked like they were already friends.

Slash didn't remove his arm from my shoulders and I could almost see the wheels in Beau's head spinning. He was curious as to what might be going on between Slash and me, but I wasn't going to launch into an explanation of our relationship at this point while covered in blood and gore. Especially since no one in my family knew yet.

Finally, Beau patted my hand and then grimaced as something gross came off on his fingers. "See you soon, sis?"

I rubbed at my cheeks. "Sure. Just tell Mom, Dad and Rock I'm okay. I'll call them as soon as I'm able."

"Will do. But if I know Mom, expect a visit in the hospital." Beau gave me one more hug and then disappeared into the crowd.

Slash walked me to an ambulance. I started to climb in when he put a hand on my arm. He leaned in for a kiss and then pulled away. "I have to leave you here, *cara*."

"You're not coming with me?"

"I can't. I'm not permitted to ride in the ambulance. Besides I need to tie up some loose ends here. I'll be at the hospital as soon as I can. Stay safe, love."

He kissed me again and then strode away. I watched him until he disappeared into a small trailer that had been set up in the school parking lot.

A medic handed me a bottle of water and a blanket and I climbed into the ambulance and sat on one of the cushioned benches. I took a swig of the water when Elvis climbed in with a blanket already draped around his shoulders and an empty water bottle in one hand.

He joined me on the bench and then took my hand, lifting it like a winning boxer in a prize fight.

"We did it, Lexi."

"We really did," I said, grinning. "Brains over brawn. Geeks rock."

"We do, indeed. Never doubted it."

"I never doubted *you*, Elvis."

"Likewise. You are the most amazing geek girl I've ever met."

His compliment warmed me. "Speaking of geeks, do you know if Piper and Brandon are okay?"

"I think so. I saw them being led out of the school. Both were walking on their own. Brandon is a real hero, you know. Disarming the bomb at the door to let the SWAT team in. Not bad for a high school kid. A good-looking guy like that should be able to milk that for a movie or book deal, or, at the very least, three dozen dates or so."

"He only has eyes for Piper."

He lifted an eyebrow. "Oh. So, you're a relationship expert now?"

"Not really. It was pretty obvious."

"Yeah, you're right. It was. First love. Something a man never gets over."

"Now who's the relationship expert?"

He fidgeted. "It was obvious, just like you said."

There was a moment of silence before Elvis spoke again. "So, speaking of relationships, where's Slash?"

"He's not allowed to ride in the ambulance." I took another sip of water. "Besides he had to tie up some loose ends or something."

"Oh. Well, I just wanted you to know that I'm proud of you."

"I'm proud of you, too, Elvis. You were a true hero back there."

"No, that's not what I meant." He leaned back against the wall of the ambulance. "I meant I'm proud of you as a person. You're growing, Lexi. You've openly confronted your weaknesses. You are more confident, self-assured. You even went on national television, for crying out loud."

"Whoa. That *so* wasn't my idea."

"It doesn't matter. You embraced it. No, you freaking *owned* it. You have a boyfriend." He cleared his throat. "You're navigating the murky waters of social relationships and moving forward with your life. Taking chances and reaping the rewards, despite the risk. I admire you."

"Hey, you're moving forward, too."

"No." His voice hardened. "No, I'm not. I've stayed in my comfort zone, hiding behind my skills. Even Xavier is emerging from his shell. He's going to Greece with a woman he's crazy about. He's taking risks. Big ones. But my life has stalled. I've let the things I want pass me by because the odds were not in my favor. I realize now that's a crappy way to live. I'm missing out on the best parts of life trapped in an emotional freezer."

I squeezed his hand. "Stop right now. You *are* growing and expanding. As someone who knows you pretty well, I can say that with full certainty. But I totally understand the freezer concept. Been there, done that, bought the T-shirt. It's cold in that freezer, but it's safe."

"It's safe, but it's stagnant and it's lonely. It's time for Elvis Zimmerman to thaw."

We glanced over as Bonnie climbed into the ambulance and sat on the other side of Elvis. She looked beyond exhausted. Elvis scooted over even closer to me to make room for her on our bench. It was almost as if we all needed to touch one another to remind ourselves we were truly alive.

"I just talked to the police," she said. "Several students got shot. We have no idea how serious their conditions are yet."

I couldn't bear to think about anyone getting hurt, especially kids. But given the arsenal in the school, I wasn't surprised. "I'm so sorry, Bonnie."

"I don't know what we would have done without you, Lexi. Without you and Elvis. It would have been much, much worse."

"You've got a couple of very bright students who played an important role, as well."

"So I understand."

Elvis stretched out his legs in front of him. "Speaking of students, I wanted to tell you Piper's bridge was ace, Lexi. That girl has some wicked skill. No, more than wicked. She's potential wizard material. Really, really good. She had linked all three systems and hidden it with some pretty sophisticated methods."

For Elvis to call someone good was significant. To call them really, *really* good was monumental.

"Do I want to know what that means?" Bonnie asked.

"No," Elvis and I said in unison and then laughed.

"Are you sure it was her work?" I asked Elvis.

"Mostly. I think Brandon helped some, but she's the true master."

I felt a tug of jealousy that he was so impressed with her ability. Then I reminded myself that I owed my life, in part, to Piper and her bridge, and also to the man sitting next to me.

I had to say it. "Elvis, I want… I want to thank you for risking your life to save mine. I don't know how to say how much that means to me."

"You don't have to explain anything. I told you I had your back. Always have and always will. You know I don't say things I don't mean."

"I know. But…you killed someone on my behalf. I'm

aware, at a firsthand level, that isn't an easy thing to live with."

The muscles in his jaw tensed. "It was easy. I didn't even have to think twice about it. I wasn't going to lose you. I'm just glad I wasn't too late."

I couldn't think of what to say to that, so I pressed my cheek against his hand and closed my eyes. A moment later, a medic climbed in with us and slammed the rear door shut. The ambulance lurched forward.

I finally left high school for good.

THIRTY-THREE

THE DOCTORS REFUSED to let me be debriefed until they were done examining me. By that time, my ribs and right knee were bandaged and my entire face had been slathered with salves and ointments. I'd been given an IV for dehydration and some excellent pain medication. I'd required two small stitches beneath my left cheekbone where Jouret had clocked me a good one. Otherwise, I'd come off really lucky in terms of injuries.

My parents and Rock were permitted a short visit. My dad nearly fractured my ribs (again) with his hugs. My mom burst into tears (again) after reminding me this was my second stay in the hospital with serious injuries in a month. My brother Rock, who is a reporter for the *Washington Post*, wanted me to promise him an inside scoop, but I had been sworn to secrecy until after my debrief. After that, I promised him whatever insights I was permitted to offer.

Slash came and went, and I saw numerous medical staff. The official debriefing happened shortly after my family left and the nurse had brought me a tray of hospital food. I managed to force down some green gelatin, but I couldn't eat anything else. I did drink half a carafe of water, despite the IV drip I'd had earlier for dehydration.

After identifying themselves as FBI agents, two men and one woman proceeded to take me through the entire chain of events. It was more painful than I'd expected to tell them about the death of Mr. Jouret, Mr. Fitzgerald's shooting and my attempted murder of one of the terrorists.

Hadim. That had been his name. The man Elvis killed in order to save me. Despite Elvis's words, I wasn't really sure how he was processing it. It was hard for *me* to process and I was the victim. Elvis had killed a man for me. Intellectually, I understood what he was going through, because I'd been through a similar situation myself. Self-defense is a good reason for causing another's death, perhaps the best reason, but it doesn't change the fact that someone dies.

I paused, swallowing hard. I must have stopped talking for longer than I expected because the woman FBI agent had to gently ask me to continue.

"Tell us more about this Ice Eyes."

"His name is Johannes Broodryk. He's a cyber mercenary from South Africa."

I spent considerable time and effort explaining everything I knew about Broodryk, his signature file and his efforts to extort the students' parents for bitcoins. Two of the agents were part of the FBI's Cyber Crimes Unit and both were surprised that I had thought of something as simple as bending the network cable to prevent the emails to the parents from going out. One of them actually slapped me on the back in excitement before realizing what he'd done.

Once they realized I knew what I was talking about in terms of computers, they began firing dozens of technical questions at me. The other agent finally had to shut them down, but at least I felt as if I had given them the big picture, even though I believed that by this point, Broodryk was long gone.

The session lasted well over an hour. At that point, the doctor told them they had to leave. The agents argued, saying they had several follow-up questions, but the doctor held firm. For today, the debriefing was done and no more visitors were allowed until the morning. After they left, I leaned back against the pillows and closed my eyes.

I must have fallen asleep, because I jerked upright with a gasp, my heart galloping. I don't remember what I'd dreamed, but my heart was racing and my hands shook. I was disoriented until I heard the bleep of the blood pressure machine hooked to my finger. I took a couple of calming breaths and then removed the clip from my finger. The room was dark, but the light from the machines provided enough visibility that I could see where I was going without tripping over anything.

I peeked out the door, startling a policeman who had been reading a newspaper. He leapt to his feet. "Hey, are you okay?"

"I'm fine. Why are you here?"

"Keeping the press at bay. There are a slew of journalists and reporters who would like to speak with you. You'll all be famous now."

I hadn't thought of that…of what it meant to my life. Oh, jeez. I couldn't stress about that now.

"Do you know if any of the terrorists survived?"

He took off his hat, put it across his knee. "As far as I know, only one made it out of the school alive. He died about an hour ago on the operating table. The rest were either shot by the SWAT team or killed themselves. It was pretty ugly, but you're safe now."

I felt sick. "Thanks. What about the students? Were any hurt?"

"No casualties yet, other than a teacher, but two students are in critical condition. I heard one student was saved by his explosive vest. How crazy is that?"

"Really crazy."

I must have paled, because he looked concerned.

"Sorry, kid. Maybe I shouldn't have provided that level of detail. I understand everyone involved will be offered counseling services."

"It's okay. Thanks for letting me know. I'm also trying to find out about one of the students who got shot. His first name is Wally, possibly short for Wallace. Can you tell me what room he's in? I just want to know how he's doing."

He stood. "Okay. I'll check with the nurse."

He walked down to the nurses' station. A nurse came around the desk and walked back to my room with him.

She frowned. "You really shouldn't be out of bed."

"I'm fine. Please, can you tell me the status of one of the students?"

"I just looked him up. Wallace Harris in Room 304. He had surgery a few hours ago to sew up damage from a bullet he took to the shoulder and to have a nasty head cut stitched up. He got banged up pretty good, but no life-threatening injuries."

"Wow. That's great news. Can I see him?"

"He's probably still unconscious from the anesthesia. His parents were here earlier and he didn't wake for them."

"I don't care if he's unconscious. I just want to see him. Please. He's…a friend."

Her face softened. "You kids were pretty amazing. All right. Come with me."

I didn't have the heart to correct her about being a kid, so I just followed her to Room 304. She opened the door and we walked in. Wally was in a room by himself, hooked up to several machines which beeped softly. I stood next to the bed and looked down at him. His eyes were closed. He looked so small in the big bed. He didn't have his glasses and his head was swathed in a white bandage. His hands were at his sides. I reached down over the bed rail and touched the top of one of them. To my surprise, he opened his eyes.

"Lara?"

"Lexi."

He blinked a couple of times. "Ah, right. Can I... have...some water?"

The nurse poured him some water and lifted him up to a sitting position so he could drink it.

"How do you feel?" she asked him after he had taken a few sips.

"Like I got run over by a stampede of buffalo."

"You're a pretty resilient kid. At least that's what your parents said when they were here earlier."

"They were here?"

"They left a few hours ago. They'll be back soon."

"I feel a bit like I'm floating. No acute pain at least."

"It's the medication. You're due to have another round soon."

"Excellent. I feel pretty happy right now."

The nurse smiled, inspected the dressings on his shoulder and head and then checked his pulse. After shining a light in his eyes and asking him to follow her finger, she tapped out something on an electronic tablet and then tucked it in a pouch around her waist.

"Okay, you're looking stable. I'll be right back. I'm going to get you some more medicine. Talk fast, kids. Visitor hours are over when I get back."

As soon as she left, I smiled at him. "You did good, Wally. Really good. A true champion."

"Damn. I always knew I was hero material."

"I knew it, too. You'll probably be a star now. Famous worldwide."

"Really? Do think it will make a difference with the chicks?"

"Undoubtedly."

"Maybe they'll make a movie about it."

"Maybe."

"Who would play me?"

"No idea."

"He'd better be a hunk."

"Good luck with that."

He smiled, before it faded. "So, you weren't a student after all, Lara... I mean, Lexi. I guess I shouldn't be surprised. You were pretty amazing at the keyboard. Superadvanced. What were you really doing there?"

"I was trying to penetrate the WOMBATs."

"What?"

My legs were still a bit shaky, so I perched on the arm of a nearby armchair. "I work for a cyberintelligence firm. Headmistress Swanson hired my company to find the students who kept breaking into the system, changing grades and causing general havoc. I was hired to figure out how to stop them. My approach was to penetrate the group from the inside."

Wally's mouth dropped open and then he laughed.

"Oh, God, that's rich. Really rich. The terrorists had no idea who you are."

"Not until the end."

"How did they find out?"

I considered. "My cover buckled, I think. I put it up pretty quickly. It was designed to fool high school students, even clever ones. But it wouldn't have withstood a wizard like Broodryk."

"So, it *was* you who put Phantomonics on the system?"

"No. My friend Elvis did. He was at the school, too, helping me when the terrorists came in. We were trapped inside Computer Central."

"That's how you knew the system so well and were able to so efficiently shut down Phantomonics."

"Yes. I'm a pretty decent hacker. I even did some hacks bordering on cracks in my younger years before I saw how dangerous it was."

He considered me for a long moment and I sat silently, waiting. He finally spoke. "So, what would you have done to those students involved in WOMBAT, had you found them?"

"I was looking primarily for the leader."

"Why?"

"Because a leader leads. People look to them for guidance."

"I see. Is that why you became friends with me? Stood up for me? You thought I was involved and would lead you to the leader?"

"No. That's not at all why I became your friend, Wally. I did that because I needed a friend and thought maybe you needed one, too. I didn't have any friends in high school the first time around. It sucked."

"None at all?"

"Not a one. Unless you count the computer."

He smiled. "So, that was the plan? You penetrate the group, find the ringleader and then suspend or arrest the students?"

"Actually, I would have explained that ruining their future wasn't worth it for the thrill of changing a couple of grades or a schedule. Believe me, I've been there. I got caught in a hack in high school that almost ended my future before it started. Fortunately, my father is a lawyer and I caught a break. Trust me when I say that there are many more interesting and lucrative ways to channel that focus and energy."

"Such as?"

"Such as becoming an intern at a local cyberintelligence firm. Mine."

He blinked in surprise. "Really? What's the trade-off?"

I leaned forward against the bed rail. "Shut down the WOMBATs. Stop hacking into the school's system and pass the word down to others that it's not worth it, especially now that the school is on to you."

"Ha. I'm flattered. You think I can do all that single-handedly?"

"I don't just think it, I *know* you can, Wally."

"That's because you think the ringleader is me."

"I *think* that honor goes to an awfully shrewd kid who was able get a bunch of other really smart kids to follow him."

A small smile touched his lips. "Wow. Nobody has ever believed in me like you. It's crazy."

"It's not crazy, it's logical. I saw something special in

you from the beginning. You've got a really, really bright future ahead of you if you play this right."

He perked up. "Okay, let me recap. Theoretically speaking, since I'm not admitting anything, if I shut down the WOMBATs, I get an internship at your company?"

"Yes."

"That's it?"

"That's it."

"Does this also mean you are going to dump that other guy for me?"

"Not a chance."

He sighed. "Well, you can't blame me for trying."

THIRTY-FOUR

SLASH BROUGHT ME HOME from the hospital. My ribs ached, my face looked as if I'd been run over by a truck and my neck had so many bruises it looked like I'd gotten a tattoo of a sprawling grapevine. I'd been able to take a shower at the hospital and my mom had brought me fresh clothes. I felt almost new again. Slash opened my apartment and led me inside.

I collapsed on the couch. "I can't believe how happy I am to be home. One thing is for certain. I'm never, *ever* going back to high school again."

Slash closed the door and joined me on the couch. "I think that's a good idea."

"I also can't wait to be a brunette again. It's the small things in life. Being blonde was so not working for me."

Slash lifted a strand of my hair. "I kind of like it."

"Ugh." I stretched my legs out, put them on the coffee table. My sore knee creaked. "So, how goes the hunt for Broodryk?"

"Cold. He vanished, not surprisingly. But thanks to your earlier cryptic message to me about your teacher pal, Willem Jouret, we had a head start on him. We were eventually able to link Jouret to the Veiled Knights, and then by extension to Broodryk. As a result, we put some peripheral pressure on Broodryk's network to keep him busier than he might have been expecting during the operation. What caused you to be suspicious of Jouret?"

I told him about stumbling across the file on Jouret's computer and how Elvis had tied it to the Veiled Knights. Slash listened without saying a word. When I was done, I shifted my feet to the couch. "So, does this mean Broodryk gets off scot-free?"

"Not at all. We're hunting him, *cara*. And not just us. He's on an international list now. Our goal is to make his cyber life a living misery. We'll do it, too, until we catch him. Trust me when I say all of his future plans will have a major crimp in them."

"Good." I shuddered when I thought of his white eyes staring at me.

"Besides, he got nothing. Not one bitcoin from the parents. Whatever he got paid by the terrorists will not have been enough for him."

"He's probably seriously pissed."

"Undoubtedly. It was a risk for him and one that back-fired badly."

"I'll bet other cyber criminals will think twice before working with him again."

"It will be a significant blow to his worldwide operation."

"Good."

He took my hand in his and began massaging my palm with his thumb. "The agents at the FBI Cyber Crimes Unit have been talking about you. Your cable-bending maneuver is going to be the stuff of legends."

I grinned. "Ha! Good to know in case I need a reference if this X-Corp gig doesn't work out."

"Ah, not to worry. I'd have far better uses of your considerable time and talent."

"Well, don't tell that to Finn." I wound my hair up into a ponytail and tied it up with the scrunchie I had on my wrist. "So, what about Operation Dove? Is it now defunct?"

"Yes and no."

"Well, that made no sense."

He laughed. "Yes, the operation is defunct. But no, in the sense that the peace process will continue. The *Mehsuds* will come to the table and the *Shahids* are left in disarray and disgrace."

"But the U.S. *was* involved secretly in the Pakistani peace process. From what I read in the newspaper this morning, the U.S. was putting pressure on the prime minister to exclude the *Shahids*."

"First of all, it isn't just the U.S. secretly involved in the process. Trust me on that. There are multiple countries from all parts of the world all offering support to the Pakistani peace process behind the scenes. You might be quite surprised if I told you who. Just suffice it to say more countries than you might imagine have a seriously vested interest in a stable Pakistan. Secondly, the *Shahids* made their own bed by engaging in terrorism to get what they want. Folding to terrorist demands is no way to run a country."

"True. But what a mess."

"Welcome to world politics." Slash rose and retrieved his duffel bag. He pulled out a bottle of wine and a plastic bag filled with goodies.

I looked at him curiously. "What's that?"

"Nonna's recipe for hot-spiced wine. You're going to like it."

"If Nonna made it, you *know* I'm going to like it. But can I drink that with my painkillers?"

"The heat boils out most of the alcohol, but I'll only give you a little."

"Sounds heavenly."

While he was in the kitchen fixing the wine, I plugged my phone into a speaker and turned on some Christmas music. I turned on my little plastic tree and felt eternally grateful that I was able to enjoy the sparkling lights.

I returned to the couch and dozed a bit as the smell of hot-spiced wine filled the apartment and an instrumental version of "Silent Night" soothed me. It felt good to be safe, alive and loved.

Slash deposited two mugs of the wine on the coffee table and sat beside me, sliding his arm around my waist. "It needs to mull a bit, but we can have a sip while we wait. I'd like to give you your Christmas present now."

"Now?" I turned around in his embrace. "But it's three days until Christmas. Your present hasn't even arrived yet."

He lifted an eyebrow. "My present? You got me something after all?"

"Of course I got you something, even though you didn't come through with any advice. It's scheduled to arrive on Christmas Eve. I thought that would be the appropriate time to exchange gifts. But I'll show it to you online instead, if you want."

"You have me intrigued. But you first."

He rooted around in the duffel bag and pulled out two wrapped boxes.

My mouth fell open. "Two presents? *What*? You didn't say there would be two of them."

He laughed. "Relax, *cara*, and let me spoil you a little. Okay?"

"Jeez. Okay."

He handed me the first present—a small box that fit

in the palm of my hand. It had lovely dark blue glittery paper and a pretty blue bow.

"It's too pretty to open."

"Go ahead."

I carefully untied the bow and then unwrapped the paper without ripping it. Then I turned my attention to a small black velvet box. I looked up at Slash and then down at the box as I slowly opened it.

Inside the box were two glittering, diamond stud earrings. I'm not an earring person, but even I liked these because they were simple, pretty and nonpretentious.

"Wow, Slash. They are…stunning."

"Do you like them? I noticed you don't often wear earrings, but thought you might like these because they aren't anything too fancy."

"I never thought I'd say this about a pair of earrings, but I love them."

He took the box from me, removing the earrings. He pushed back the hair from my ear and slid one in the hole on my ear, fastening it. He did the other one and then leaned back to get a better look.

"Perfect. Don't take them off, okay?"

"Shouldn't be a problem. It's not like I'm an earring fashionista."

He laughed and kissed me behind my right ear. "Good."

He handed me the second box. This rectangle-shaped box was much bigger and heavier. It had the same wrapping paper, but instead of a midnight blue bow, this one had a pretty silver one.

I gave it back to him. "How about you save this one for my birthday?"

He growled and pushed it back at me. "Open it."

"Can we negotiate?"

"No."

"Fine. But I only got you one present."

"Good."

I took it back and began the slow, painstaking process of opening the present without tearing the wrapping paper.

"You can rip the paper, you know."

"I know. But it's so pretty."

"I'll buy you a dozen rolls. Just open it already."

I glanced sideways at him. "I bet you were the first one in your family to open all your presents on Christmas morning."

"We open them on Christmas Eve in Italy."

"Oh." I had almost removed all the paper. I pulled the last piece free, but before I could neatly fold it and set it aside, Slash snatched it from my hand.

"Go ahead. Look inside."

The brown box had no markings. I carefully lifted the lid and then gasped.

"A gun? You bought me a gun for Christmas?"

"It's a 9 mm semiautomatic pistol."

"You bought me a pistol? A semiautomatic? For Christmas?"

"Given the recent events in your life, I figured it was time you learned how to protect yourself properly. I actually purchased this before the school incident. Now the gift seems even more fortuitous. I'm going to take you shooting as soon as you're feeling up to it. Somehow I feel like we shouldn't wait another minute."

"I... I can't own a gun. I can't go shooting. I'm a computer geek."

He spread his hands. "So am I."

I hesitantly picked up the pistol. It was heavier than I expected and the metal was cold. I wasn't sure how I felt about it. On the one hand, knowing how to handle a gun was a practical skill. Practical skills were useful. On the other hand, owning a gun meant dealing with the reality that I might one day actually need to point it at someone and use it. Then I remembered how Elvis had said he was taking shooting lessons and how I'd almost choked Hadim to death to save Wally and myself. Maybe learning how to use a gun wasn't such a bad idea, the way my life was going.

"Thank you, Slash."

Slash tucked a finger under my chin and nudged it up. "You'll be a natural."

"I'll likely be a danger to all of society and myself with a loaded weapon. But I'm willing to give it a try, especially in light of what just happened. It's thoughtful of you. I mean it. The earrings and the gun are nice presents. I never expected anything like this."

"I'm glad you like them."

"I do."

We kissed while the song "White Christmas" played in the background. After a bit, I pulled back and stood up. "Would you like to see what I got you for Christmas?"

"I actually had something else on my mind, but given your injuries, exchanging additional presents might be best." He smiled.

"Well, I hope you like it."

"I've already received my Christmas gift. When I heard you were trapped in that school…" His voice wavered and he cleared his throat. "Let's just say it was the worst day of my life."

"I knew you were out there, Slash. It gave me strength."

"I wanted to tear down the walls of that school and pull you out. It was all I could do to maintain my composure and sanity."

"It helped knowing you were so close. I mean that."

"Good." He leaned over and kissed me again. "Mine. Always."

I smiled against his lips and then pulled away. "So, are you ready to see your present…at least the online version of it?"

"If you insist. I told you a present wasn't necessary."

"Reciprocity is an important part of the relationship foundation. Didn't we already have this conversation?"

"*Si*, we did. I eagerly await the presentation of my gift."

I retrieved my laptop from my bedroom and returned to the couch. I booted it up and then found the photo of his gift, turning the screen so he couldn't see it yet.

"I tried to think of something you might enjoy, Slash, but also something functional. Despite its origins a thousand years ago, you can still use it today."

I turned the screen so he could see and heard the catch of his breath. He looked at the screen but didn't say anything.

I continued nervously. "I thought an astrolabe would be fitting for a guy who likes math and numbers as much as me. I bought you a replica of one created by the Italian craftsman Prezioso in 1522. It's made of pressed gold and metal and can measure most angles associated with navigational and astronomical sightings. There were other varieties, but Prezioso's Western version was my favorite and he was also Italian, so I had a winner. So, if you're ever without your GPS, you'll be able to navigate just like travelers did a thousand years ago."

After a moment, Slash plucked the laptop from my lap and set it on the coffee table. I stood as he pulled me toward him.

"No one has ever given me such a thoughtful gift. You surprise me. It is magnificent. Thank you."

He gave me a long, deep kiss. "Merry Christmas, *cara*," he whispered against my cheek.

"Merry Christmas, Slash."

THIRTY-FIVE

FINN VISITED ME the next day at my apartment after forbidding me to come to work. He gave me a careful hug when I opened the door.

"Lexi. I can't tell you how good it is to see you. How are you feeling?"

"Pretty good actually. The ribs and knee are feeling much better. My face needs some more healing, however. I'm not entering a beauty contest any time soon."

"Ha. I'm never, *ever* giving you an assignment outside the office again."

I thought about it for a moment. "Actually, the odds of being trapped in a school with terrorists a second time are so incredibly small it's almost not worth calculating. I wouldn't worry about it."

He grinned. "Good to know. Sit down and I'll make you some tea. If you're up to it, I'd like to hear what happened from the beginning."

He took off his suit jacket and hung it over the back of the kitchen chair. My cell phone rang. I checked the number and put it aside.

Finn poured the hot water in the mug. "Aren't you going to answer that?"

"It's probably another reporter. I've already gotten fifty-two calls today, including three from *People* magazine and two from the *New York Times*. I stopped answering if I don't recognize the number."

"I can have the office issue a press release with a statement from you so they'll stop bothering you."

"That would be great, Finn. I'll give Glinda a call later."

We took the tea to the living room and sat on the couch. I quickly took him through an abbreviated version of the events, skimming over Willem Jouret's death, the brutal execution of Mr. Fitzgerald and the part where I tried to choke a man to death. They weren't things I wanted to keep dwelling on for the rest of my life.

"But, Finn, the best part is that I believe the WOM-BAT problem has been solved."

He shook his head. "Solved? How did you manage to do that in the midst of all of this insanity?"

"Well, it's complicated and involves an internship at X-Corp...or three."

His eyebrows rose. "Three?"

"Yes, one for the leader and two more for some of the most innovative kids on a keyboard that I've ever met. You won't be sorry."

"I'm sure I won't."

He reached across the table and took my hand. "I want you to take until after New Year's Day to recover, Lexi. Don't come in to work for the next two weeks. Stay home, enjoy the holidays, visit with family and friends and get some rest. Now, before you argue with me, it's the prescription required for the addition of three new high school interns at X-Corp. It's my Christmas gift to you, so take it, please."

I smiled. "You know, you're a really good friend, Finn. For a girl who never had many friends in her life, I'm lucky to have made some pretty good ones lately."

"Good. So listen to your boss and rest, okay?"

He rose from his chair, washed out his mug and put it in my dish drainer. He kissed me on the cheek before he left.

After he was gone, I fielded a brief call from my mother. I assured her I was fine and thanked her sincerely for doing my laundry and restocking my refrigerator.

Shortly thereafter, Basia called me from LAX airport, ready to head out on her trip for Greece to meet up with Xavier. By this time, I was exhausted from all the talking.

"Lexi, are you sure you are okay? I can come home if you need me."

"I'm fine. Really. Go to Greece. I've got my family, Slash and Elvis here. I have no life-threatening injuries. I'm actually overdosing on people and attention. I need some downtime. Please, just assure Xavier that Elvis and I are in good shape and not to worry, okay?"

"I can't imagine what you've been through. Will you tell me all about it?"

"Someday. Just not today, okay?"

"Okay. I love you, Lexi."

"Ditto. Have a great time in Greece."

"And?"

I frowned. "And what?"

"Well, you figure it out."

I pressed my hand to my forehead. "Wait. Is this the part where I'm supposed say I want to hear about your sex life when you get back? Because in all honesty, I really don't."

She laughed. "Ah, now that's the Lexi I know. Talk to you soon, sweetie."

I hung up the phone and took a nap. I'd awakened

from a good three-hour rest and was headed into the kitchen for a cup of coffee when I heard the knock on my door. Wow. I had never been so popular and I felt a bit cranky about it.

I peeked through the keyhole before stepping back and opening the door. Brandon and Piper stood in my apartment hallway, clad in their winter coats. Brandon wore no hat while Piper sported a red beret. Brandon had both hands shoved in his pockets and Piper shifted nervously on boot-clad feet.

"Uh, hey, Lexi. Good to see you." Brandon held out his fist and I gave it a bump.

"Hey, Brandon, Piper. Wow. It's really great to see you."

Brandon nodded. "Likewise. Can we come in?"

I opened the door wider. "Of course. After seeing your skills at the keyboard, I'm not going to ask how you know my address."

Piper grinned as I stepped aside and they entered.

"We won't take much of your time," she said. "We just want to talk to you."

"Sure. You can take as much time as you want. Want anything to drink or eat?"

"You got any soda?" Brandon asked.

"Diet Coke."

"It'll have to do."

Piper removed her hat. "I'll take some hot tea, if you have some."

"Yep. Go drop your coats on the couch while I fix everything. We'll sit here and chat in the kitchen."

They did as instructed. After I'd fixed everything, we sat around my kitchen table, staring at each other and sipping our drinks. No one spoke. I figured I'd have to be the one who broke the ice.

"So, how are you guys feeling? I'm surprised your parents let you out of their sight."

Brandon smiled. "We told them we had to do this."

"Do what?

"Thank you. For everything. For holding us together. For saving our lives." His voice wavered and he quickly drank a gulp of his Coke.

I shrugged. "If I recall correctly, you and Piper are the true heroes of this operation. Disarming bombs and leading the way to the security system via a secret and totally ace bridge is pretty impressive. By the way, Piper, Elvis said you have true wizard potential. Coming from him, that is seriously high praise."

She smiled shyly. "He was incredible, just like you said. Lexi, you should have seen him work. I've never seen anything like it in my life."

"I have seen him in action. I agree his methods are truly breathtaking."

"He was nothing short of amazing. He knew just what to do and how to communicate with the police undetected. He was so calm and focused. But when he saw you being attacked on the monitor, he grabbed my jacket and ran out of the office without a word. I had no idea what he was going to do. He just lost it. He didn't have a single thought in his head for his own safety…for anything except you. It was all about you. I thought… I worried he might be too late."

I swallowed hard, those moments still fresh in my mind. I couldn't speak.

Piper continued. "It was brilliant how you figured the way the terrorists had wired the remotes to blow the vests. How did you know we were monitoring the security cameras?"

"I knew that if you got Elvis in via the bridge, he'd find a way. He sent me a message in the form of a double blip on the camera. I was looking for a signal and I found it. I'm just glad you knew sign language to help him out."

"Well, I translated your words, but I didn't have a clue what you were getting at. But Elvis did. Right away. You guys are really on the same wavelength."

"Yeah, I guess we are."

"Lexi, I also wanted to thank you for something else. My parents, well, my dad…he said he met you. He said you told him you were a lot like me in high school."

"Yes, I met him, and yes, I said I was a lot like you. I was into computers just like you. Except I didn't have a boyfriend in high school…especially not a guy as great at Brandon."

He grinned at me while Piper blushed.

"But you've got Elvis now," she said. "You're really lucky, you know. He's a great guy. Amazing actually."

"I, um—Elvis isn't my boyfriend."

"He's not? But I thought you guys are perfect for each other."

Brandon put a hand on hers. "Pip, it doesn't matter."

"Sure, okay." She looked confused. "Anyway, I guess I just wanted to thank you for everything. You were amazing. I wish you were really in high school. I think we could have been good friends."

I would have given anything to have had a friend like Piper when I'd really been in high school.

"We can still be friends."

Piper's face lit up. "Really, Lexi? That would be prime."

A warm glow spread through me. There was something special about the idea of having a friendship with another geek girl. Especially one in whom I saw so much of myself.

"Sure, as long as your parents approve."

Piper's happy expression faded. "Well, my dad doesn't approve of the way I spend a lot of time online."

Boy, did I understand that. "Look, Piper, your dad is just worried about you. He wants you to get out in the world, meet people and be more socially involved."

I stopped cold as soon as the words came out of my mouth.

Oh. My. Freaking. Goodness.

I sounded *exactly* like my mother.

I sighed. "My best advice is to introduce Brandon to your folks. I bet that will definitely give your dad something else to worry about. Then just let him have some time to come around."

"That's what I wanted to tell you, Lexi. He already has. When I told him what happened, how you and Elvis had saved us, he said he never realized how important my skills could be. I owe you a big thank-you for that."

"First of all, I didn't save you. We all worked together as a team to save each other. Which reminds me…" I glanced at Brandon. "How did you get stuck disarming the booby trap on the door?"

He took a sip of his drink and sat it down. "I was the brawn of this group. Elvis and Piper were maintaining communications with the police. They didn't need me behind the keyboard. So the police explained exactly what I had to do. Elvis set up the camera view in a loop so it appeared that no one was at the exit. Then, it was just a matter of me getting there undetected and working as quickly as I could."

"That's pretty darn heroic."

He looked down at his Coke. "It wasn't too hard, except I was pretty scared and my hands kept shaking. I was completely exposed for about four minutes. If a guard had gone that way, I would have been dead. Plus, I had to use scissors instead of wire clippers, and that alone was rather nerve-racking because one wrong snip and kaboom. But I… I shouldn't have left you in the stairwell, Lexi. I'm sorry."

I placed my hands on the table. "Don't be sorry. I told you to do it, and it was the right thing to do for all of our safety. What sense did it make for two of us to be captured?"

"I could have helped you."

I shook my head. "No, you couldn't have. There was no time. You would have been caught with me."

"But you could have been killed."

"We *all* could have been killed. At any moment. I'm thankful you left, and more importantly, you listened to me when I asked you to do so. Look how things worked out. It was exactly the right thing to do, Brandon. So put it away and pack it up. That includes what happened with Mr. Jouret, okay?"

He nodded. "Okay."

Piper reached across the table and took his hand. "By the way, Brandon and I talked to Wally. We know why you were at the school and that you're some kind of cybersecurity expert for a company named X-Corp."

"And?"

"And we're going to shut down the WOMBATs. We weren't the only three, you know, but we'll be able to convince the others to stop. We were bored. I know we shouldn't have done it. But Wally…he can be persuasive. Plus, it was mind-numbingly easy. The teachers were effortless targets."

I smiled at that. "The weakest link in cybersecurity is the people. Keep that in mind when you're on the other side of the fence."

"Are we in trouble?"

"I'll see what I can do. In the meantime, I'd like to put your considerable talents to use on other, more intriguing matters."

Brandon leaned forward. "Such as?"

"How do you guys feel about an internship at X-Corp?"

THIRTY-SIX

AFTER THEY LEFT, I made my coffee and went to watch television. My mind needed to heal as much as my body. For me there was comfort, as well as reprieve, in the familiar and routine. Given the trauma I'd been through, I needed a lot of both.

My phone chirped, so I checked it. I had a text from Slash.

Will be tied up until eleven o'clock. Is that too late to come over?

I thought about it and texted him back.

No, come when you are able.

Okay, will do. You okay?

Sure. Fine.

I fixed myself a bowl of chicken noodle soup from a can and ate it in front of the television. But I was still hungry and restless. I couldn't find anything to watch.

I had a sudden urge for pizza. Avanti's pizza. Thinking of all that gooey cheese, pepperoni and anchovies made my stomach growl.

I threw my coat over my yoga pants and sweatshirt

and grabbed my purse. I drove to Avanti's and put in my order for carryout. The smell of baking yeast and pizza was heavenly. I sat and waited, basking in the warmth of the restaurant and the great smells until it was ready.

Maybe it was just habit, but I found myself pulling into Elvis's driveway, next to his red pickup, a few minutes later. I got out of the car, bringing the pizza with me, balancing it on one hand as I rang the bell.

There was a noise and the door abruptly opened. Elvis stared at me in shock, his blue eyes widening. His hair was wet and his chest naked. He had a white towel wrapped around his waist.

"Lexi?"

My cheeks heated. "I caught you in the shower. I'm sorry. I should have called first. It's just I ordered a pizza from Avanti's. I was going to go home, but then I realized I didn't want to eat alone. I thought you might not want to be alone either. So I figured you might be up for some pizza, company and a bit of gaming."

He started to say something when I heard a voice.

"Elvis? Who is it?"

The door opened a bit wider and Bonnie stepped into view behind him. Her blonde hair was wet. She clutched a white towel around her torso with one hand, while she placed the other one on Elvis's naked shoulder.

"Lexi? What are you doing here?"

My mouth fell open as I looked between her and Elvis.

"Bonnie? I... I'm really sorry. I interrupted. I had no idea that you...that he...that Elvis had company."

Bonnie smiled. "Well, I'm so glad you stopped by. I wanted to thank you again for everything you did for our school. You and Elvis were truly amazing. I can't think of how I could possibly repay you two."

"It looks like you found one way."

Before she could answer, I shoved the pizza in Elvis's hands. "I'm sorry. I've… I've got to go. You guys enjoy the pizza."

"Lexi—" Elvis started, but I turned on my heel and fled to my car.

I pushed the key in the ignition and pulled out of his driveway as quickly as I could. I drove through at least one stop sign and a red light before I pulled over to the side of the road, leaning my head against the steering wheel and trying to think.

I was surprised, that was all. Stunned. Maybe a little dazed. Who could blame me?

I hadn't expected anyone to be at Elvis's.

Definitely not a girl.

Definitely not a *nude* girl.

Definitely not Bonnie.

I'd just been taken off guard to see them naked… together. I was entitled to a bit of shock.

So what if they'd been in the shower together? It was none of my business. He was a grown man, and Bonnie was a grown woman. A very pretty woman, not that it mattered. Consenting adults could take showers together…and do more if they wanted. Jeez, it was what I was doing with Slash. I should be happy that Elvis was emerging from his freezer and getting on with his life just like he'd vowed he'd do.

He was moving forward.

If I were any kind of best friend, I'd be thrilled for him. So why did I feel like I'd just had my guts yanked out?

Confusion throbbed behind my eyes. I wanted to puke and hit something at the same time.

Instead, to my horror, I burst into tears, crying with big honking sobs and blubbering all over the steering wheel. What in the world was wrong with me? Maybe I was suffering from some kind of post-traumatic stress. I was traumatized by recent events. That's all.

I swiped at the tears with the back of my hands, willing myself to calm down. I needed to talk to someone. Unfortunately, Basia was out. I wasn't sure I wanted to tell Slash. I didn't want to embarrass myself in front of my very first boyfriend. He would probably think I was completely out of my mind if I started babbling about pizza and towels. Besides—even though I'm not intuitive with these kinds of things—I felt like this should be a conversation between girls.

So, who?

The answer came easier than expected. I fumbled in the glove compartment for a tissue. I wiped my eyes and then blew my nose. When I felt composed enough, I retrieved the phone from my purse and punched in the number.

I waited as it rang twice, three times.

"Hello?"

I closed my eyes. Funny that it had taken me until now to realize this was something I should have done a long time ago.

Still, better late than never.

I took a deep breath.

"Hi, Mom. It's me, Lexi. Can I come over?"

THIRTY-SEVEN

I ARRIVED HOME from my parents' house about eleven o'clock. Slash was already inside waiting for me. He'd turned on the Christmas tree and holiday music played softly in the background.

He rose from the couch when I came in. *"Cara?"*

Without a word, I walked into his arms. He held me for a moment and then pulled back, searching my face.

"What happened?" He ran the pads of his thumbs under my eyes. "You've been crying."

"Yes."

He took my hand and made me sit on the couch. "Want to talk about it?"

"That's all I've been doing for the past few hours with my mom."

An eyebrow shot up. "Your mom?"

"Yes. I guess we had what you could call 'girl talk.' There's a first time for everything."

"I'm…astonished. Is there something I can do to help?"

I rubbed my eyes. "I don't think so. I just…well, things are changing so fast, I can't keep up."

"What things?"

"Everything. I barely have time to figure out how to have a boyfriend and then…"

Slash waited a beat and when I didn't say anything, he leaned forward. "Then what?"

"I think I'm losing my best friend," I blurted out.

He looked confused. "Basia?"

"No. Elvis. He said he was going to thaw and then he thawed. I can't go over there unannounced anymore. I don't even know if it's appropriate to call him. I've always been able to call him when I need him."

"I'm not following you."

I cleared my throat. "He was…with Bonnie."

Slash let out a breath and leaned back against the cushions. "Ah."

My hands were trembling. "Our friendship, mine and Elvis's, it's changing and I don't want it to."

"Relationships don't ever stay the same. They will either evolve and grow or they will wilt and die."

"So, you're saying our friendship is dying?"

He put a hand on my back, rubbing it slightly. "Perhaps it's just evolving."

I felt a tear leak from my eye and hastily brushed it aside. "I don't want it to change. It hurts."

"*Si*, it will. If something really matters, then it will hurt. Hearts are strange like that."

"Life was better without all these complications. I'm not sure I can handle this."

He tucked a strand of hair behind my ear. "This coming from the woman who just outwitted a group of terrorists with her feet? I think you're much stronger than that."

I put my head on his shoulder. "I just don't know what to do, Slash."

He shifted on the couch, putting an arm around me. "So, are you accepting candidates for the position of best friend?"

I'd been worried that having a boyfriend would be too stressful and complicated for it to be worth the risk.

And now here Slash was, offering me companionship, comfort and much more.

I lifted my head and studied his face. "Why, are you interested in applying?"

He looked directly into my eyes. "Damn right I am."

* * * * *

ABOUT THE AUTHOR

JULIE MOFFETT IS a bestselling author and writes in the genres of historical romance, paranormal romance and mystery. She has won numerous awards, including the prestigious PRISM Award for Best Romantic Time-Travel and Best of the Best Paranormal Books of 2002. She has also garnered several nominations for the Daphne du Maurier Award and the Holt Medallion. Julie is a military brat (Air Force) and has traveled extensively. Her more exciting exploits include attending high school in Okinawa, Japan; backpacking around Europe and Scandinavia for several months; a year-long college graduate study in Warsaw, Poland; and a wonderful trip to Scotland and Ireland where she fell in love with castles, kilts and brogues. Julie has a B.A. in Political Science and Russian language from Colorado College and an M.A. in international affairs from The George Washington University in Washington, D.C. She has worked as a journalist, teacher, and researcher. Julie speaks Russian and Polish and has two sons.

REQUEST YOUR FREE BOOKS!
2 FREE NOVELS PLUS 2 FREE GIFTS!

HARLEQUIN®

INTRIGUE

BREATHTAKING ROMANTIC SUSPENSE

YES! Please send me 2 FREE Harlequin® Intrigue novels and my 2 FREE gifts (gifts are worth about $10). After receiving them, if I don't wish to receive any more books, I can return the shipping statement marked "cancel." If I don't cancel, I will receive 6 brand-new novels every month and be billed just $4.74 per book in the U.S. or $5.49 per book in Canada. That's a savings of at least 12% off the cover price! It's quite a bargain! Shipping and handling is just 50¢ per book in the U.S. and 75¢ per book in Canada.* I understand that accepting the 2 free books and gifts places me under no obligation to buy anything. I can always return a shipment and cancel at any time. Even if I never buy another book, the two free books and gifts are mine to keep forever.

182/382 HDN GH3D

Name _____ (PLEASE PRINT)

Address _____ Apt. #

City _____ State/Prov. _____ Zip/Postal Code

Signature (if under 18, a parent or guardian must sign)

Mail to the **Reader Service:**
IN U.S.A.: P.O. Box 1867, Buffalo, NY 14240-1867
IN CANADA: P.O. Box 609, Fort Erie, Ontario L2A 5X3

**Are you a subscriber to Harlequin® Intrigue books
and want to receive the larger-print edition?
Call 1-800-873-8635 or visit www.ReaderService.com.**

* Terms and prices subject to change without notice. Prices do not include applicable taxes. Sales tax applicable in N.Y. Canadian residents will be charged applicable taxes. Offer not valid in Quebec. This offer is limited to one order per household. Not valid for current subscribers to Harlequin Intrigue books. All orders subject to credit approval. Credit or debit balances in a customer's account(s) may be offset by any other outstanding balance owed by or to the customer. Please allow 4 to 6 weeks for delivery. Offer available while quantities last.

Your Privacy—The Reader Service is committed to protecting your privacy. Our Privacy Policy is available online at www.ReaderService.com or upon request from the Reader Service.

We make a portion of our mailing list available to reputable third parties that offer products we believe may interest you. If you prefer that we not exchange your name with third parties, or if you wish to clarify or modify your communication preferences, please visit us at www.ReaderService.com/consumerschoice or write to us at Reader Service Preference Service, P.O. Box 9062, Buffalo, NY 14240-9062. Include your complete name and address.

I-III5

REQUEST YOUR FREE BOOKS!
2 FREE NOVELS PLUS 2 FREE GIFTS!

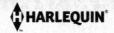

ROMANTIC suspense

Sparked by danger, fueled by passion

YES! Please send me 2 FREE Harlequin® Romantic Suspense novels and my 2 FREE gifts (gifts are worth about $10). After receiving them, if I don't wish to receive any more books, I can return the shipping statement marked "cancel." If I don't cancel, I will receive 4 brand-new novels every month and be billed just $4.74 per book in the U.S. or $5.49 per book in Canada. That's a savings of at least 12% off the cover price! It's quite a bargain! Shipping and handling is just 50¢ per book in the U.S. and 75¢ per book in Canada.* I understand that accepting the 2 free books and gifts places me under no obligation to buy anything. I can always return a shipment and cancel at any time. Even if I never buy another book, the two free books and gifts are mine to keep forever.

240/340 HDN GH3P

Name	(PLEASE PRINT)	
Address		Apt. #
City	State/Prov.	Zip/Postal Code

Signature (if under 18, a parent or guardian must sign)

Mail to the **Reader Service:**

IN U.S.A.: P.O. Box 1867, Buffalo, NY 14240-1867
IN CANADA: P.O. Box 609, Fort Erie, Ontario L2A 5X3

Want to try two free books from another line?
Call 1-800-873-8635 or visit www.ReaderService.com.

* Terms and prices subject to change without notice. Prices do not include applicable taxes. Sales tax applicable in N.Y. Canadian residents will be charged applicable taxes. Offer not valid in Quebec. This offer is limited to one order per household. Not valid for current subscribers to Harlequin Romantic Suspense books. All orders subject to credit approval. Credit or debit balances in a customer's account(s) may be offset by any other outstanding balance owed by or to the customer. Please allow 4 to 6 weeks for delivery. Offer available while quantities last.

Your Privacy—The Reader Service is committed to protecting your privacy. Our Privacy Policy is available online at www.ReaderService.com or upon request from the Reader Service.

We make a portion of our mailing list available to reputable third parties that offer products we believe may interest you. If you prefer that we not exchange your name with third parties, or if you wish to clarify or modify your communication preferences, please visit us at www.ReaderService.com/consumerschoice or write to us at Reader Service Preference Service, P.O. Box 9062, Buffalo, NY 14240-9062. Include your complete name and address.

HRS15

REQUEST YOUR FREE BOOKS!

2 FREE NOVELS
FROM THE SUSPENSE COLLECTION
PLUS 2 FREE GIFTS!

YES! Please send me 2 FREE novels from the Suspense Collection and my 2 FREE gifts (gifts are worth about $10). After receiving them, if I don't wish to receive any more books, I can return the shipping statement marked "cancel." If I don't cancel, I will receive 4 brand-new novels every month and be billed just $6.49 per book in the U.S. or $6.99 per book in Canada. That's a savings of at least 19% off the cover price. It's quite a bargain! Shipping and handling is just 50¢ per book in the U.S. and 75¢ per book in Canada.* I understand that accepting the 2 free books and gifts places me under no obligation to buy anything. I can always return a shipment and cancel at any time. Even if I never buy another book, the two free books and gifts are mine to keep forever.

191/391 MDN GH4Z

Name _____ (PLEASE PRINT) _____

Address _____ Apt. # _____

City _____ State/Prov. _____ Zip/Postal Code _____

Signature (if under 18, a parent or guardian must sign)

Mail to the **Reader Service**:
IN U.S.A.: P.O. Box 1867, Buffalo, NY 14240-1867
IN CANADA: P.O. Box 609, Fort Erie, Ontario L2A 5X3

Want to try two free books from another line?
Call 1-800-873-8635 or visit www.ReaderService.com.

* Terms and prices subject to change without notice. Prices do not include applicable taxes. Sales tax applicable in N.Y. Canadian residents will be charged applicable taxes. Offer not valid in Quebec. This offer is limited to one order per household. Not valid for current subscribers to the Suspense Collection or the Romance/Suspense Collection. All orders subject to credit approval. Credit or debit balances in a customer's account(s) may be offset by any other outstanding balance owed by or to the customer. Please allow 4 to 6 weeks for delivery. Offer available while quantities last.

Your Privacy—The Reader Service is committed to protecting your privacy. Our Privacy Policy is available online at www.ReaderService.com or upon request from the Reader Service.

We make a portion of our mailing list available to reputable third parties that offer products we believe may interest you. If you prefer that we not exchange your name with third parties, or if you wish to clarify or modify your communication preferences, please visit us at www.ReaderService.com/consumerschoice or write to us at Reader Service Preference Service, P.O. Box 9062, Buffalo, NY 14240-9062. Include your complete name and address.

READERSERVICE.COM

Manage your account online!

- Review your order history
- Manage your payments
- Update your address

*We've designed the
Reader Service website
just for you.*

Enjoy all the features!

- Discover new series available to you, and read excerpts from any series.
- Respond to mailings and special monthly offers.
- Connect with favorite authors at the blog.
- Browse the Bonus Bucks catalog and online-only exculsives.
- Share your feedback.

Visit us at:
ReaderService.com